THE WOULDBEGOODS

When EDITH NESBIT (1858–1924) was in her teens, the family moved to a large house in Kent called Halstead Hall. Although she lived here for only three years, they were the happiest years of a happy childhood, and echoes of Halstead Hall recur in many of her books. There was, for instance, a railway cutting near the house, which the young Edith used to explore.

She was a mischievous, tomboyish child who grew into an unconventional adult. With her husband, Hubert Bland, she was one of the founder members of the socialist Fabian Society; their household became a centre of the socialist and literary circles of the times. The chaos of their Bohemian home, managed by the restless 'Daisy' (as she was known to her friends), was regularly increased by the presence of numerous friends, among whom were George Bernard Shaw and H. G. Wells. And apart from their own children, Edith looked after two children born as a result of her husband's affairs!

Her clothing, haircut, lifestyle and habit of expressing herself forcefully and in public proclaimed her to be a woman who was trying to break out of the mould which English society demanded at the time. She was no armchair socialist, however; in fact, despite her success as a writer, late in life her charitable deeds brought her close to bankruptcy.

E. Nesbit – she always used the plain initial for her writing, with the result that she was occasionally thought to be a man – turned late to children's writing, after a number of years as a successful writer of short pieces for adult magazines. The first children's book, *The Treasure Seekers*, was published in 1899 to great acclaim. She never looked back. *The Wouldbegoods* (1901) was just the first of the sequels about the Bastable children, and she also wrote a popular series of magical fantasy books (including *Five Children and It*) and the much-loved *The Railway Children*.

Some other Puffin Classics to enjoy

LITTLE LORD FAUNTLEROY
A LITTLE PRINCESS
THE LOST PRINCE
THE SECRET GARDEN
Frances Hodgson Burnett

THE CUCKOO CLOCK   Mrs Molesworth

THE ENCHANTED CASTLE
FIVE CHILDREN AND IT
THE HOUSE OF ARDEN
THE LAST OF THE DRAGONS AND SOME OTHERS
THE MAGIC WORLD
THE STORY OF THE TREASURE SEEKERS
NEW TREASURE SEEKERS
THE PHOENIX AND THE CARPET
THE RAILWAY CHILDREN
THE STORY OF THE AMULET
E Nesbit

E. NESBIT

THE WOULDBEGOODS

BEING THE FURTHER ADVENTURES
OF THE TREASURE SEEKERS

WITH ILLUSTRATIONS BY
Cecil Leslie

PUFFIN BOOKS

PUFFIN BOOKS

Published by the Penguin Group
Penguin Books Ltd, 27 Wrights Lane, London W8 5TZ, England
Penguin Books USA Inc., 375 Hudson Street, New York, New York 10014, USA
Penguin Books Australia Ltd, Ringwood, Victoria, Australia
Penguin Books Canada Ltd, 10 Alcorn Avenue, Toronto, Ontario, Canada M4V 3B2
Penguin Books (NZ) Ltd, 182–190 Wairau Road, Auckland 10, New Zealand

Penguin Books Ltd, Registered Offices: Harmondsworth, Middlesex, England

First published 1901
Published in Puffin Books 1958
23 25 27 29 30 28 26 24 22

Printed in England by Clays Ltd, St Ives plc
Set in Monotype Baskerville

To
MY DEAR SON
FABIAN BLAND

CONTENTS

LIST OF ILLUSTRATIONS

CHAPTER I

THE JUNGLE

CHILDREN are like jam: all very well in the proper place, but you can't stand them all over the shop – eh, what?

These were the dreadful words of our Indian uncle. They made us feel very young and angry; and yet we could not be comforted by calling him names to ourselves, as you do when nasty grown-ups say nasty things, because he is not nasty, but quite the exact opposite when not irritated. And we could not think it ungentlemanly of him to say we were like jam, because, as Alice says, jam is very nice indeed – only not on furniture and improper places like that. My father said, 'Perhaps they had better go to boarding-school.' And that was awful, because we know Father disapproves of boarding-schools. And he looked at us and said, 'I am ashamed of them, sir!'

Your lot is indeed a dark and terrible one when your father is ashamed of you. And we all knew this, so that we felt in our chests just as if we had swallowed a hard-boiled egg whole. At least, this is what Oswald felt, and Father said once that Oswald, as the eldest, was the representative of the family, so, of course, the others felt the same.

And then everybody said nothing for a short time. At last Father said –

'You may go – but remember . . .' The words that followed I am not going to tell you. It is no use telling you what you know before – as they do in schools. And you must all have had such words said to you many times. We went away when it was over. The girls cried, and we boys got out books and began to read, so that nobody should think we cared. But we felt it deeply in our interior hearts, especially Oswald, who is the eldest and the representative of the family.

We felt it all the more because we had not really meant to do anything wrong. We only thought perhaps the grown-ups would not be quite pleased if they knew, and that is quite different. Besides, we meant to put all the things back in their proper places when we had done with them before anyone found out about it. But I must not anticipate (that means telling the end of the story before the beginning. I tell you this because it is so sickening to have words you don't know in a story, and to be told to look it up in the dicker).

We are the Bastables – Oswald, Dora, Dicky, Alice, Noël, and H. O. If you want to know why we call our youngest brother H. O. you can jolly well read *The Treasure Seekers* and find out. We were the Treasure Seekers, and we sought it high and low, and quite regularly, because we particularly wanted to find it. And at last we did not find it, but we were found by a good, kind Indian uncle, who helped Father with his business, so that Father was able to take us all to live in a jolly big red house on Blackheath, instead of in the Lewisham Road, where we lived when we were only poor but honest Treasure Seekers. When we were poor but honest we always used to think that if only Father had plenty of business, and we did not have to go short of pocket money and wear shabby clothes (I don't mind this myself, but the girls do), we should be happy and very, very good.

And when we were taken to the beautiful big Blackheath house we thought now all would be well, because it was a house with vineries and pineries, and gas and water, and shrubberies and stabling, and replete with every modern convenience, like it says in Dyer & Hilton's list of Eligible House Property. I read all about it, and I have copied the words quite right.

It is a beautiful house, all the furniture solid and strong, no casters off the chairs, and the tables not scratched, and the silver not dented; and lots of servants, and the most decent meals every day – and lots of pocket-money.

But it is wonderful how soon you get used to things, even the things you want most. Our watches, for instance. We wanted them frightfully; but when I had mine a week or two, after the mainspring got broken and was repaired at Bennett's in the village, I hardly cared to look at the works at all, and it did not make me feel happy in my heart any more, though, of course, I should have been very unhappy if it had been taken away from me. And the same with new clothes and nice dinners and having enough of everything. You soon get used to it all, and it does not make you extra happy, although, if you had it all taken away, you would be very dejected. (That is a good word, and one I have never used before.) You get used to everything, as I said, and then you want something more. Father says this is what people mean by the deceitfulness of riches; but Albert's uncle says it is the spirit of progress, and Mrs Leslie said some people called it 'divine discontent'. Oswald asked them all what they thought one Sunday at dinner. Uncle said it was rot, and what we wanted was bread and water and a licking; but he meant it for a joke. This was in the Easter holidays.

We went to live at the Red House at Christmas. After the holidays the girls went to the Blackheath High

School, and we boys went to the Prop. (that means the Proprietary School). And we had to swot rather during term; but about Easter we knew the deceitfulness of riches in the vac., when there was nothing much on, like pantomimes and things. Then there was the summer term, and we swotted more than ever; and it was boiling hot, and masters' tempers got short and sharp, and the girls used to wish the exams came in cold weather. I can't think why they don't. But I suppose schools don't think of sensible thinks like that. They teach botany at girls' schools.

Then the Midsummer holidays came, and we breathed again – but only for a few days. We began to feel as if we had forgotten something, and did not know what it was. We wanted something to happen – only we didn't exactly know what. So we were very pleased when Father said –

'I've asked Mr Foulkes to send his children here for a week or two. You know – the kids who came at Christmas. You must be jolly to them, and see that they have a good time, don't you know.'

We remembered them right enough – they were little pinky, frightened things, like white mice, with very bright eyes. They had not been to our house since Christmas, because Denis, the boy, had been ill, and they had been with an aunt at Ramsgate.

Alice and Dora would have liked to get the bedrooms ready for the honoured guests, but a really good housemaid is sometimes more ready to say 'Don't' than even a general. So the girls had to chuck it. Jane only let them put flowers in the pots on the visitors' mantelpieces, and then they had to ask the gardener which kind they might pick, because nothing worth gathering happened to be growing in our own gardens just then.

Their train got in at 12.27. We all went to meet them.

Afterwards I thought that was a mistake, because their aunt was with them, and she wore black with beady things and a tight bonnet, and she said, when we took our hats off –

'Who are you?' quite crossly.

We said, 'We are the Bastables; we've come to meet Daisy and Denny.'

The aunt is a very rude lady, and it made us sorry for Daisy and Denny when she said to them –

'*Are* these the children? Do you remember them?'

We weren't very tidy, perhaps, because we'd been playing brigands in the shrubbery; and we knew we should have to wash for dinner as soon as we got back, anyhow. But still –

Denny said he thought he remembered us. But Daisy said, 'Of course they are,' and then looked as if she was going to cry.

So then the aunt called a cab, and told the man where to drive, and put Daisy and Denny in, and then she said –

'You two little girls may go too, if you like, but you little boys must walk.'

So the cab went off, and we were left. The aunt turned to us to say a few last words. We knew it would have been about brushing your hair and wearing gloves, so Oswald said, 'Good-bye', and turned haughtily away, before she could begin, and so did the others. No one but that kind of black beady tight lady would say 'little boys'. She is like Miss Murdstone in *David Copperfield*. I should like to tell her so; but she would not understand. I don't suppose she has ever read anything but *Markham's History* and *Mangnall's Questions* – improving books like that.

When we got home we found all four of those who had ridden in the cab sitting in our sitting-room – we don't call it nursery now – looking very thoroughly washed, and our girls were asking polite questions and the others were saying 'Yes' and 'No', and 'I don't know'. We boys did not say anything. We stood at the window and looked out till the gong went for our dinner. We felt it was going to be awful – and it was. The newcomers would never have done for knight-errants, or to carry the Cardinal's sealed message through the heart of France on a horse; they would never have thought of anything to say to throw the enemy off the scent when they got into a tight place.

They said 'Yes, please', and 'No, thank you'; and they ate very neatly, and always wiped their mouths before they drank, as well as after, and never spoke with them full.

And after dinner it got worse and worse.

We got out all our books and they said 'Thank you', and didn't look at them properly. And we got out all our toys, and they said 'Thank you, it's very nice' to everything. And it got less and less pleasant, and towards teatime it came to nobody saying anything except Noël and H. O. – and they talked to each other about cricket.

After tea Father came in, and he played 'Letters' with them and the girls, and it was a little better; but while late dinner was going on – I shall never forget it. Oswald felt like the hero of a book – 'almost at the end of his resources'. I don't think I was ever glad of bed-time before, but that time I was.

When they had gone to bed (Daisy had to have all her strings and buttons undone for her, Dora told me, though she is nearly ten, and Denny said he couldn't sleep without the gas being left a little bit on) we held a council in the girls' room. We all sat on the bed – it is a mahogany fourposter with green curtains very good for tents, only the housekeeper doesn't allow it, and Oswald said –

'This is jolly nice, isn't it?'

'They'll be better to-morrow,' Alice said, 'they're only shy.'

Dicky said shy was all very well, but you needn't behave like a perfect idiot.

'They're frightened. You see we're all strange to them,' Dora said.

'We're not wild beasts or Indians; we shan't eat them. What have they got to be frightened of?' Dicky said this.

Noël told us he thought they were an enchanted prince and princess who'd been turned into white rabbits, and their bodies had got changed back but not their insides.

But Oswald told him to dry up.

'It's no use making things up about them,' he said. 'The thing is: what are we going to *do*? We can't have our holidays spoiled by these snivelling kids.'

'No,' Alice said, 'but they can't possibly go on snivelling for ever. Perhaps they've got into the habit of it with that Murdstone aunt. She's enough to make anyone snivel.'

'All the same,' said Oswald, 'we jolly well aren't going to have another day like today. We must do something to rouse them from their snivelling leth – what's its name? – something sudden and – what is it? – decisive.'

'A booby trap,' said H. O., 'the first thing when they get up, and an apple-pie bed at night.'

But Dora would not hear of it, and I own she was right.

'Suppose,' she said, 'we could get up a good play – like we did when we were Treasure Seekers.'

We said, well what? But she did not say.

'It ought to be a good long thing – to last all day,' Dicky said, 'and if they like they can play, and if they don't – '

'If they don't, I'll read to them,' Alice said.

But we all said 'No, you don't – if you begin that way you'll have to go on.' And Dicky added, 'I wasn't going to say that at all. I was going to say if they didn't like it they could jolly well do the other thing.'

We all agreed that we must think of something, but we none of us could, and at last the council broke up in confusion because Mrs Blake – she is the housekeeper – came up and turned off the gas.

But next morning when we were having breakfast, and the two strangers were sitting there so pink and clean, Oswald suddenly said –

'I know; we'll have a jungle in the garden.'

And the others agreed, and we talked about it till brek was over. The little strangers only said 'I don't know' whenever we said anything to them.

After brekker Oswald beckoned his brothers and sisters mysteriously apart and said –

'Do you agree to let me be captain today, because I thought of it?'

And they said they would.

Then he said, 'We'll play *Jungle Book*, and I shall be Mowgli. The rest of you can be what you like – Mowgli's father and mother, or any of the beasts.'

'I don't suppose they know the book,' said Noël. 'They don't look as if they read anything, except at lesson times.'

'Then they can go on being beasts all the time,' Oswald said. 'Anyone can be a beast.'

So it was settled.

And now Oswald – Albert's uncle has sometimes said he is clever at arranging things – began to lay his plans for the jungle. The day was indeed well chosen. Our Indian uncle was away; Father was away; Mrs Blake was going away, and the housemaid had an afternoon off. Oswald's first conscious act was to get rid of the white mice – I mean the little good visitors. He explained to them that there would be a play in the afternoon, and they could be what they liked, and gave them the *Jungle Book* to read the stories he told them to – all the ones about Mowgli. He led the strangers to a secluded spot among the sea-kale pots in the kitchen garden and left them. Then he went back to the others, and we had a jolly morning under the cedar talking about what we would do when Blakie was gone. She went just after our dinner.

When we asked Denny what he would like to be in the play, it turned out he had not read the stories Oswald told him at all, but only the 'White Seal' and 'Rikki Tikki'.

We then agreed to make the jungle first and dress up for our parts afterwards. Oswald was a little uncomfortable about leaving the strangers alone all the morning, so he said Denny should be his aide-de-camp, and he was really quite useful. He is rather handy with his fingers, and things that he does up do not come untied. Daisy might have come too, but she wanted to go on reading, so we let her, which is the truest manners to a visitor. Of course the shrubbery was to be the jungle, and the lawn under the cedar a forest glade, and then we began to collect the things. The cedar lawn is just nicely out of the way of the windows. It was a jolly hot day – the kind of day when the sunshine is white and the shadows are dark grey, not black like they are in the evening.

Up to now all was not

We all thought of different things. Of course first we
dressed up pillows in the skins of beasts and set them
about on the grass to look as natural as we could. And
then we got Pincher, and rubbed him all over with
powdered slate-pencil, to make him the right colour
for Grey Brother. But he shook it all off, and it had taken
an awful time to do. Then Alice said –

'Oh, I know!' and she ran off to Father's dressing-
room, and came back with the tube of *crème d'amande
pour la barbe et les mains*, and we squeezed it on Pincher
and rubbed it in, and then the slate-pencil stuff stuck
all right, and he rolled in the dust-bin of his own accord,
which made him just the right colour. He is a very
clever dog, but soon after he went off and we did not

lost beyond recall

find him till quite late in the afternoon. Denny helped with Pincher, and with the wild-beast skins, and when Pincher was finished he said –

'Please, may I make some paper birds to put in the trees? I know how.'

And of course we said 'Yes', and he only had red ink and newspapers, and quickly he made quite a lot of large paper birds with red tails. They didn't look half bad on the edge of the shrubbery.

While he was doing this he suddenly said, or rather screamed, 'Oh?'

And we looked, and it was a creature with great horns and a fur rug – something like a bull and something like a minotaur – and I don't wonder

Denny was frightened. It was Alice, and it was first-class.

Up to now all was not yet lost beyond recall. It was the stuffed fox that did the mischief – and I am sorry to own it was Oswald who thought of it. He is not ashamed of having *thought* of it. That was rather clever of him. But he knows now that it is better not to take other people's foxes and things without asking, even if you live in the same house with them.

It was Oswald who undid the back of the glass case in the hall and got out the fox with the green and grey duck in its mouth, and when the others saw how awfully like life they looked on the lawn, they all rushed off to fetch the other stuffed things. Uncle has a tremendous lot of stuffed things. He shot most of them himself – but not the fox, of course. There was another fox's mask, too, and we hung that in a bush to look as if the fox was peeping out. And the stuffed birds we fastened on to the trees with string. The duck-bill – what's its name? – looked very well sitting on his tail with the otter snarling at him. Then Dicky had an idea; and though not nearly so much was said about it afterwards as there was about the stuffed things, I think myself it was just as bad, though it was a good idea, too. He just got the hose and put the end over a branch of the cedar-tree. Then we got the steps they clean windows with, and let the hose rest on the top of the steps and run. It was to be a waterfall, but it ran between the steps and was only wet and messy; so we got Father's mackintosh and uncle's and covered the steps with them, so that the water ran down all right and was glorious, and it ran away in a stream across the grass where we had dug a little channel for it – and the otter and the duck-bill-thing were as if in their native haunts. I hope all this is not very dull to read about. I know it was jolly good fun to do. Taking one thing with another, I don't know that we ever had a better time while it lasted.

We got all the rabbits out of the hutches and put pink paper tails on to them, and hunted them with horns made out of *The Times*. They got away somehow, and before they were caught next day they had eaten a good many lettuces and other things. Oswald is very sorry for this. He rather likes the gardener.

Denny wanted to put paper tails on the guinea-pigs, and it was no use our telling him there was nothing to tie the paper on to. He thought we were kidding until we showed him, and then he said, 'Well, never mind', and got the girls to give him bits of the blue stuff left over from their dressing-gowns.

'I'll make them sashes to tie round their little middles,' he said. And he did, and the bows stuck up on the tops of their backs. One of the guinea-pigs was never seen again, and the same with the tortoise when we had done his shell with vermilion paint. He crawled away and returned no more. Perhaps someone collected him and thought he was an expensive kind unknown in these cold latitudes.

The lawn under the cedar was transformed into a dream of beauty, what with the stuffed creatures and the paper-tailed things and the waterfall. And Alice said –

'I wish the tigers did not look so flat.' For of course with pillows you can only pretend it is a sleeping tiger getting ready to make a spring out at you. It is difficult to prop up tiger-skins in a life-like manner when there are no bones inside them, only pillows and sofa cushions. 'What about the beer-stands?' I said. And we got two out of the cellar. With bolsters and string we fastened insides to the tigers – and they were really fine. The legs of the beer-stands did for tigers' legs. It was indeed the finishing touch.

Then we boys put on just our bathing drawers and vests – so as to be able to play with the waterfall without hurting our clothes. I think this was thoughtful. The girls only tucked up their frocks and took their shoes and stockings off. H. O. painted his legs and his hands with Condy's fluid – to make him brown, so that he might be Mowgli, although Oswald was captain and had plainly said he was going to be Mowgli himself. Of course the others weren't going to stand that. So Oswald said –

'Very well. Nobody asked you to brown yourself like that. But now you've done it, you've simply got to go and be a beaver, and live in the dam under the waterfall till it washes off.'

He said he didn't want to be beavers. And Noël said –

'Don't make him. Let him be the bronze statue in the palace gardens that the fountain plays out of.'

So we let him have the hose and hold it up over his head. It made a lovely fountain, only he remained brown. So then Dicky and Oswald and I did ourselves brown too, and dried H. O. as well as we could with our handkerchiefs, because he was just beginning to snivel. The brown did not come off any of us for days.

Oswald was to be Mowgli, and we were just beginning to arrange the different parts. The rest of the hose that was on the ground was Kaa, the Rock Python, and Pincher was Grey Brother, only we couldn't find him. And while most of us were talking, Dicky and Noël got messing about with the beer-stand tigers.

And then a really sad event instantly occurred, which was not really our fault, and we did not mean to.

That Daisy girl had been mooning indoors all the afternoon with the *Jungle Books*, and now she came suddenly out, just as Dicky and Noël had got under the tigers and were shoving them along to fright each other. Of course, this is not in the Mowgli book at all: but they did look jolly like real tigers, and I am very far from wishing to blame the girl, though she little knew what would be the awful consequence of her rash act. But for her we might have got out of it all much better than we did.

What happened was truly horrid.

As soon as Daisy saw the tigers she stopped short, and uttering a shriek like a railway whistle she fell flat on the ground.

'Fear not, gentle Indian maid,' Oswald cried, thinking with surprise that perhaps after all she did know how to play, 'I myself will protect thee.' And he sprang forward with the native bow and arrows out of uncle's study.

The gentle Indian maiden did not move.

'Come hither,' Dora said, 'let us take refuge in yonder covert while this good knight does battle for us.'

Dora might have remembered that we were savages, but she did not. And that is Dora all over. And still the Daisy girl did not move.

Then we were truly frightened. Dora and Alice lifted her up, and her mouth was a horrid violet-colour and her eyes half shut. She looked horrid. Not at all like fair fainting damsels, who are always of an interesting pallor. She was green, like a cheap oyster on a stall.

We did what we could, a prey to alarm as we were. We rubbed her hands and let the hose play gently but perseveringly on her unconscious brow. The girls loosened her dress, though it was only the kind that comes down straight without a waist. And we were all doing what we could as hard as we could, when we heard the click of the front gate. There was no mistake about it.

'I hope whoever it is will go straight to the front

door,' said Alice. But whoever it was did not. There were feet on the gravel, and there was the uncle's voice, saying in his hearty manner –

'This way. This way. On such a day as this we shall find our young barbarians all at play somewhere about the grounds.'

And then, without further warning, the uncle, three other gentlemen and two ladies burst upon the scene.

We had no clothes on to speak of – I mean us boys. We were all wet through. Daisy was in a faint or a fit, or dead, none of us then knew which. And all the stuffed animals were there staring the uncle in the face. Most of them had got a sprinkling, and the otter and the duck-bill brute were simply soaked. And three of us were dark brown. Concealment, as so often happens, was impossible.

The quick brain of Oswald saw, in a flash, exactly how it would strike the uncle, and his brave young blood ran cold in his veins. His heart stood still.

'What's all this – eh, what?' said the tones of the wronged uncle.

Oswald spoke up and said it was jungles we were playing, and he didn't know what was up with Daisy. He explained as well as anyone could, but words were now in vain.

The uncle had a Malacca cane in his hand, and we were but ill prepared to meet the sudden attack. Oswald and H. O. caught it worst. The other boys were under the tigers – and of course my uncle would not strike a girl. Denny was a visitor and so got off. But it was bread and water for us for the next three days, and our own rooms. I will not tell you how we sought to vary the monotonousness of imprisonment. Oswald thought of taming a mouse, but he could not find one. The reason of the wretched captives might have given

24

way but for the gutter that you can crawl along from our room to the girls'. But I will not dwell on this because you might try it yourselves, and it really is dangerous. When my father came home we got the talking to, and we said we were sorry – and we really were – especially about Daisy, though she had behaved with muffishness, and then it was settled that we were to go into the country and stay till we had grown into better children.

Albert's uncle was writing a book in the country; we were to go to his house. We were glad of this – Daisy and Denny too. This we bore nobly. We knew we had deserved it. We were all very sorry for everything, and we resolved that for the future we *would* be good.

I am not sure whether we kept this resolution or not. Oswald thinks now that perhaps we made a mistake in trying so very hard to be good all at once. You should do everything by degrees.

P.S. – It turned out Daisy was not really dead at all. It was only fainting – so like a girl.

N.B. – Pincher was found on the drawing-room sofa.

Appendix. – I have not told you half the things we did for the jungle – for instance, about the elephants' tusks and the horse-hair sofa-cushions, and uncle's fishing-boots.

CHAPTER 2

THE WOULDBEGOODS

WHEN we were sent down into the country to learn to be good we felt it was rather good business, because we knew our being sent there was really only to get us out of the way for a little while, and we knew right enough that it wasn't a punishment, though Mrs Blake said it was, because we had been punished thoroughly for taking the stuffed animals out and making a jungle on the lawn with them, and the garden hose. And you cannot be punished twice for the same offence. This is the English law; at least I think so. And at any rate no one would punish you three times, and we had had the Malacca cane and the solitary confinement; and the uncle had kindly explained to us that all ill-feeling between him and us was wiped out entirely by the bread and water we had endured. And what with the bread and water and being prisoners, and not being able to tame any mice in our prisons, I quite feel that we had suffered it up thoroughly, and now we could start fair.

I think myself that descriptions of places are generally dull, but I have sometimes thought that was because the authors do not tell you what you truly want to know. However, dull or not, here goes – because you won't understand anything unless I tell you what the place was like.

The Moat House was the one we went to stay at. There has been a house there since Saxon times. It is a manor, and a manor goes on having a house on it whatever happens. The Moat House was burnt down once or twice in ancient centuries – I don't remember which – but they always built a new one, and Cromwell's soldiers smashed it about, but it was patched up again. It is a very odd house: the front door opens

The Moat House with a brick bridge leading to the front door

straight into the dining-room, and there are red curtains and a black-and-white marble floor like a chess-board, and there is a secret staircase, only it is not secret now – only rather rickety. It is not very big, but there is a watery moat all round it with a brick bridge that leads to the front door. Then, on the other side of the moat there is the farm, with barns and oast houses and stables, or things like that. And the other way the garden lawn goes on till it comes to the churchyard. The churchyard is not divided from the garden at all except by a little grass bank. In the front of the house there is more garden, and the big fruit garden is at the back.

The man the house belongs to likes new houses, so he built a big one with conservatories and a stable with a clock in a turret on the top, and he left the Moat House. And Albert's uncle took it, and my father was to come down sometimes from Saturday to Monday, and Albert's uncle was to live with us all the time, and he would be writing a book, and we were not to bother him, but he would give an eye to us. I hope all this is plain. I have said it as short as I can.

We got down rather late, but there was still light enough to see the big bell hanging at the top of the house. The rope belonging to it went right down the house, through our bedroom to the dining-room. H. O. saw the rope and pulled it while he was washing his hands for supper, and Dicky and I let him, and the bell tolled solemnly. Father shouted to him not to, and we went down to supper. But presently there were many feet trampling on the gravel, and Father went out to see. When he came back he said –

'The whole village, or half of it, has come up to see why the bell rang. It's only rung for fire or burglars. Why can't you kids let things alone?'

Albert's uncle said –

'Bed follows supper as the fruit follows the flower. They'll do no more mischief to-night, sir. To-morrow I will point out a few of the things to be avoided in this bucolic retreat.'

So it was bed directly after supper, and that was why we did not see much that night.

But in the morning we were all up rather early, and we seemed to have awakened in a new world rich in surprises beyond the dreams of anybody, as it says in the quotation.

We went everywhere we could in the time, but when it was breakfast-time we felt we had not seen half or a quarter. The room we had breakfast in was exactly like in a story – black oak panels and china in corner cupboards with glass doors. These doors were locked. There were green curtains, and honeycomb for breakfast. After brekker my father went back to town, and Albert's uncle went too, to see publishers. We saw them to the station, and Father gave us a long list of what we weren't to do. It began with 'Don't pull ropes unless you're quite sure what will happen at the other end,' and it finished with 'For goodness sake, try to keep out of mischief till I come down on Saturday'. There were lots of other things in between.

We all promised we would. And we saw them off, and waved till the train was quite out of sight. Then we started to walk home. Daisy was tired so Oswald carried her home on his back. When we got home she said –

'I do like you, Oswald.'

She is not a bad little kid; and Oswald felt it was his duty to be nice to her because she was a visitor. Then we looked all over everything. It was a glorious place. You did not know where to begin.

We were all a little tired before we found the hay-loft, but we pulled ourselves together to make a fort with the trusses of hay – great square things – and we were having a jolly good time, all of us, when suddenly a trap-door opened and a head bobbed up with a straw in its mouth. We knew nothing about the country then, and the head really did scare us rather, though, of course, we found out directly that the feet belonging to it were standing on the bar of the loose-box underneath. The head said –

'Don't you let the governor catch you a-spoiling of that there hay, that's all.' And it spoke thickly because of the straw.

It is strange to think how ignorant you were in the past. We can hardly believe now that once we really did not know that it spoiled hay to mess about with it. Horses don't like to eat it afterwards. Always remember this.

When the head had explained a little more it went away, and we turned the handle of the chaff-cutting machine, and nobody got hurt, though the head *had* said we should cut our fingers off if we touched it.

And then we sat down on the floor, which is dirty with the nice clean dirt that is more than half chopped hay, and those there was room for hung their legs down out of the top door, and we looked down at the farmyard, which is very slushy when you get down into it, but most interesting.

Then Alice said –

'Now we're all here, and the boys are tired enough to sit still for a minute, I want to have a council.'

We said what about? And she said, 'I'll tell you. H. O., don't wriggle so; sit on my frock if the straws tickle your legs.'

You see he wears socks, and so he can never be quite as comfortable as anyone else.

'Promise not to laugh,' Alice said, getting very red, and looking at Dora, who got red too.

We did, and then she said: 'Dora and I have talked this over, and Daisy too, and we have written it down because it is easier than saying it. Shall I read it? or will you, Dora?'

Dora said it didn't matter; Alice might. So Alice read it, and though she gabbled a bit we all heard it. I copied it afterwards. This is what she read:

'NEW SOCIETY FOR BEING GOOD IN

'I, Dora Bastable, and Alice Bastable, my sister, being of sound mind and body, when we were shut up with bread and water on that jungle day, we thought a great deal about our naughty sins, and we made our minds up to be good for ever after. And we talked to Daisy about it, and she had an idea. So we want to start a society for being good in. It is Daisy's idea, but we think so too.'

'You know,' Dora interrupted, 'when people want to do good things they always make a society. There are thousands – there's the Missionary Society.'

'Yes,' Alice said, 'and the Society for the Prevention of something or other, and the Young Men's Mutual Improvement Society, and the S.P.G.'

'What's S.P.G.?' Oswald asked.

'Society for the Propagation of the Jews, of course,' said Noël, who cannot always spell.

'No, it isn't; but do let me go on.'

Alice did go on.

'We propose to get up a society, with a chairman and a treasurer and secretary, and keep a journal-book saying what we've done. If that doesn't make us good it won't be my fault.

'The aim of the society is nobleness and goodness, and great and unselfish deeds. We wish not to be such a nuisance to grown-up people and to perform prodigies of real goodness. We wish to spread our wings' – here Alice read very fast. She told me afterwards Daisy had helped her with that part, and she thought when she came to the wings they sounded rather silly – 'to spread our wings and rise above the kind of interesting things that you ought not to do, but to do kindnesses to all, however low and mean.'

Denny was listening carefully. Now he nodded three or four times.

> '*Little words of kindness*' (he said),
>   '*Little deeds of love,*
> *Make this earth an eagle*
> *Like the one above.*'

This did not sound right, but we let it pass, because an eagle *does* have wings, and we wanted to hear the rest of what the girls had written. But there was no rest.

'That's all,' said Alice, and Daisy said –

'Don't you think it's a good idea?'

'That depends,' Oswald answered, 'who is president and what you mean by being good.' Oswald did not care very much for the idea himself, because being good is not the sort of thing he thinks it is proper to talk about, especially before strangers. But the girls and Denny seemed to like it, so Oswald did not say exactly what he thought, especially as it was Daisy's idea. This was true politeness.

'I think it would be nice,' Noël said, 'if we made it a sort of play. Let's do the *Pilgrim's Progress*.'

We talked about that for some time, but it did not come to anything, because we all wanted to be Mr Greatheart, except H. O., who wanted to be the lions, and you could not have lions in a Society for Goodness.

Dicky said he did not wish to play if it meant reading books about children who die; he really felt just as Oswald did about it, he told me afterwards. But the girls were looking as if they were in Sunday school, and we did not wish to be unkind.

At last Oswald said, 'Well, let's draw up the rules of

the society, and choose the president and settle the name.'

Dora said Oswald should be president, and he modestly consented. She was secretary, and Denny treasurer if we ever had any money.

Making the rules took us all the afternoon. They were these:

RULES

1. Every member is to be as good as possible.
2. There is to be no more jaw than necessary about being good. (Oswald and Dicky put that rule in.)
3. No day must pass without our doing some kind action to a suffering fellow-creature.
4. We are to meet every day, or as often as we like.
5. We are to do good to people we don't like as often as we can.
6. No one is to leave the Society without the consent of all the rest of us.
7. The Society is to be kept a profound secret from all the world except us.
8. The name of our Society is –

And when we got as far as that we all began to talk at once. Dora wanted it called the Society for Humane Improvement; Denny said the Society for Reformed Outcast Children; but Dicky said, No, we really were not so bad as all that. Then H. O. said, 'Call it the Good Society.'

'Or the Society for Being Good In,' said Daisy.

'Or the Society of Goods,' said Noël.

'That's priggish,' said Oswald; 'besides, we don't know whether we shall be so very.'

'You see,' Alice explained, 'we only said if we *could* we would be good.'

'Well, then,' Dicky said, getting up and beginning to dust the chopped hay off himself, 'call it the Society of the Wouldbegoods and have done with it.'

Oswald thinks Dicky was getting sick of it and wanted to make himself a little disagreeable. If so, he was doomed to disappointment. For everyone else clapped hands and called out, 'That's the very thing!' Then the girls went off to write out the rules, and took H. O. with them, and Noël went to write some poetry to put in the minute book. That's what you call the book that a society's secretary writes what it does in. Denny went with him to help. He knows a lot of poetry. I think he went to a lady's school where they taught nothing but that. He was rather shy of us, but he took to Noël. I can't think why. Dicky and Oswald walked round the garden and told each other what they thought of the new society.

'I'm not sure we oughtn't to have put our foot down at the beginning,' Dicky said. 'I don't see much in it, anyhow.'

'It pleases the girls,' Oswald said, for he is a kind brother.

'But we're not going to stand jaw, and "words in season", and "loving sisterly warnings". I tell you what it is, Oswald, we'll have to run this thing our way, or it'll be jolly beastly for everybody.'

Oswald saw this plainly.

'We must do something,' Dicky said; 'it's very very hard, though. Still, there must be *some* interesting things that are not wrong.'

'I suppose so,' Oswald said, 'but being good is so much like being a muff, generally. Anyhow I'm not going to smooth the pillows of the sick, or read to the aged poor, or any rot out of *Ministering Children*.'

'No more am I,' Dicky said. He was chewing a straw

like the head had in its mouth, 'but I suppose we must play the game fair. Let's begin by looking out for something useful to do – something like mending things or cleaning them, not just showing off.'

'The boys in books chop kindling wood and save their pennies to buy tea and tracts.'

'Little beasts!' said Dick. 'I say, let's talk about something else.' And Oswald was glad to, for he was beginning to feel jolly uncomfortable.

We were all rather quiet at tea, and afterwards Oswald played draughts with Daisy and the others yawned. I don't know when we've had such a gloomy evening. And everyone was horribly polite, and said 'Please' and 'Thank you' far more than requisite.

Albert's uncle came home after tea. He was jolly, and told us stories, but he noticed us being a little dull, and asked what blight had fallen on our young lives. Oswald could have answered and said, 'It is the Society of the Wouldbegoods that is the blight,' but of course he didn't; and Albert's uncle said no more, but he went up and kissed the girls when they were in bed, and asked them if there was anything wrong. And they told him no, on their honour.

The next morning Oswald awoke early. The refreshing beams of the morning sun shone on his narrow white bed and on the sleeping forms of his dear little brothers and Denny, who had got the pillow on top of his head and was snoring like a kettle when it sings. Oswald could not remember at first what was the matter with him, and then he remembered the Wouldbegoods, and wished he hadn't. He felt at first as if there was nothing you could do, and even hesitated to buzz a pillow at Denny's head. But he soon saw that this could not be. So he chucked his boot and caught Denny right in the waistcoat part, and thus the day began more brightly than he had expected.

Oswald had not done anything out of the way good the night before, except that when no one was looking he polished the brass candlestick in the girls' bedroom with one of his socks. And he might just as well have let it alone, for the servants cleaned it again with the other things in the morning, and he could never find the sock afterwards. There were two servants. One of them had to be called Mrs Pettigrew instead of Jane and Eliza like others. She was cook and managed things.

After breakfast Albert's uncle said –

'I now seek the retirement of my study. At your peril violate my privacy before 1.30 sharp. Nothing short of bloodshed will warrant the intrusion, and nothing short of man – or rather boy – slaughter shall avenge it.'

So we knew he wanted to be quiet, and the girls decided that we ought to play out of doors so as not to disturb him; we should have played out of doors anyhow on a jolly fine day like that.

But as we were going out Dicky said to Oswald –

'I say, come along here a minute, will you?'

So Oswald came along, and Dicky took him into the other parlour and shut the door, and Oswald said –

'Well, spit it out: what is it?' He knows that is vulgar, and he would not have said it to anyone but his own brother.

Dicky said –

'It's a pretty fair nuisance. I told you how it would be.'

And Oswald was patient with him, and said –

'What is? Don't be all day about it.'

Dicky fidgeted about a bit, and then he said –

'Well, I did as I said. I looked about for something useful to do. And you know that dairy window that wouldn't open – only a little bit like that? Well, I mended the catch with wire and whipcord and it opened wide.'

'And I suppose they didn't want it mended,' said Oswald. He knew but too well that grown-up people sometimes like to keep things far different from what we would, and you catch it if you try to do otherwise.

'I shouldn't have minded *that*,' Dicky said, 'because I could easily have taken it all off again if they'd only said so. But the sillies went and propped up a milk-pan against the window. They never took the trouble to notice I had mended it. So the wretched thing pushed the window open all by itself directly they propped it up, and it's tumbled through into the moat, and they are most awfully waxy. All the men are out in the fields and they haven't any spare milk-pans. If I were a farmer, I must say I wouldn't stick at an extra milk-pan or two. Accidents must happen sometimes. I call it mean.'

Dicky spoke in savage tones. But Oswald was not so unhappy, first because it wasn't his fault, and next because he is a far-seeing boy.

'Never mind,' he said kindly. 'Keep your tail up. We'll get the beastly milk-pan out all right. Come on.'

He rushed hastily to the garden and gave a low, signifying whistle, which the others know well enough to mean something extra being up.

And when they were all gathered round him he spoke.

'Fellow countrymen,' he said, 'we're going to have a rousing good time.'

'It's nothing naughty, is it,' Daisy asked,' like the last time you had that was rousingly good?'

Alice said 'Shish', and Oswald pretended not to hear.

'A precious treasure,' he said, 'has inadvertently been laid low in the moat by one of us.'

'The rotten thing tumbled in by itself,' Dicky said.

Oswald waved his hand and said, 'Anyhow, it's there. It's our duty to restore it to its sorrowing owners. I say, look here – we're going to drag the moat.'

Everyone brightened up at this. It was our duty and it was interesting too. This is very uncommon.

So we went out to where the orchard is, at the other side of the moat. There were gooseberries and things on the bushes, but we did not take any till we had asked if we might. Alice went and asked. Mrs Pettigrew said, 'Law! I suppose so; you'd eat 'em anyhow, leave or no leave.'

She little knows the honourable nature of the house of Bastable. But she has much to learn.

The orchard slopes gently down to the dark waters of the moat. We sat there in the sun and talked about dragging the moat, till Denny said, 'How *do* you drag moats?'

And we were speechless, because, though we had read many times about a moat being dragged for missing heirs and lost wills, we really had never thought about exactly how it was done.

'Grappling-irons are right, I believe,' Denny said, 'but I don't suppose they'd have any at the farm.'

And we asked, and found they had never even heard of them. I think myself he meant some other word, but he was quite positive.

So then we got a sheet off Oswald's bed, and we all took our shoes and stockings off, and we tried to see if the sheet would drag the bottom of the moat, which is shallow at that end. But it would keep floating on the top of the water, and when we tried sewing stones into one end of it, it stuck on something in the bottom, and when we got it up it was torn. We were very sorry, and the sheet was in an awful mess; but the girls said they were sure they could wash it in the basin in their room, and we thought as we had torn it anyway, we might as well go on. That washing never came off.

'No human being,' Noël said, 'knows half the treasures hidden in this dark tarn.'

And we decided we would drag a bit more at that end, and work gradually round to under the dairy window where the milk-pan was. We could not see that part very well, because of the bushes that grow between the cracks of the stones where the house goes down into the moat. And opposite the dairy window the barn goes straight down into the moat too. It is like pictures of Venice; but you cannot get opposite the dairy window anyhow.

We got the sheet down again when we had tied the torn parts together in a bunch with string, and Oswald was just saying –

'Now then, my hearties, pull together, pull with a will! One, two, three,' when suddenly Dora dropped her bit of the sheet with a piercing shriek and cried out –

'Oh! it's all wormy at the bottom. I felt them wriggle.' And she was out of the water almost before the words were out of her mouth. The other girls all scuttled out too, and they let the sheet go in such a hurry that we had no time to steady ourselves, and one of us went right in, and the rest got wet up to our waistbands. The one who went right in was only H. O.; but Dora made an awful fuss and said it was our fault. We told her what we thought, and it ended in the girls going in with H. O. to change his things. We had some more goose-berries while they were gone. Dora was in an awful wax when she went away, but she is not of a sullen disposition though sometimes hasty, and when they all came back we saw it was all right, so we said –

'What shall we do now?'

Alice said, 'I don't think we need drag any more. It *is* wormy. I felt it when Dora did. And besides, the milk-pan is sticking a bit of itself out of the water. I saw it through the dairy window.'

'Couldn't we get it up with fish-hooks?' Noël said. But Alice explained that the dairy was now locked up and the key taken out.

So then Oswald said –

'Look here, we'll make a raft. We should have to do it some time, and we might as well do it now. I saw an old door in that corner stable that they don't use. You know. The one where they chop the wood.'

We got the door.

We had never made a raft, any of us, but the way to make rafts is better described in books, so we knew what to do.

We found some nice little tubs stuck up on the fence of the farm garden, and nobody seemed to want them for anything just then, so we took them. Denny had a box of tools someone had given him for his last birthday; they were rather rotten little things, but the gimlet worked all right, so we managed to make holes in the edges of the tubs and fasten them with string under the four corners of the old door. This took us a long time. Albert's uncle asked us at dinner what we had been playing at, and we said it was a secret, and it was nothing wrong. You see we wished to atone for Dicky's mistake before anything more was said. The house has no windows in the side that faces the orchard.

The rays of the afternoon sun were beaming along the orchard grass when at last we launched the raft. She floated out beyond reach with the last shove of the launching. But Oswald waded out and towed her back; he is not afraid of worms. Yet if he had known of the other things that were in the bottom of that moat he would have kept his boots on. So would the others, especially Dora, as you will see.

At last the gallant craft rode upon the waves. We manned her, though not up to our full strength, because if more than four got on the water came up too near our knees, and we feared she might founder if over-manned.

Daisy and Denny did not want to go on the raft, white mice that they were, so that was all right. And as H.O. had been wet through once he was not very keen. Alice promised Noël her best paint-brush if he'd give up and not go, because we knew well that the voyage was fraught with deep dangers, though the exact danger that lay in wait for us under the dairy window we never even thought of.

So we four elder ones got on the raft very carefully; and even then, every time we moved the water swished up over the raft and hid our feet. But I must say it was a jolly decent raft.

Dicky was captain, because it was his adventure. We had hop-poles from the hop-garden beyond the orchard to punt with. We made the girls stand together in the middle and hold on to each other to keep steady. Then we christened our gallant vessel. We called it the *Richard*, after Dicky, and also after the splendid admiral who used to eat wine-glasses and died after the Battle of the *Revenge* in Tennyson's poetry.

Then those on shore waved a fond adieu as well as they could with the dampness of their handkerchiefs, which we had had to use to dry our legs and feet when we put on our stockings for dinner, and slowly and stately the good ship moved away from shore, riding on the waves as though they were her native element.

We kept her going with the hop-poles, and we kept her steady in the same way, but we could not always keep her steady enough, and we could not always keep her in the wind's eye. That is to say, she went where we did not want, and once she bumped her corner against the barn wall, and all the crew had to sit down suddenly to avoid falling overboard into a watery grave. Of course then the waves swept her decks, and when we got up again we said that we should have to change completely before tea.

But we pressed on undaunted, and at last our saucy craft came into port, under the dairy window and there was the milk-pan, for whose sake we had endured such hardships and privations, standing up on its edge quite quietly.

The girls did not wait for orders from the captain, as they ought to have done; but they cried out, 'Oh, here it is!' and then both reached out to get it. Anyone who has pursued a naval career will see that of course the raft capsized. For a moment it felt like standing on the roof of the house, and the next moment the ship stood up on end and shot the whole crew into the dark waters.

We boys can swim all right. Oswald has swum three times across the Ladywell Swimming Baths at the shallow end, and Dicky is nearly as good; but just then we did not think of this; though, of course, if the water had been deep we should have.

As soon as Oswald could get the muddy water out of his eyes he opened them on a horrid scene.

Dicky was standing up to his shoulders in the inky waters; the raft had righted itself, and was drifting gently away towards the front of the house, where the bridge is, and Dora and Alice were rising from the deep,

A great noise of splashing, and 'Lord love the children!'

with their hair all plastered over their faces – like Venus in the Latin verses.

There was a great noise of splashing. And besides that a feminine voice, looking out of the dairy window and screaming –

'Lord love the children!'

It was Mrs Pettigrew. She disappeared at once, and we were sorry we were in such a situation that she would be able to get at Albert's uncle before we could. Afterwards we were not so sorry.

Before a word could be spoken about our desperate position Dora staggered a little in the water, and suddenly shrieked, 'Oh, my foot! oh, it's a shark! I know it is – or a crocodile!'

The others on the bank could hear her shrieking, but they could not see us properly; they did not know what was happening. Noël told me afterwards he never could care for that paint-brush.

Of course we knew it could not be a shark, but I thought of pike, which are large and very angry always, and I caught hold of Dora. She screamed without stopping. I shoved her along to where there was a ledge of brickwork, and shoved her up, till she could sit on it, then she got her foot out of the water, still screaming.

It was indeed terrible. The thing she thought was a shark came up with her foot, and it was a horrid, jagged, old meat-tin, and she had put her foot right into it. Oswald got it off, and directly he did so blood began to pour from the wounds. The tin edges had cut it in several spots. It was very pale blood, because her foot was wet, of course.

She stopped screaming, and turned green, and I thought she was going to faint, like Daisy did on the Jungle day.

Oswald held her up as well as he could, but it really was one of the least agreeable moments in his life. For the raft was gone, and she couldn't have waded back anyway, and we didn't know how deep the moat might be in other places.

But Mrs Pettigrew had not been idle. She is not a bad sort really.

Just as Oswald was wondering whether he could swim after the raft and get it back, a boat's nose shot out from under a dark archway a little further up under the house. It was the boathouse, and Albert's uncle had got the punt and took us back in it. When we had regained the dark arch where the boat lives we had to go up the cellar stairs. Dora had to be carried.

There was but little said to us that day. We were sent to bed – those who had not been on the raft the same as the others, for they owned up all right, and Albert's uncle is the soul of justice.

Next day but one was Saturday. Father gave us a talking to – with other things.

The worst was when Dora couldn't get her shoe on, so they sent for the doctor, and Dora had to lie down for ever so long. It was indeed poor luck.

When the doctor had gone Alice said to me –

'It *is* hard lines, but Dora's very jolly about it. Daisy's been telling her about how we should all go to her with our little joys and sorrows and things, and about the sweet influence from a sick bed that can be felt all over the house, like in *What Katy Did*, and Dora said she hoped she might prove a blessing to us all while she's laid up.'

Oswald said he hoped so, but he was not pleased. Because this sort of jaw was exactly the sort of thing he and Dicky didn't want to have happen.

The thing we got it hottest for was those little tubs

off the garden railings. They turned out to be butter-tubs that had been put out there 'to sweeten'.

But as Denny said, 'After the mud in that moat not all the perfumes of somewhere or other could make them fit to use for butter again.'

I own this was rather a bad business. Yet we did not do it to please ourselves, but because it was our duty. But that made no difference to our punishment when Father came down. I have known this mistake occur before.

CHAPTER 3

BILL'S TOMBSTONE

THERE were soldiers riding down the road, on horses
two and two. That is the horses were two and two, and
the men not. Because each man was riding one horse
and leading another. To exercise them. They came from
Chatham Barracks. We all drew up in a line outside
the churchyard wall, and saluted as they went by,
though we had not read *Toady Lion* then. We have
since. It is the only decent book I have ever read
written by *Toady Lion*'s author. The others are mere
piffle. But many people like them.

In *Sir Toady Lion* the officer salutes the child.

There was only a lieutenant with those soldiers, and
he did not salute me. He kissed his hand to the girls;
and a lot of the soldiers behind kissed theirs too. We
waved ours back.

Next day we made a Union Jack out of pocket-
handkerchiefs and part of a red flannel petticoat of the
White Mouse's, which she did not want just then, and
some blue ribbon we got at the village shop.

Then we watched for the soldiers, and after three
days they went by again, by twos and twos as before. It
was A1.

We waved our flag, and we shouted. We gave them
three cheers. Oswald can shout loudest. So as soon as
the first man was level with us (not the advance guard,
but the first of the battery) – he shouted –

'Three cheers for the Queen and the British Army!'

47

And then we waved the flag, and bellowed. Oswald stood on the wall to bellow better, and Denny waved the flag because he was a visitor, and so politeness made us let him enjoy the fat of whatever there was going.

The soldiers did not cheer that day; they only grinned and kissed their hands.

The next day we all got up as much like soldiers as we could. H. O. and Noël had tin swords, and we asked Albert's uncle to let us wear some of the real arms that are on the wall in the dining-room. And he said, 'Yes', if we would clean them up afterwards. But we jolly well cleaned them up first with Brooke's soap and brick dust and vinegar, and the knife polish (invented by the great and immortal Duke of Wellington in his spare time when he was not conquering Napoleon. Three cheers for our Iron Duke!), and with emery paper and wash leather and whitening. Oswald wore a cavalry sabre in its sheath. Alice and the Mouse had pistols in their belts, large old flint-locks, with bits of red flannel behind the flints. Denny had a naval cutlass, a very beautiful blade, and old enough to have been at Trafalgar. I hope it was. The others had French sword-bayonets that were used in the Franco-German war. They are very bright when you get them bright, but the sheaths are hard to polish. Each sword-bayonet has the name on the blade of the warrior who once wielded it. I wonder where they are now. Perhaps some of them died in the war. Poor chaps! But it is a very long time ago.

I should like to be a soldier. It is better than going to the best schools, and to Oxford afterwards, even if it is Balliol you go to. Oswald wanted to go to South Africa for a bugler, but father would not let him. And it is true that Oswald does not yet know how to bugle, though he can play the infantry 'advance', and the 'charge' and the 'halt' on a penny whistle. Alice taught them to him with the piano, out of the red book Father's cousin had when he was in the Fighting Fifth. Oswald cannot play the 'retire', and he would scorn to do so. But I suppose a bugler has to play what he is told, no matter how galling to the young boy's proud spirit.

The next day, being thoroughly armed, we put on everything red, white and blue that we could think of -- night-shirts are good for white, and you don't know what you can do with red socks and blue jerseys till you try -- and we waited by the churchyard wall for the soldiers. When the advance guard (or whatever you call it of artillery -- it's that for infantry, I know) came by, we got ready, and when the first man of the first battery was level with us Oswald played on his penny whistle the 'advance' and the 'charge' -- and then shouted --

'Three cheers for the Queen and the British Army!'

This time they had the guns with them. And every man of the battery cheered too. It was glorious. It made you tremble all over. The girls said it made them want to cry -- but no boy would own to this, even if it were true. It is babyish to cry. But it was glorious, and Oswald felt differently to what he ever did before.

Then suddenly the officer in front said, 'Battery! Halt!' and all the soldiers pulled their horses up, and the great guns stopped too. Then the officer said, 'Sit at ease,' and something else, and the sergeant repeated it, and some of the men got off their horses and lit their pipes, and some sat down on the grass edge of the road, holding their horses' bridles.

We could see all the arms and accoutrements as plain as plain.

Then the officer came up to us. We were all standing on the wall that day, except Dora, who had to sit, because her foot was bad, but we let her have the three-edged rapier to wear, and the blunderbuss to hold as well – it has a brass mouth and is like in Mr Caldecott's pictures.

He was a beautiful man the officer. Like a Viking. Very tall and fair, with moustaches very long, and bright blue eyes.

He said –

'Good morning.'

So did we.

Then he said –

'You seem to be a military lot.'

We said we wished we were.

'And patriotic,' said he.

Alice said she should jolly well think so.

Then he said he had noticed us there for several days, and he had halted the battery because he thought we might like to look at the guns.

Alas! there are but too few grown-up people so far-seeing and thoughtful as this brave and distinguished officer.

We said, 'Oh, yes', and then we got off the wall, and that good and noble man showed us the string that moves the detonator and the breech-block (when you take it out and carry it away the gun is in vain to the enemy, even if he takes it); and he let us look down the gun to see the rifling, all clean and shiny; and he showed us the ammunition boxes, but there was nothing in them. He also told us how the gun was unlimbered (this means separating the gun from the ammunition carriage), and how quick it could be done – but he did not make the men do this then, because they were resting. There were six guns. Each had painted on the carriage, in white letters, 15 Pr., which the captain told us meant fifteen-pounder.

'I should have thought the gun weighed more than fifteen pounds,' Dora said. 'It would if it was beef, but I suppose wood and gun are lighter.'

And the officer explained to her very kindly and patiently that 15 Pr. meant the gun could throw a *shell* weighing fifteen pounds.

When we had told him how jolly it was to see the soldiers go by so often, he said –

'You won't see us many more times. We're ordered to the front; and we sail on Tuesday week; and the guns will be painted mud-colour, and the men will wear mud-colour too, and so shall I.'

The men looked very nice, though they were not wearing their busbies, but only Tommy caps, put on all sorts of ways.

We were very sorry they were going, but Oswald, as well as others, looked with envy on those who would soon be allowed – being grown up, and no nonsense about your education – to go and fight for their Queen and country.

Then suddenly Alice whispered to Oswald, and he said –

'All right; but tell him yourself.'

So Alice said to the captain –

'Will you stop next time you pass?'

He said, 'I'm afraid I can't promise that.'

Alice said, 'You might; there's a particular reason.'

He said, 'What?' which was a natural remark; not rude, as it is with children.

Alice said –

'We want to give the soldiers a keepsake and will write to ask my father. He is very well off just now. Look here – if we're not on the wall when you come by, don't stop; but if we are, *please*, PLEASE do!'

The officer pulled his moustache and looked as if he

He showed us all the cuts, thrusts, and guards

did not quite know; but at last he said 'Yes', and we were very glad, though but Alice and Oswald knew the dark but pleasant scheme at present fermenting in their youthful nuts.

The captain talked a lot to us. At last Noël said –

'I think you are like Diarmid of the Golden Collar. But I should like to see your sword out, and shining in the sun like burnished silver.'

The captain laughed and grasped the hilt of his good blade. But Oswald said hurriedly –

'Don't. Not yet. We shan't ever have a chance like this. If you'd only show us the pursuing practice! Albert's uncle knows it; but he only does it on an arm-chair, because he hasn't a horse.'

And that brave and swagger captain did really do it. He rode his horse right into our gate when we opened it, and showed us all the cuts, thrusts, and guards. There are four of each kind. It was splendid. The morning sun shone on his flashing blade, and his good steed stood with all its legs far apart and stiff on the lawn. Then we opened the paddock gate, and he did it again, while the horse galloped as if upon the bloody battlefield among the fierce foes of his native land, and this was far more ripping still.

Then we thanked him very much, and he went away, taking his men with him. And the guns of course.

Then we wrote to my father, and he said 'Yes', as we knew he would, and next time the soldiers came by – but they had no guns this time, only the captive Arabs of the desert – we had the keepsakes ready in a wheelbarrow, and we were on the churchyard wall.

And the bold captain called an immediate halt.

Then the girls had the splendid honour and pleasure of giving a pipe and four whole ounces of tobacco to each soldier.

Then we shook hands with the captain, and the sergeant and the corporals, and the girls kissed the captain – I can't think why girls will kiss everybody – and we all cheered for the Queen.

It was grand. And I wish my father had been there

to see how much you can do with £12 if you order the things from the Stores.

We have never seen those brave soldiers again.

I have told you all this to show you how we got so keen about soldiers, and why we sought to aid and abet the poor widow at the white cottage in her desolate and oppressedness.

Her name was Simpkins, and her cottage was just beyond the churchyard, on the other side from our house. On the different military occasions which I have remarked upon this widow woman stood at her garden gate and looked on. And after the cheering she rubbed her eyes with her apron. Alice noticed this slight but signifying action.

We feel quite sure Mrs Simpkins liked soldiers, and so we felt friendly to her. But when we tried to talk to her she would not. She told us to go along with us, do, and not bother her. And Oswald, with his usual delicacy and good breeding, made the others do as she said.

But we were not to be thus repulsed with impunity. We made complete but cautious inquiries, and found out that the reason she cried when she saw soldiers was that she had only one son, a boy. He was twenty-two, and he had gone to the War last April. So that she thought of him when she saw the soldiers, and that was why she cried. Because when your son is at the wars you always think he is being killed. I don't know why. A great many of them are not. If I had a son at the wars I should never think he was dead till I heard he was, and perhaps not then, considering everything.

After we had found this out we held a council.

Dora said, 'We must do something for the soldier's widowed mother.'

We all agreed, but added 'What?'

Alice said, 'The gift of money might be deemed an insult by that proud, patriotic spirit. Besides, we haven't more than eighteenpence among us.'

We had put what we had to father's £12 to buy the baccy and pipes.

The Mouse then said, 'Couldn't we make her a flannel petticoat and leave it without a word upon her doorstep?'

But everyone said, 'Flannel petticoats in this weather?' so that was no go.

Noël said he would write her a poem, but Oswald had a deep, inward feeling that Mrs Simpkins would not understand poetry. Many people do not.

H. O. said, 'Why not sing "Rule Britannia" under her window after she had gone to bed, like waits,' but no one else thought so.

Denny thought we might get up a subscription for her among the wealthy and affluent, but we said again that we knew money would be no balm to the haughty mother of a brave British soldier.

'What we want,' Alice said, 'is something that will be a good deal of trouble to us and some good to her.'

'A little help is worth a deal of poetry,' said Denny. I should not have said that myself. Noël did look sick.

'What *does* she do that we can help in?' Dora asked. 'Besides, she won't let us help.'

H. O. said, 'She does nothing but work in the garden. At least if she does anything inside you can't see it, because she keeps the door shut.'

Then at once we saw. And we agreed to get up the very next day, ere yet the rosy dawn had flushed the east, and have a go at Mrs Simpkins's garden.

We got up. We really did. But too often when you mean to, overnight, it seems so silly to do it when you come to waking in the dewy morn. We crept downstairs with our boots in our hands. Denny is rather unlucky, though a most careful boy. It was he who dropped his boot, and it went blundering down the stairs, echoing like thunderbolts, and waking up Albert's uncle. But when we explained to him that we were going to do some gardening he let us, and went back to bed.

Everything is very pretty and different in the early morning, before people are up. I have been told this is because the shadows go a different way from what they do in the awake part of the day. But I don't know. Noël says the fairies have just finished tidying up then. Anyhow it all feels quite otherwise.

We put on our boots in the porch, and we got our gardening tools and we went down to the white cottage. It is a nice cottage, with a thatched roof, like in the drawing copies you get at girls' schools, and you do the thatch – if you can – with a B.B. pencil. If you cannot, you just leave it. It looks just as well, somehow, when it is mounted and framed.

We looked at the garden. It was very neat. Only one patch was coming up thick with weeds. I could see groundsel and chickweed, and others that I did not know. We set to work with a will. We used all our tools – spades, forks, hoes, and rakes – and Dora worked with the trowel, sitting down, because her foot was hurt. We cleared the weedy patch beautifully, scraping off all the nasty weeds and leaving the nice clean brown dirt. We worked as hard as ever we could. And we were happy, because it was unselfish toil, and no one thought then of putting it in the Book of Golden Deeds, where we had agreed to write down our virtuous actions and the good doings of each other, when we happen to notice them.

We had just done, and we were looking at the beautiful production of our honest labour, when the cottage door burst open, and the soldier's widowed mother came out like a wild tornado, and her eyes looked like upas trees – death to the beholder.

'You wicked, meddlesome, nasty children!' she said, 'ain't you got enough of your own good ground to runch up and spoil, but you must come into *my* little lot?'

Some of us we were deeply alarmed, but we stood firm.

'We have only been weeding your garden,' Dora said; 'we wanted to do something to help you.'

'Dratted little busybodies,' she said. It was indeed hard, but everyone in Kent says 'dratted' when they are cross. 'It's my turnips,' she went on, 'you've hoed up, and my cabbages. My turnips that my boy sowed afore he went. There, get along with you do, afore I come at you with my broom-handle.'

She did come at us with her broom-handle as she spoke, and even the boldest turned and fled. Oswald was even the boldest.

'They looked like weeds right enough,' he said.

And Dicky said, 'It all comes of trying to do golden deeds.'

This was when we were out in the road.

As we went along, in a silence full of gloomy remorse, we met the postman. He said –

'Here's the letters for the Moat,' and passed on hastily. He was a bit late.

When we came to look through the letters, which were nearly all for Albert's uncle, we found there was a postcard that had got stuck in a magazine wrapper. Alice pulled it out. It was addressed to Mrs Simpkins. We honourably only looked at the address, although it is allowed by the rules of honourableness to read postcards that come to your house if you like, even if they are not for you.

After a heated discussion, Alice and Oswald said they were not afraid, whoever was, and they retraced their steps, Alice holding the postcard right way up, so that we should not look at the lettery part of it, but only the address.

With quickly-beating heart, but outwardly unmoved, they walked up to the white cottage door.

It opened with a bang when we knocked.

'Well?' Mrs Simpkins said, and I think she said it what people in books call 'sourly'.

Oswald said, 'We are very, very sorry we spoiled your turnips, and we will ask my father to try and make it up to you some other way.'

She muttered something about not wanting to be beholden to anybody.

'We came back,' Oswald went on, with his always unruffled politeness, 'because the postman gave us a postcard in mistake with our letters, and it is addressed to you.'

'We haven't read it,' Alice said quickly. I think she needn't have said that. Of course we hadn't. But perhaps girls know better than we do what women are likely to think you capable of.

The soldier's mother took the postcard (she snatched it really, but 'took' is a kinder word, considering everything) and she looked at the address a long time. Then she turned it over and read what was on the back. Then she drew her breath in as far as it would go, and caught hold of the door-post. Her face got awful. It was like the wax face of a dead king I saw once at Madame Tussaud's.

Alice understood. She caught hold of the soldier's mother's hand and said –

'Oh, *no* – it's *not* your boy Bill!'

And the woman said nothing, but shoved the postcard into Alice's hand, and we both read it – and it *was* her boy Bill.

Alice gave her back the card. She had held on to the woman's hand all the time, and now she squeezed the hand, and held it against her face. But she could not say a word because she was crying so. The soldier's mother took the card again and she pushed Alice away, but it was not an unkind push, and she went in and shut the door; and as Alice and Oswald went down the road Oswald looked back, and one of the windows of the cottage had a white blind. Afterwards the other windows had too. There were no blinds really to the cottage. It was aprons and things she had pinned up.

Alice cried most of the morning, and so did the other girls. We wanted to do something for the soldier's mother, but you can do nothing when people's sons are shot. It is the most dreadful thing to want to do something for people who are unhappy, and not to know what to do.

It was Noël who thought of what we *could* do at last.

He said, 'I suppose they don't put up tombstones to soldiers when they die in war. But there – I mean —'

Oswald said, 'Of course not.'

Noël said, 'I daresay you'll think it's silly, but I don't care. Don't you think she'd like it, if we put one up to *him*? Not in the churchyard, of course, because we shouldn't be let, but in our garden, just where it joins on to the churchyard?'

And we all thought it was a first-rate idea.

This is what we meant to put on the tombstone:

'Here lies

BILL SIMPKINS

Who died fighting for Queen and Country.'

———

59

> '*A faithful son,*
> *A son so dear,*
> *A soldier brave*
> *Lies buried here.*'

Then we remembered that poor brave Bill was really buried far away in the Southern hemisphere, if at all.

So we altered it to –

> '*A soldier brave*
> *We weep for here.*'

Then we looked out a nice flagstone in the stable-yard, and we got a cold chisel out of the Dentist's tool-box, and began.

But stone-cutting is difficult and dangerous work.

Oswald went at it a bit, but he chipped his thumb, and it bled so he had to chuck it. Then Dicky tried, and then Denny, but Dicky hammered his finger, and Denny took all day over every stroke, so that by tea-time we had only done the H, and about half the E – and the E was awfully crooked. Oswald chipped his thumb over the H.

We looked at it the next morning, and even the most sanguinary of us saw that it was a hopeless task.

Then Denny said, 'Why not wood and paint?' and he showed us how. We got a board and two stumps from the carpenter's in the village, and we painted it all white, and when that was dry Denny did the words on it.

It was something like this:

> 'IN MEMORY OF
> BILL SIMPKINS
> DEAD FOR QUEEN AND COUNTRY.
> HONOUR TO HIS NAME AND ALL
> OTHER BRAVE SOLDIERS.'

We could not get in what we meant to at first, so we had to give up the poetry.

We fixed it up when it was dry. We had to dig jolly deep to get the posts to stand up, but the gardener helped us.

Then the girls made wreaths of white flowers, roses and canterbury bells, and lilies and pinks, and sweet-peas and daisies, and put them over the posts. And I think if Bill Simpkins had known how sorry we were, he would have been glad. Oswald only hopes if *he* falls on the wild battlefield, which is his highest ambition, that somebody will be as sorry about him as he was about Bill, that's all!

When all was done, and what flowers there were over from the wreaths scattered under the tombstone between the posts, we wrote a letter to Mrs Simpkins, and said –

DEAR MRS SIMPKINS – We are very, very sorry about the turnips and things, and we beg your pardon humbly. We have put up a tombstone to your brave son.

And we signed our names.

Alice took the letter.

The soldier's mother read it, and said something about our oughting to know better than to make fun of people's troubles with our tombstones and tomfoolery.

Alice told me she could not help crying.

She said –

'It's *not!* it's NOT! Dear, *dear* Mrs Simpkins, do come with me and see! You don't know how sorry we are about Bill. Do come and see. We can go through the churchyard, and the others have all gone in, so as to leave it quiet for you. Do come.'

And Mrs Simpkins did. And when she read what we had put up, and Alice told her the verse we had not had room for, she leant against the wall by the grave – I mean the tombstone – and Alice hugged her, and they both cried bitterly. The poor soldier's mother was very, very pleased, and she forgave us about the turnips, and we were friends after that, but she always liked Alice the best. A great many people do, somehow.

After that we used to put fresh flowers every day on Bill's tombstone, and I do believe his mother *was* pleased, though she got us to move it away from the churchyard edge and put it in a corner of our garden under a laburnum, where people could not see it from the church. But you could from the road, though I think she thought you couldn't. She came every day to look at the new wreaths. When the white flowers gave out we put coloured, and she liked it just as well.

About a fortnight after the erecting of the tombstone the girls were putting fresh wreaths on it when a soldier in a red coat came down the road, and he stopped and looked at us. He walked with a stick, and he had a bundle in a blue cotton handkerchief, and one arm in a sling.

And he looked again, and he came nearer, and he leaned on the wall, so that he could read the black printing on the white paint.

And he grinned all over his face, and he said –

'Well, I *am* blessed!'

And he read it all out in a sort of half whisper, and when he came to the end, where it says, 'and all such brave soldiers', he said –

'Well, I really *am*!' I suppose he meant he really was blessed.

Oswald thought it was like the soldier's cheek, so he said –

'I daresay you aren't so very blessed as you think. What's it to do with you, anyway, eh, Tommy?'

Of course Oswald knew from Kipling that an infantry soldier is called that. The soldier said –

'Tommy yourself, young man. That's *me*!' and he pointed to the tombstone.

We stood rooted to the spot. Alice spoke first.

'Then you're Bill, and you're not dead,' she said. 'Oh, Bill, I am so glad! Do let *me* tell your mother.'

She started running, and so did we all. Bill had to go slowly because of his leg, but I tell you he went as fast as ever he could.

We all hammered at the soldier's mother's door, and shouted –

'Come out! come out!' and when she opened the door we were going to speak, but she pushed us away, and went tearing down the garden path like winking. I never saw a grown-up woman run like it, because she saw Bill coming.

She met him at the gate, running right into him, and caught hold of him, and she cried much more than when she thought he was dead.

And we all shook his hand and said how glad we were.

The soldier's mother kept hold of him with both hands, and I couldn't help looking at her face. It was like wax that had been painted on both pink cheeks, and the eyes shining like candles. And when we had all said how glad we were, she said –

'Thank the dear Lord for His mercies,' and she took her boy Bill into the cottage and shut the door.

We went home and chopped up the tombstone with the wood-axe and had a blazing big bonfire, and cheered till we could hardly speak.

The postcard was a mistake; he was only missing. There was a pipe and a whole pound of tobacco left over from our keepsake to the other soldiers. We gave it to Bill. Father is going to have him for under-gardener when his wounds get well. He'll always be a bit lame, so he cannot fight any more.

CHAPTER 4

THE TOWER OF MYSTERY

It was very rough on Dora having her foot bad, but we took it in turns to stay in with her, and she was very decent about it. Daisy was most with her. I do not dislike Daisy, but I wish she had been taught how to play. Because Dora is rather like that naturally, and sometimes I have thought that Daisy makes her worse.

I talked to Albert's uncle about it one day, when the others had gone to church, and I did not go because of ear-ache, and he said it came from reading the wrong sort of books partly – she has read *Ministering Children*, and *Anna Ross, or The Orphan of Waterloo*, and *Ready Work for Willing Hands*, and *Elsie, or Like a Little Candle*, and even a horrid little blue book about the something or other of Little Sins. After this conversation Oswald took care she had plenty of the right sort of books to read, and he was surprised and pleased when she got up early one morning to finish *Monte Cristo*. Oswald felt that he was really being useful to a suffering fellow-creature when he gave Daisy books that were not all about being good.

A few days after Dora was laid up, Alice called a council of the Wouldbegoods, and Oswald and Dicky attended with darkly-clouded brows. Alice had the minute-book, which was an exercise-book that had not much written in it. She had begun at the other end. I hate doing that myself, because there is so little room at the top compared with right way up.

Dora and a sofa had been carried out on to the lawn, and we were on the grass. It was very hot and dry. We had sherbet. Alice read:

' "Society of the Wouldbegoods.
' "We have not done much. Dicky mended a window, and we got the milk-pan out of the moat that dropped through where he mended it. Dora, Oswald, Dicky and me got upset in the moat. This was not goodness. Dora's foot was hurt. We hope to do better next time." '

Then came Noël's poem:

> '*We are the Wouldbegoods Society,*
> *We are not good yet, but we mean to try,*
> *And if we try, and if we don't succeed,*
> *It must mean we are very bad indeed.*'

This sounded so much righter than Noël's poetry generally does, that Oswald said so, and Noël explained that Denny had helped him.

'He seems to know the right length for lines of poetry. I suppose it comes of learning so much at school,' Noël said.

Then Oswald proposed that anybody should be allowed to write in the book if they found out anything good that anyone else had done, but not things that were public acts; and nobody was to write about themselves, or anything other people told them, only what they found out.

After a brief jaw the others agreed, and Oswald felt, not for the first time in his young life, that he would have made a good diplomatic hero to carry despatches and outwit the other side. For now he had put it out of the minute-book's power to be the kind of thing readers of *Ministering Children* would have wished.

'And if anyone tells other people any good thing he's done he is to go to Coventry for the rest of the day.' And Denny remarked, 'We shall do good by stealth, and blush to find it shame.'

After that nothing was written in the book for some time. I looked about, and so did the others, but I never caught anyone in the act of doing anything extra; though several of the others have told me since of things they did at this time, and really wondered nobody had noticed.

I think I said before that when you tell a story you cannot tell everything. It would be silly to do it. Because ordinary kinds of play are dull to read about; and the only other thing is meals, and to dwell on what you eat is greedy and not like a hero at all. A hero is always contented with a venison pasty and a horn of sack. All the same, the meals *were* very interesting; with things you do not get at home – Lent pies with custard and currants in them, sausage rolls and flede cakes, and raisin cakes and apple turnovers, and honeycomb and syllabubs, besides as much new milk as you cared about, and cream now and then, and cheese always on the table for tea. Father told Mrs Pettigrew to get what meals she liked, and she got these strange but attractive foods.

In a story about Wouldbegoods it is not proper to tell of times when only some of us were naughty, so I will pass lightly over the time when Noël got up the kitchen chimney and brought three bricks and an old starling's nest and about a ton of soot down with him when he fell. They never use the big chimney in the summer, but cook in the wash-house. Nor do I wish to dwell on what H. O. did when he went into the dairy. I do not know what his motive was. But Mrs Pettigrew said *she* knew; and she locked him in, and said if it was cream he wanted he should have enough, and she wouldn't let him out till tea-time. The cat had also got into the dairy for some reason of her own, and when H. O. was tired of whatever he went in for he poured all the milk into the churn and tried to teach the cat to swim in it. He must have been desperate. The cat did not even try to learn, and H. O. had the scars on his hands for weeks. I do not wish to tell tales of H. O., for he is very young, and whatever he does he always catches it for; but I will just allude to our being told not to eat the greengages in the garden. And we did not. And whatever H. O. did was Noël's fault – for Noël told H. O. that greengages would grow again all right if you did not bite as far as the stone, just as wounds are not mortal except when you are pierced through the heart. So the two of them bit bites out of every green-gage they could reach. And of course the pieces did not grow again.

Oswald did not do things like these, but then he is older than his brothers. The only thing he did just about then was making a booby-trap for Mrs Pettigrew when she had locked H. O. up in the dairy, and un-fortunately it was the day she was going out in her best things, and part of the trap was a can of water. Oswald was not willingly vicious; it was but a light and thought-less act which he had every reason to be sorry for after-wards. And he is sorry even without those reasons, because he knows it is ungentlemanly to play tricks on women.

I remember Mother telling Dora and me when we were little that you ought to be very kind and polite to servants, because they have to work very hard, and do not have so many good times as we do. I used to think about Mother more at the Moat House than I did at Blackheath, especially in the garden. She was very fond of flowers, and she used to tell us about the big garden where she used to live; and I remember Dora and I helped her to plant seeds. But it is no use wishing. She would have liked that garden, though.

The girls and the white mice did not do anything boldly wicked – though of course they used to borrow Mrs Pettigrew's needles, which made her very nasty. Needles that are borrowed might just as well be stolen. But I say no more.

I have only told you these things to show the kind of events which occurred on the days I don't tell you about. On the whole, we had an excellent time.

It was on the day we had the pillow-fight that we went for the long walk. Not the Pilgrimage – that is another story. We did not mean to have a pillow-fight. It is not usual to have them after breakfast, but Oswald had come up to get his knife out of the pocket of his Etons, to cut some wire we were making rabbit snares of. It is a very good knife, with a file in it, as well as a corkscrew and other things – and he did not come down at once, because he was detained by having to make an apple-pie bed for Dicky. Dicky came up after him to see what we was up to, and when he did see he buzzed a pillow at Oswald, and the fight began. The others, hearing the noise of battle from afar, hastened to the field of action, all except Dora, who couldn't because of being laid up with her foot, and Daisy, because she is a little afraid of us still, when we are all together. She thinks we are rough. This comes of having only one brother.

Well, the fight was a very fine one. Alice backed me up, and Noël and H. O. backed Dicky, and Denny heaved a pillow or two; but he cannot shy straight, so I don't know which side he was on.

And just as the battle raged most fiercely, Mrs Pettigrew came in and snatched the pillows away, and shook those of the warriors who were small enough for it. *She* was rough if you like. She also used language I should have thought she would be above. She said, 'Drat you!' and 'Drabbit you!' The last is a thing I have never heard said before. She said –

'There's no peace of your life with you children. Drat your antics! And that poor, dear, patient gentleman right underneath, with his headache and his handwriting: and you rampaging about over his head like young bull-calves. I wonder you haven't more sense, a great girl like you.'

She said this to Alice, and Alice answered gently, as we are told to do –

'I really am awfully sorry; we forgot about the headache. Don't be cross, Mrs Pettigrew; we didn't mean to; we didn't think.'

'You never do,' she said, and her voice, though grumpy, was no longer violent. 'Why on earth you can't take yourselves off for the day I don't know.'

We all said, 'But may we?'

She said, 'Of course you may. Now put on your boots and go for a good long walk. And I'll tell you what – I'll put you up a snack, and you can have an egg to your tea to make up for missing your dinner. Now don't go clattering about the stairs and passages, there's good children. See if you can't be quiet this once, and give the good gentleman a chance with his copying.'

She went off. Her bark is worse than her bite. She does not understand anything about writing books, though. She thinks Albert's uncle copies things out of printed books, when he is really writing new ones. I wonder how she thinks printed books get made first of all. Many servants are like this.

She gave us the 'snack' in a basket, and sixpence to

buy milk with. She said any of the farms would let us
have it, only most likely it would be skim. We thanked
her politely, and she hurried us out of the front door as
if we'd been chickens on a pansy bed.

(I did not know till after I had left the farm gate
open, and the hens had got into the garden, that these
feathered bipeds display a great partiality for the young
buds of plants of the genus *viola*, to which they are
extremely destructive. I was told that by the gardener.
I looked it up in the gardening book afterwards to be
sure he was right. You do learn a lot of things in the
country.)

We went through the garden as far as the church,
and then we rested a bit in the porch, and just looked
into the basket to see what the 'snack' was. It proved to
be sausage rolls and queen cakes, and a Lent pie in a
round tin dish, and some hard-boiled eggs, and some
apples. We all ate the apples at once, so as not to have to
carry them about with us. The churchyard smells
awfully good. It is the wild thyme that grows on the
graves. This is another thing we did not know before
we came into the country.

Then the door of the church tower was ajar, and we
all went up; it had always been locked before when we
had tried it.

We saw the ringers' loft where the ends of the bell-
ropes hang down with long, furry handles to them like
great caterpillars, some red, and some blue and white,
but we did not pull them. And then we went up to where
the bells are, very big and dusty among large dirty
beams; and four windows with no glass, only shutters
like Venetian blinds, but they won't pull up. There
were heaps of straws and sticks on the window ledges.
We think they were owls' nests, but we did not see any
owls.

Then the tower stairs got very narrow and dark, and we went on up, and we came to a door and opened it suddenly, and it was like being hit in the face, the light was so sudden. And there we were on the top of the tower, which is flat, and people have cut their names on it, and a turret at one corner, and a low wall all round, up and down, like castle battlements. And we looked down and saw the roof of the church, and the leads, and the churchyard, and our garden, and the Moat House, and the farm, and Mrs Simpkins's cottage, looking very small, and other farms looking like toy things out of boxes, and we saw corn-fields and meadows and pastures. A pasture is not the same thing as a meadow, whatever you may think. And we saw the tops of trees and hedges, looking like the map of the United States, and villages, and a tower that did not look very far away standing by itself on the top of a hill.

Alice pointed to it, and said –

'What's that?'

'It's not a church,' said Noël, 'because there's no churchyard. Perhaps it's a tower of mystery that covers the entrance to a subterranean vault with treasure in it.'

Dicky said, 'Subterranean fiddlestick!' and 'A water-works, more likely.'

Alice thought perhaps it was a ruined castle, and the rest of its crumbling walls were concealed by ivy, the growth of years.

Oswald could not make his mind up what it was, so he said, 'Let's go and see! We may as well go there as anywhere.'

So we got down out of the church tower and dusted ourselves, and set out.

The Tower of Mystery showed quite plainly from the road, now that we knew where to look for it, because it was on the top of a hill. We began to walk. But the tower did not seem to get any nearer. And it was very hot.

So we sat down in a meadow where there was a stream in the ditch and ate the 'snack'. We drank the pure water from the brook out of our hands, because there was no farm to get milk at just there, and it was too much fag to look for one – and, besides, we thought we might as well save the sixpence.

Then we started again, and still the tower looked as far off as ever. Denny began to drag his feet, though he had brought a walking-stick which none of the rest of us had, and said –

'I wish a cart would come along. We might get a lift.'

He knew all about getting lifts, of course, from having been in the country before. He is not quite the white mouse we took him for at first. Of course when you live in Lewisham or Blackheath you learn other things. If you asked for a lift in Lewisham, High Street, your only reply would be jeers. We sat down on a heap of stones, and decided that we would ask for a lift from the next cart, whichever way it was going. It was while we were waiting that Oswald found out about plantain seeds being good to eat.

When the sound of wheels came we remarked with joy that the cart was going towards the Tower of Mystery. It was a cart a man was going to fetch a pig home in. Denny said –

'I say, you might give us a lift. Will you?'

The man who was going for the pig said –

'What, all that little lot?' but he winked at Alice, and we saw that he meant to aid us on our way. So we climbed up, and he whipped up the horse and asked us where we were going. He was a kindly old man, with a face like a walnut shell, and white hair and beard like a jack-in-the-box.

'We want to get to the tower,' Alice said. 'Is it a ruin, or not?'

'It ain't no ruin,' the man said; 'no fear of that! The man wot built it he left so much a year to be spent on repairing of it! Money that might have put bread in honest folks' mouths.'

We asked was it a church then, or not.

'Church?' he said. 'Not it. It's more of a tombstone, from all I can make out. They do say there was a curse on him that built it, and he wasn't to rest in earth or sea. So he's buried half-way up the tower – if you can call it buried.'

'Can you go up it?' Oswald asked.

'Lord love you! yes; a fine view from the top they say. I've never been up myself, though I've lived in sight of it, boy and man, these sixty-three years come harvest.'

Alice asked whether you had to go past the dead and buried person to get to the top of the tower, and could you see the coffin.

'No, no,' the man said; 'that's all hid away behind a slab of stone, that is, with reading on it. You've no call to be afraid, missy. It's daylight all the way up. But I wouldn't go there after dark, so I wouldn't. It's always open, day and night, and they say tramps sleep there now and again. Anyone who likes can sleep there, but it wouldn't be me.'

We thought that it would not be us either, but we wanted to go more than ever, especially when the man said –

'My own great-uncle of the mother's side, he was one of the masons that set up the stone slab. Before then it was thick glass, and you could see the dead man lying inside, as he'd left it in his will. He was lying there in a glass coffin with his best clothes – blue satin and silver, my uncle said, such as was all the go in his day, with his wig on, and his sword beside him, what he used to wear. My uncle said his hair had grown out from under his wig, and his beard was down to the toes of him. My uncle he always upheld that that dead man was no deader than you and me, but was in a sort of fit, a transit, I think they call it, and looked for him to waken into life again some day. But the doctor said not. It was only something done to him like Pharaoh in the Bible afore he was buried.'

Alice whispered to Oswald that we should be late for tea, and wouldn't it be better to go back now directly. But he said –

'If you're afraid, say so; and you needn't come in anyway – but I'm going on.'

The man who was going for the pig put us down at a gate quite near the tower – at least it looked so until we began to walk again. We thanked him, and he said –

'Quite welcome,' and drove off.

We were rather quiet going through the wood. What we had heard made us very anxious to see the tower – all except Alice, who would keep talking about tea, though not a greedy girl by nature. None of the others encouraged her, but Oswald thought himself that we had better be home before dark.

As we went up the path through the wood we saw a poor wayfarer with dusty bare feet sitting on the bank.

He stopped us and said he was a sailor, and asked for a trifle to help him to get back to his ship.

I did not like the look of him much myself, but Alice said, 'Oh, the poor man, do let's help him, Oswald.' So we held a hurried council, and decided to give him the milk sixpence. Oswald had it in his purse, and he had to empty the purse into his hand to find the sixpence, for that was not all the money he had, by any means. Noël said afterwards that he saw the wayfarer's eyes fastened greedily upon the shining pieces as Oswald returned them to his purse. Oswald has to own that he purposely let the man see that he had more money, so that the man might not feel shy about accepting so large a sum as sixpence.

The man blessed our kind hearts and we went on.

The sun was shining very brightly, and the Tower of Mystery did not look at all like a tomb when we got to it. The bottom storey was on arches, all open, and ferns and things grew underneath. There was a round stone stair going up in the middle. Alice began to gather ferns while we went up, but when we had called out to her that it was as the pig-man had said, and daylight all the way up, she said –

'All right. I'm not afraid. I'm only afraid of being late home,' and came up after us. And perhaps, though not downright manly truthfulness, this was as much as you could expect from a girl.

There were holes in the little tower of the staircase to let light in. At the top of it was a thick door with iron bolts. We shot these back, and it was not fear but caution that made Oswald push open the door so very slowly and carefully.

Because, of course, a stray dog or cat might have got shut up there by accident, and it would have startled Alice very much if it had jumped out on us.

When the door was opened we saw that there was no such thing. It was a room with eight sides. Denny says it is the shape called octagenarian; because a man named Octagius invented it. There were eight large arched windows with no glass, only stone-work, like in churches. The room was full of sunshine, and you could see the blue sky through the windows, but nothing else, because they were so high up It was so bright we began to think the pig-man had been kidding us. Under one of the windows was a door. We went through, and there was a little passage and then a turret-twisting stair, like in the church, but quite light with windows. When we had gone some way up this, we came to a sort of landing, and there was a block of stone let into the wall – polished – Denny said it was Aberdeen graphite, with gold letters cut in it. It said –

'Here lies the body of Mr Richard Ravenal
Born 1720. Died 1779.'

and a verse of poetry:

> 'Here lie I, between earth and sky,
> Think upon me, dear passers-by,
> And you who do my tombstone see
> Be kind to say a prayer for me.'

'How horrid!' Alice said. 'Do let's get home.'

'We may as well go to the top,' Dicky said, 'just to say we've been.'

And Alice is no funk – so she agreed; though I could see she did not like it.

Up at the top it was like the top of the church tower, only octagenarian in shape, instead of square.

Alice got all right there; because you cannot think much about ghosts and nonsense when the sun is shining bang down on you at four o'clock in the afternoon, and you can see red farm-roofs between the trees, and the safe white roads, with people in carts like black ants crawling.

It was very jolly, but we felt we ought to be getting

back, because tea is at five, and we could not hope to find lifts both ways.

So we started to go down. Dicky went first, then Oswald, then Alice – and H. O. had just stumbled over the top step and saved himself by Alice's back, which nearly upset Oswald and Dicky, when the hearts of all stood still, and then went on by leaps and bounds, like the good work in missionary magazines.

For, down below us, in the tower where the man whose beard grew down to his toes after he was dead was buried, there was a noise – a loud noise. And it was like a door being banged and bolts fastened. We tumbled over each other to get back into the open sunshine on the top of the tower, and Alice's hand got jammed between the edge of the doorway and H. O.'s boot; it was bruised black and blue, and another part bled, but she did not notice it till long after.

We looked at each other, and Oswald said in a firm voice (at least, I hope it was) –

'What was that?'

'He *has* waked up,' Alice said. 'Oh, I know he has. Of course there is a door for him to get out by when he wakes. He'll come up here. I know he will.'

Dicky said, and his voice was not at all firm (I noticed that at the time), 'It doesn't matter, if he's *alive*.'

'Unless he's come to life a raving lunatic,' Noël said, and we all stood with our eyes on the doorway of the turret – and held our breath to hear.

But there was no more noise.

Then Oswald said – and nobody ever put it in the Golden Deed book, though they own that it was brave and noble of him – he said –

'Perhaps it was only the wind blowing one of the doors to. I'll go down and see, if you will, Dick.'

Dicky only said –

77

'*I'm not afraid. I'll go and see*'

'The wind doesn't shoot bolts.'

'A bolt from the blue,' said Denny to himself, looking up at the sky. His father is a sub-editor. He had gone very red, and he was holding on to Alice's hand. Suddenly he stood up quite straight and said –

'I'm not afraid. I'll go and see.'

This was afterwards put in the Golden Deed book. It ended in Oswald and Dicky and Denny going. Denny went first because he said he would rather – and Oswald understood this and let him. If Oswald had pushed first it would have been like Sir Lancelot refusing to let a young knight win his spurs. Oswald took good care to go second himself, though. The others never understood this. You don't expect it from girls; but I did think father would have understood without Oswald telling him, which of course he never could.

We all went slowly.

At the bottom of the turret stairs we stopped short. Because the door there was bolted fast and would not yield to shoves, however desperate and united.

Only now somehow we felt that Mr Richard Ravenal was all right and quiet, but that some one had done it for a lark, or perhaps not known about anyone being up there. So we rushed up, and Oswald told the others in a few hasty but well-chosen words, and we all leaned over between the battlements, and shouted, 'Hi! you there!'

Then from under the arches of the quite-downstairs part of the tower a figure came forth – and it was the sailor who had had our milk sixpence. He looked up and he spoke to us. He did not speak loud, but he spoke loud enough for us to hear every word quite plainly. He said –

'Drop that.'

Oswald said, 'Drop what?'

He said, 'That row.'

Oswald said, 'Why?'

He said, 'Because if you don't I'll come up and make you, and pretty quick too, so I tell you.'

Dicky said, 'Did you bolt the door?'

The man said, 'I did so, my young cock.'

Alice said – and Oswald wished to goodness she had held her tongue, because he saw right enough the man was not friendly – 'Oh, do come and let us out – do, please.'

While she was saying it Oswald suddenly saw that he did not want the man to come up. So he scurried down the stairs because he thought he had seen something on the door on the top side, and sure enough there were two bolts, and he shot them into their sockets. This bold act was not put in the Golden Deed book, because when Alice wanted to, the others said it was not *good* of Oswald to think of this, but only *clever*. I think sometimes, in moments of danger and disaster, it is as good to be clever as it is to be good. But Oswald would never demean himself to argue about this.

When he got back the man was still standing staring up. Alice said –

'Oh, Oswald, he says he won't let us out unless we give him all our money. And we might be here for days and days and all night as well. No one knows where we are to come and look for us. Oh, do let's give it him *all*.'

She thought the lion of the English nation, which does not know when it is beaten, would be ramping in her brother's breast. But Oswald kept calm. He said –

'All right,' and he made the others turn out their pockets. Denny had a bad shilling, with a head on both sides, and three halfpence. H. O. had a halfpenny. Noël had a French penny, which is only good for chocolate machines at railway stations. Dicky had tenpence-half-penny, and Oswald had a two-shilling piece of his own that he was saving up to buy a gun with. Oswald tied the whole lot up in his handkerchief, and looking over the battlements, he said –

'You are an ungrateful beast. We gave you sixpence freely of our own will.'

The man did look a little bit ashamed, but he mumbled something about having his living to get.

Then Oswald said –

'Here you are. Catch!' and he flung down the hand-kerchief with the money in it.

The man muffed the catch – butter-fingered idiot! – but he picked up the handkerchief and undid it, and when he saw what was in it he swore dreadfully. The cad!

'Look here,' he called out, 'this won't do, young shaver. I want those there shiners I see in your pus! Chuck 'em along!'

Then Oswald laughed. He said –

'I shall know you again anywhere, and you'll be put in prison for this. Here are the *shiners*.' And he was so angry he chucked down purse and all. The shiners were not real ones, but only card-counters that looked like sovereigns on one side. Oswald used to carry them in his purse so as to look affluent. He does not do this now.

When the man had seen what was in the purse he disappeared under the tower, and Oswald was glad of what he had done about the bolts – and he hoped they were as strong as the ones on the other side of the door.

They were.

We heard the man kicking and pounding at the door,

and I am not ashamed to say that we were all holding on to each other very tight. I am proud, however, to relate that nobody screamed or cried.

After what appeared to be long years, the banging stopped, and presently we saw the brute going away among the trees.

Then Alice did cry, and I do not blame her.

Then Oswald said –

'It's no use. Even if he's undone the door, he may be in ambush. We must hold on here till somebody comes.'

Then Alice said, speaking chokily because she had not quite done crying –

'Let's wave a flag.'

By the most fortunate accident she had on one of her Sunday petticoats, though it was Monday. This petticoat is white. She tore it out at the gathers, and we tied it to Denny's stick, and took turns to wave it. We had laughed at his carrying a stick before, but we were very sorry now that we had done so.

And the tin dish the Lent pie was baked in we polished with our handkerchiefs, and moved it about in the sun so that the sun might strike on it and signal our distress to some of the outlying farms.

This was perhaps the most dreadful adventure that had then ever happened to us. Even Alice had now stopped thinking of Mr Richard Ravenal, and thought only of the lurker in ambush.

We all felt our desperate situation keenly. I must say Denny behaved like anything but a white mouse. When it was the others' turn to wave, he sat on the leads of the tower and held Alice's and Noël's hands, and said poetry to them – yards and yards of it. By some strange fatality it seemed to comfort them. It wouldn't have me.

He said 'The Battle of the Baltic', and 'Gray's

Elegy', right through, though I think he got wrong in places, and the 'Revenge', and Macaulay's thing about Lars Porsena and the Nine Gods. And when it was his turn he waved like a man.

I will try not to call him a white mouse any more. He was a brick that day, and no mouse.

The sun was low in the heavens, and we were sick of waving and very hungry, when we saw a cart in the road below. We waved like mad, and shouted, and Denny screamed exactly like a railway whistle, a thing none of us had known before that he could do.

And the cart stopped. And presently we saw a figure with a white beard among the trees. It was our Pig-man.

We bellowed the awful truth to him, and when he had taken it in – he thought at first we were kidding – he came up and let us out.

He had got the pig; luckily it was a very small one – and we were not particular. Denny and Alice sat on the front of the cart with the Pig-man, and the rest of us got in with the pig, and the man drove us right home. You may think we talked it over on the way. Not us. We went to sleep, among the pig, and before long the Pig-man stopped and got us to make room for Alice and Denny. There was a net over the cart. I never was so sleepy in my life, though it was not more than bed-time.

Generally, after anything exciting, you are punished – but this could not be, because we had only gone for a walk, exactly as we were told.

There was a new rule made, though. No walks except on the high-roads, and we were always to take Pincher and either Lady, the deer-hound, or Martha, the bull-dog. We generally hate rules, but we did not mind this one.

Father gave Denny a gold pencil-case because he was first to go down into the tower. Oswald does not grudge Denny this, though some might think he deserved at least a silver one.

But Oswald is above such paltry jealousies.

CHAPTER 5

THE WATERWORKS

THIS is the story of one of the most far-reaching and influentially naughty things we ever did in our lives. We did not mean to do such a deed. And yet we did do it. These things will happen with the best-regulated consciences.

The story of this rash and fatal act is intimately involved – which means all mixed up anyhow – with a private affair of Oswald's, and the one cannot be revealed without the other. Oswald does not particularly want his story to be remembered, but he wishes to tell the truth, and perhaps it is what father calls a wholesome discipline to lay bare the awful facts.

It was like this.

On Alice's and Noël's birthday we went on the river for a picnic. Before that we had not known that there was a river so near us. Afterwards father said he wished we had been allowed to remain on our pristine ignorance, whatever that is. And perhaps the dark hour did dawn when we wished so too. But a truce to vain regrets.

It was rather a fine thing in birthdays. The uncle sent a box of toys and sweets, things that were like a vision from another and a brighter world. Besides that Alice had a knife, a pair of shut-up scissors, a silk handkerchief, a book – it was *The Golden Age* and is A1 except where it gets mixed with grown-up nonsense. Also a work-case lined with pink plush, a boot-bag, which no one in their senses would use because it had flowers in wool all over it. And she had a box of chocolates and a musical box that played 'The Man who broke' and two other tunes, and two pairs of kid gloves for church, and a box of writing-paper – pink – with 'Alice' on it in gold writing, and an egg coloured red that said 'A. Bastable' in ink on one side. These gifts were the offerings of Oswald, Dora, Dicky, Albert's uncle, Daisy, Mr Foulkes (our own robber), Noël, H. O., father and Denny. Mrs Pettigrew gave the egg. It was a kindly housekeeper's friendly token.

I shall not tell you about the picnic on the river because the happiest times form but dull reading when they are written down. I will merely state that it was prime. Though happy, the day was uneventful. The only thing exciting enough to write about was in one of the locks, where there was a snake – a viper. It was asleep in a warm sunny corner of the lock gate, and when the gate was shut it fell off into the water.

Alice and Dora screamed hideously. So did Daisy, but her screams were thinner.

The snake swam round and round all the time our boat was in the lock. It swam with four inches of itself – the head end – reared up out of the water, exactly like Kaa in the *Jungle Book* – so we know Kipling is a true author and no rotter. We were careful to keep our hands well inside the boat. A snake's eyes strike terror into the boldest breast.

When the lock was full father killed the viper with a boat-hook. I was sorry for it myself. It was indeed a venomous serpent. But it was the first we had ever seen, except at the Zoo. And it did swim most awfully well.

Directly the snake had been killed H. O. reached out for its corpse, and the next moment the body of our little brother was seen wriggling conclusively on the boat's edge. This exciting spectacle was not of a lasting nature. He went right in. Father clawed him out. He is very unlucky with water.

Being a birthday, but little was said. H. O. was wrapped in everybody's coats, and did not take any cold at all.

This glorious birthday ended with an iced cake and ginger wine, and drinking healths. Then we played whatever we liked. There had been rounders during the afternoon. It was a day to be for ever marked by memory's brightest what's-its-name.

I should not have said anything about the picnic but for one thing. It was the thin edge of the wedge. It was the all-powerful lever that moved but too many events. You see, *we were now no longer strangers to the river*.

And we went there whenever we could. Only we had to take the dogs, and to promise no bathing without grown-ups. But paddling in back waters was allowed. I say no more.

I have not numerated Noël's birthday presents because I wish to leave something to the imagination of my young readers. (The best authors always do this.) If you will take the large, red catalogue of the Army and Navy Stores, and just make a list of about fifteen of the things you would like best – prices from 2s. to 25s. – you will get a very good idea of Noël's presents, and it will help you to make up your mind in case you are asked just before your next birthday what you really *need*.

One of Noël's birthday presents was a cricket ball. He cannot bowl for nuts, and it was a first-rate ball. So some days after the birthday Oswald offered him to exchange it for a coconut he had won at the fair, and two pencils (new), and a brand-new note-book. Oswald thought, and he still thinks, that this was a fair exchange, and so did Noël at the time, and he agreed to it, and was quite pleased till the girls said it wasn't fair, and Oswald had the best of it. And then that young beggar Noël wanted the ball back, but Oswald, though not angry, was firm.

'You said it was a bargain, and you shook hands on it,' he said, and he said it quite kindly and calmly.

Noël said he didn't care. He wanted his cricket ball back.

And the girls said it was a horrid shame.

If they had not said that, Oswald might yet have consented to let Noël have the beastly ball, but now, of course, he was not going to. He said –

'Oh, yes, I daresay. And then you would be wanting the coconut and things again the next minute.'

'No, I shouldn't,' Noël said. It turned out afterwards he and H. O. had eaten the coconut, which only made it worse. And it made them worse too – which is what the book calls poetic justice.

Dora said, 'I don't think it was fair,' and even Alice said –

'Do let him have it back, Oswald.' I wish to be just to Alice. She did not know then about the coconut having been secretly wolfed up.

We were in the garden. Oswald felt all the feelings of the hero when the opposing forces gathered about him are opposing as hard as ever they can. He knew he was not unfair, and he did not like to be jawed at just because Noël had eaten the coconut and wanted the ball back. Though Oswald did not know then about the eating of the coconut, but he felt the injustice in his soul all the same.

Noël said afterwards he meant to offer Oswald something else to make up for the coconut, but he said nothing about this at the time.

'Give it me, I say.' Noël said.

And Oswald said, 'Shan't!'

Then Noël called Oswald names, and Oswald did not answer back but just kept smiling pleasantly, and carelessly throwing up the ball and catching it again with an air of studied indifference.

It was Martha's fault that what happened happened. She is the bull-dog, and very stout and heavy. She had just been let loose and she came bounding along in her clumsy way, and jumped up on Oswald, who is beloved by all dumb animals. (You know how sagacious they are.) Well, Martha knocked the ball out of Oswald's hands, and it fell on the grass, and Noël pounced on it like a hooded falcon on its prey. Oswald would scorn to deny that he was not going to stand this, and the next moment the two were rolling over on the grass, and very soon Noël was made to bite the dust. And serve him right. He is old enough to know his own mind.

Then Oswald walked slowly away with the ball, and the others picked Noël up, and consoled the beaten, but Dicky would not take either side.

And Oswald went up into his own room and lay on his bed, and reflected gloomy reflections about unfairness.

Presently he thought he would like to see what the others were doing without their knowing he cared. So he went into the linen-room and looked out of its window, and he saw they were playing Kings and Queens – and Noël had the biggest paper crown and the longest stick sceptre.

Oswald turned away without a word, for it really was sickening.

Then suddenly his weary eyes fell upon something they had not before beheld. It was a square trap-door in the ceiling of the linen-room.

Oswald never hesitated. He crammed the cricket ball into his pocket and climbed up the shelves and un-bolted the trap-door, and shoved it up, and pulled himself up through it. Though above all was dark and smelt of spiders, Oswald fearlessly shut the trap-door down again before he struck a match. He always carries matches. He is a boy fertile in every subtle expedient. Then he saw he was in the wonderful, mysterious place between the ceiling and the roof of the house. The roof is beams and tiles. Slits of light show through the tiles here and there. The ceiling, on its other and top side, is made of rough plaster and beams. If you walk on the beams it is all right – if you walk on the plaster you go through with your feet. Oswald found this out later, but some fine instinct now taught the young explorer where he ought to tread and where not. It was splendid. He was still very angry with the others and he was glad he had found out a secret they jolly well didn't know.

He walked along a dark, narrow passage. Every now and then cross-beams barred his way, and he had to creep under them. At last a small door loomed before him with cracks of light under and over. He drew back the rusty bolts and opened it. It opened straight on to the leads, a flat place between two steep red roofs, with a parapet two feet high back and front, so that no one could see you. It was a place no one could have in-vented better than, if they had tried, for hiding in.

Oswald spent the whole afternoon there. He happened to have a volume of *Percy's Anecdotes* in his pocket, the one about lawyers, as well as a few apples. While he read he fingered the cricket ball, and presently it rolled away, and he thought he would get it by-and-by.

When the tea-bell rang he forgot the ball and went

hurriedly down, for apples do not keep the inside from the pangs of hunger.

Noël met him on the landing, got red in the face, and said –

'It wasn't *quite* fair about the ball, because H. O. and I had eaten the coconut. *You* can have it.'

'I don't want your beastly ball,' Oswald said, 'only I hate unfairness. However, I don't know where it is just now. When I find it you shall have it to bowl with as often as you want.'

'Then you're not waxy?'

And Oswald said 'No' and they went in to tea together. So that was all right. There were raisin cakes for tea.

Next day we happened to want to go down to the river quite early. I don't know why; this is called Fate, or Destiny. We dropped in at the 'Rose and Crown' for some ginger-beer on our way. The landlady is a friend of ours and lets us drink it in her back parlour, instead of in the bar, which would be improper for girls.

We found her awfully busy, making pies and jellies, and her two sisters were hurrying about with great hams, and pairs of chickens, and rounds of cold beef and lettuces, and pickled salmon and trays of crockery and glasses.

'It's for the angling competition,' she said.

We said, 'What's that?'

'Why,' she said, slicing cucumber like beautiful machinery while she said it, 'a lot of anglers come down some particular day and fish one particular bit of the river. And the one that catches most fish gets the prize. They're fishing the pen above Stoneham Lock. And they all come here to dinner. So I've got my hands full and a trifle over.'

We said, 'Couldn't we help?'

But she said, 'Oh, no, thank you. Indeed not, please. I really am so I don't know which way to turn. Do run along, like dears.'

So we ran along like these timid but graceful animals.

Need I tell the intellectual reader that we went straight off to the pen above Stoneham Lock to see the anglers competing? Angling is the same thing as fishing.

I am not going to try and explain locks to you. If you've never seen a lock you could never understand even if I wrote it in words of one syllable and pages and pages long. And if you have, you'll understand without my telling you. It is harder than Euclid if you don't know beforehand. But you might get a grown-up person to explain it to you with books or wooden bricks.

I will tell you what a pen is because that is easy. It is the bit of river between one lock and the next. In some rivers 'pens' are called 'reaches', but pen is the proper word.

We went along the towing-path; it is shady with willows, aspens, alders, elders, oaks and other trees. On the banks are flowers – yarrow, meadow-sweet, willow herb, loosestrife, and lady's bed-straw. Oswald learned the names of all these trees and plants on the day of the picnic. The others didn't remember them, but Oswald did. He is a boy of what they call relenting memory.

The anglers were sitting here and there on the shady bank among the grass and the different flowers I have named. Some had dogs with them, and some umbrellas, and some had only their wives and families.

We should have liked to talk to them and ask how they liked their lot, and what kinds of fish there were, and whether they were nice to eat, but we did not like to.

Denny had seen anglers before and he knew they

liked to be talked to, but though he spoke to them quite like to equals he did not ask the things we wanted to know. He just asked whether they'd had any luck, and what bait they used.

And they answered him back politely. I am glad I am not an angler. It is an immovable amusement, and, as often as not, no fish to speak of after all.

Daisy and Dora had stayed at home: Dora's foot was nearly well but they seem really to like sitting still. I think Dora likes to have a little girl to order about. Alice never would stand it. When we got to Stoneham Lock Denny said he should go home and fetch his fishing-rod. H. O. went with him. This left four of us – Oswald, Alice, Dicky, and Noël. We went on down the towing-path.

The lock shuts up (that sounds as if it was like the lock on a door, but it is very otherwise) between one pen of the river and the next; the pen where the anglers were was full right up over the roots of the grass and flowers.

But the pen below was nearly empty.

'You can see the poor river's bones,' Noël said.

And so you could.

Stones and mud and dried branches, and here and there an old kettle or a tin pail with no bottom to it, that some bargee had chucked in.

From walking so much along the river we knew many of the bargees. Bargees are the captains and crews of the big barges that are pulled up and down the river by slow horses. The horses do not swim. They walk on the towing-path, with a rope tied to them, and the other end to the barge. So it gets pulled along. The bargees we knew were a good friendly sort, and used to let us go all over the barges when they were in a good temper. They were not at all the sort of bullying, cowardly fiends in human form that the young hero at Oxford fights a crowd of, single-handed, in books.

The river does not smell nice when its bones are showing. But we went along down, because Oswald wanted to get some cobbler's wax in Falding village for a bird-net he was making.

But just above Falding Lock, where the river is narrow and straight, we saw a sad and gloomy sight – a big barge sitting flat on the mud because there was not water enough to float her.

There was no one on board, but we knew by a red flannel waistcoat that was spread out to dry on top that the barge belonged to friends of ours.

Then Alice said, 'They have gone to find the man who turns on the water to fill the pen. I daresay they won't find him. He's gone to his dinner, I shouldn't wonder. What a lovely surprise it would be if they came back to find their barge floating high and dry on a lot of water! *Do* let's do it. It's a long time since any of us did a kind action deserving of being put in the Book of Golden Deeds.'

We had given that name to the minute-book of that beastly 'Society of the Wouldbegoods'. Then you could think of the book if you wanted to without remembering the Society. I always tried to forget both of them.

Oswald said, 'But how? *You* don't know how. And if you did we haven't got a crowbar.'

I cannot help telling you that locks are opened with crowbars. You push and push till a thing goes up and the water runs through. It is rather like the little sliding door in the big door of a hen-house.

'I know where the crowbar is,' Alice said. 'Dicky and I were down here yesterday when you were su –' She was going to say sulking, I know, but she remembered manners ere too late so Oswald bears her no malice. She went on: 'Yesterday, when you were upstairs. And we saw the water-tender open the lock and the weir sluices. It's quite easy, isn't it, Dicky?'

'As easy as kiss your hand,' said Dicky; 'and what's more, I know where he keeps the other thing he opens the sluices with. I votes we do.'

'Do let's, if we can,' Noël said, 'and the bargees will bless the names of their unknown benefactors. They might make a song about us, and sing it on winter nights as they pass round the wassail bowl in front of the cabin fire.'

Noël wanted to very much; but I don't think it was altogether for generousness, but because he wanted to see how the sluices opened. Yet perhaps I do but wrong the boy.

We sat and looked at the barge a bit longer, and then Oswald said, well, he didn't mind going back to the lock and having a look at the crowbars. You see Oswald did not propose this; he did not even care very much about it when Alice suggested it.

But when we got to Stoneham Lock, and Dicky dragged the two heavy crowbars from among the elder bushes behind a fallen tree, and began to pound away at the sluice of the lock, Oswald felt it would not be manly to stand idly apart. So he took his turn.

It was very hard work but we opened the lock sluices, and we did not drop the crowbar into the lock either, as I have heard of being done by older and sillier people.

The water poured through the sluices all green and solid, as if it had been cut with a knife, and where it fell on the water underneath the white foam spread like a moving counterpane. When we had finished the lock we did the weir – which is wheels and chains – and the water pours through over the stones in a magnificent waterfall and sweeps out all round the weir-pool.

The sight of the foaming waterfalls was quite enough reward for our heavy labours, even without the thought of the unspeakable gratitude that the bargees would feel to us when they got back to their barge and found her no longer a stick-in-the-mud, but bounding on the free bosom of the river.

When we had opened all the sluices we gazed awhile on the beauties of Nature, and then went home, because we thought it would be more truly noble and good not to wait to be thanked for our kind and devoted action – and besides, it was nearly dinner-time and Oswald thought it was going to rain.

On the way home we agreed not to tell the others, because it would be like boasting of our good acts.

'They will know all about it,' Noël said, 'when they hear us being blessed by the grateful bargees, and the tale of the Unknown Helpers is being told by every village fireside. And then they can write it in the Golden Deed book.'

So we went home. Denny and H. O. had thought better of it, and they were fishing in the moat. They did not catch anything.

Oswald is very weather-wise – at least, so I have heard it said, and he had thought there would be rain. There was. It came on while we were at dinner – a great, strong, thundering rain, coming down in sheets – the first rain we had had since we came to the Moat House.

We went to bed as usual. No presentiment of the coming awfulness clouded our young mirth. I remember Dicky and Oswald had a wrestling match, and Oswald won.

In the middle of the night Oswald was awakened by

a hand on his face. It was a wet hand and very cold.
Oswald hit out, of course, but a voice said, in a hoarse,
hollow whisper –

'Don't be a young ass! Have you got any matches?
My bed's full of water; it's pouring down from the
ceiling.'

Oswald's first thoughts was that perhaps by opening
those sluices we had flooded some secret passage which
communicated with the top of Moat House, but when
he was properly awake he saw that this could not be, on
account of the river being so low.

He had matches. He is, as I said before, a boy full of
resources. He struck one and lit a candle, and Dicky,
for it was indeed he, gazed with Oswald at the amazing
spectacle.

Our bedroom floor was all wet in patches. Dicky's
bed stood in a pond, and from the ceiling water was
dripping in rich profusion at a dozen different places.
There was a great wet patch in the ceiling, and that was
blue, instead of white like the dry part, and the water
dripped from different parts of it.

In a moment Oswald was quite unmanned.

'Krikey!' he said, in a heart-broken tone, and
remained an instant plunged in thought.

'What on earth are we to do?' Dicky said.

And really for a short time even Oswald did not know.
It was a blood-curdling event, a regular facer. Albert's
uncle had gone to London that day to stay till the next.
Yet something must be done.

The first thing was to rouse the unconscious others
from their deep sleep, because the water was beginning to drip on to their beds, and though as yet
they knew it not, there was quite a pool on Noël's bed,
just in the hollow behind where his knees were doubled
up, and one of H. O.'s boots was full of water, that

surged wildly out when Oswald happened to kick it over.

We woke them – a difficult task, but we did not shrink from it.

Then we said, 'Get up, there is a flood! Wake up, or you will be drowned in your beds! And it's half past two by Oswald's watch.'

They awoke slowly and very stupidly. H. O. was the slowest and stupidest.

The water poured faster and faster from the ceiling.

We looked at each other and turned pale, and Noël said –

'Hadn't we better call Mrs Pettigrew?'

But Oswald simply couldn't consent to this. He could not get rid of the feeling that this was our fault somehow for meddling with the river, though of course the clear star of reason told him it could not possibly be the case.

We all devoted ourselves, heart and soul, to the work before us. We put the bath under the worst and wettest place, and the jugs and basins under lesser streams, and we moved the beds away to the dry end of the room. Ours is a long attic that runs right across the house.

But the water kept coming in worse and worse. Our nightshirts were wet through, so we got into our other shirts and knickerbockers, but preserved bareness in our feet. And the floor kept on being half an inch deep in water, however much we mopped it up.

We emptied the basins out of the window as fast as they filled, and we baled the bath with a jug without pausing to complain how hard the work was. All the same, it was more exciting than you can think. But in Oswald's dauntless breast he began to see that they would *have* to call Mrs Pettigrew.

A new waterfall broke out between the fire-grate and the mantelpiece, and spread in devastating floods.

Oswald is full of ingenious devices. I think I have said this before, but it is quite true; and perhaps even truer this time than it was last time I said it.

He got a board out of the box-room next door, and rested one end in the chink between the fireplace and the mantelpiece, and laid the other end on the back of a chair, then we stuffed the rest of the chink with our nightgowns, and laid a towel along the plank, and behold, a noble stream poured over the end of the board right into the bath we put there ready. It was like Niagara, only not so round in shape. The first lot of water that came down the chimney was very dirty. The wind whistled outside. Noël said, 'If it's pipes burst, and not the rain, it will be nice for the water-rates.' Perhaps it was only natural after this for Denny to begin with his everlasting poetry. He stopped mopping up the water to say:

> *'By this the storm grew loud apace,*
> *The water-rats were shrieking,*
> *And in the howl of Heaven each face*
> *Grew black as they were speaking.'*

Our faces were black, and our hands too, but we did not take any notice; we only told him not to gas but to go on mopping. And he did. And we all did.

But more and more water came pouring down. You would not believe so much could come off one roof.

When at last it was agreed that Mrs Pettigrew must be awakened at all hazards, we went and woke Alice to do the fatal errand.

When she came back, with Mrs Pettigrew in a night-cap and red flannel petticoat, we held our breath.

But Mrs Pettigrew did not even say, 'What on earth have you children been up to *now*?' as Oswald had feared.

Up all night, with water pouring through the roof

She simply sat down on my bed and said –

'Oh, dear! oh, dear! oh, dear!' ever so many times.

Then Denny said, 'I once saw holes in a cottage roof. The man told me it was done when the water came through the thatch. He said if the water lies all about on the top of the ceiling, it breaks it down, but if you make holes the water will only come through the holes and you can put pails under the holes to catch it.'

So we made nine holes in the ceiling with the poker, and put pails, baths and tubs under, and now there was not so much water on the floor. But we had to keep on working like niggers, and Mrs Pettigrew and Alice worked the same.

About five in the morning the rain stopped; about seven the water did not come in so fast, and presently it only dripped slowly. Our task was done.

This is the only time I was ever up all night. I wish it happened oftener. We did not go back to bed then, but dressed and went down. We all went to sleep in the afternoon, though. Quite without meaning to.

Oswald went up on the roof, before breakfast, to see if he could find the hole where the rain had come in. He did not find any hole, but he found the cricket ball jammed in the top of a gutter pipe which he afterwards knew ran down inside the wall of the house and ran into the moat below. It seems a silly dodge, but so it was.

When the men went up after breakfast to see what had caused the flood they said there must have been a good half-foot of water on the leads the night before for it to have risen high enough to go above the edge of the lead, and of course when it got above the lead there was nothing to stop it running down under it, and soaking through the ceiling. The parapet and the roofs kept it from tumbling off down the sides of the house in the natural way. They said there must have been some obstruction in the pipe which ran down into the house, but whatever it was the water had washed it away, for they put wires down, and the pipe was quite clear.

While we were being told this Oswald's trembling fingers felt at the wet cricket ball in his pocket. And he *knew*, but he *could* not tell. He heard them wondering what the obstruction could have been, and all the time he had the obstruction in his pocket, and never said a single word.

I do not seek to defend him. But it really was an awful thing to have been the cause of; and Mrs Pettigrew is but harsh and hasty. But this, as Oswald knows too well, is no excuse for his silent conduct.

That night at tea Albert's uncle was rather silent too. At last he looked upon us with a glance full of intelligence, and said –

'There was a queer thing happened yesterday. You know there was an angling competition. The pen was kept full on purpose. Some mischievous busybody went and opened the sluices and let all the water out. The anglers' holiday was spoiled. No, the rain wouldn't have spoiled it anyhow, Alice; anglers *like* rain. The 'Rose and Crown' dinner was half of it wasted because the anglers were so furious that a lot of them took the next train to town. And this is the worst of all – a barge, that was on the mud in the pen below, was lifted and jammed across the river and the water tilted her over, and her cargo is on the river bottom. It was coals.'

During this speech there were four of us who knew not where to turn our agitated glances. Some of us tried bread-and-butter, but it seemed dry and difficult, and those who tried tea choked and spluttered and were sorry they had not let it alone.

When the speech stopped Alice said, 'It was us.'

And with deepest feelings she and the rest of us told

all about it. Oswald did not say much. He was turning the obstruction round and round in his pocket, and wishing with all his sentiments that he had owned up like a man when Albert's uncle asked him before tea to tell him all about what had happened during the night.

When they had told all, Albert's uncle told us four still more plainly, and exactly, what we had done, and how much pleasure we had spoiled, and how much of my father's money we had wasted – because he would have to pay for the coals being got up from the bottom of the river, if they could be, and if not, for the price of the coals. And we saw it all.

And when he had done Alice burst out crying over her plate and said –

'It's no use! We have tried to be good since we've been down here. You don't know how we've tried! And it's all no use. I believe we are the wickedest children in the whole world, and I wish we were all dead!'

This was a dreadful thing to say, and of course the rest of us were all very shocked. But Oswald could not help looking at Albert's uncle to see how he would take it.

He said very gravely, 'My dear kiddie, you ought to be sorry, and I wish you to be sorry for what you've done. And you will be punished for it.' (We were; our pocket-money was stopped and we were forbidden to go near the river, besides impositions miles long.) 'But,' he went on, 'you mustn't give up trying to be good. You are extremely naughty and tiresome, as you know very well.'

Alice, Dicky, and Noël began to cry at about this time.

'But you are not the wickedest children in the world by any means.'

Then he stood up and straightened his collar, and put his hands in his pockets.

'You're very unhappy now,' he said, 'and you deserve to be. But I will say one thing to you.'

Then he said a thing which Oswald at least will never forget (though but little he deserved it, with the obstruction in his pocket, unowned up to all the time).

He said, 'I have known you all for four years – and you know as well as I do how many scrapes I've seen you in and out of – but I've never known one of you tell a lie, and I've never known one of you do a mean or dishonourable action. And when you have done wrong you are always sorry. Now this is something to stand firm on. You'll learn to be good in the other ways some day.'

He took his hands out of his pockets, and his face looked different, so that three of the four guilty creatures knew he was no longer adamant, and they threw themselves into his arms. Dora, Denny, Daisy, and H. O., of course, were not in it, and I think they thanked their stars.

Oswald did not embrace Albert's uncle. He stood there and made up his mind he would go for a soldier. He gave the wet ball one last squeeze, and took his hand out of his pocket, and said a few words before going to enlist. He said –

'The others may deserve what you say. I hope they do, I'm sure. But I don't, because it was my rotten cricket ball that stopped up the pipe and caused the midnight flood in our bedroom. And I knew it quite early this morning. And I didn't own up.'

Oswald stood there covered with shame, and he could feel the hateful cricket ball heavy and cold against the top of his leg, through the pocket.

Albert's uncle said – and his voice made Oswald hot all over, but not with shame – he said –

I shall not tell you what he said. It is no one's business but Oswald's; only I will own it made Oswald not quite so anxious to run away for a soldier as he had been before.

That owning up was the hardest thing I ever did. They did put that in the Book of Golden Deeds, though it was not a kind or generous act, and did no good to anyone or anything except Oswald's own inside feelings. I must say I think they might have let it alone. Oswald would rather forget it. Especially as Dicky wrote it in and put this:

'Oswald acted a lie, which, he knows, is as bad as telling one. But he owned up when he needn't have, and this condones his sin. We think he was a thorough brick to do it.'

Alice scratched this out afterwards and wrote the record of the incident in more flattering terms. But Dicky had used Father's ink, and she used Mrs Pettigrew's, so anyone can read *his* underneath the scratching outs.

The others were awfully friendly to Oswald, to show they agreed with Albert's uncle in thinking I deserved as much share as anyone in any praise there might be going.

It was Dora who said it all came from my quarrelling with Noël about that rotten cricket ball; but Alice, gently yet firmly, made her shut up.

I let Noël have the ball. It had been thoroughly soaked, but it dried all right. But it could never be the same to me after what *it* had done and what I had done.

I hope you will try to agree with Albert's uncle and not think foul scorn of Oswald because of this story. Perhaps you have done things nearly as bad yourself sometimes. If you have, you will know how 'owning up' soothes the savage breast and alleviates the gnawings of remorse.

If you have never done naughty acts I expect it is only because you never had the sense to think of anything.

CHAPTER 6

THE CIRCUS

THE ones of us who had started the Society of the Wouldbegoods began, at about this time, to bother.

They said we had not done anything really noble – not worth speaking of, that is – for over a week, and that it was high time to begin again – 'with earnest endeavour', Daisy said. So then Oswald said –

'All right; but there ought to be an end to everything. Let's each of us think of one really noble and unselfish act, and the others shall help to work it out, like we did when we were Treasure Seekers. Then when everybody's had their go-in we'll write every single thing down in the Golden Deed book, and we'll draw two lines in red ink at the bottom, like Father does at the end of an account. And after that, if anyone wants to be good they can jolly well be good on our own, if at all.'

The ones who had made the Society did not welcome this wise idea, but Dicky and Oswald were firm.

So they had to agree. When Oswald is really firm, opposingness and obstinacy have to give way.

Dora said, 'It would be a noble action to have all the school-children from the village and give them tea and games in the paddock. They would think it so nice and good of us.'

But Dicky showed her that this would not be *our* good act, but Father's, because he would have to pay for the tea, and he had already stood us the keepsakes for the soldiers, as well as having to stump up heavily over the coal barge. And it is in vain being noble and generous when someone else is paying for it all the time, even if it happens to be your father. Then three others had ideas at the same time and began to explain what they were.

We were all in the dining-room, and perhaps we were making a bit of a row. Anyhow, Oswald for one, does not blame Albert's uncle for opening his door and saying

'I suppose I must not ask for complete silence. That were too much. But if you could whistle, or stamp with your feet, or shriek or howl – anything to vary the monotony of your well-sustained conversation.'

Oswald said kindly, 'We're awfully sorry. Are you busy?'

'Busy?' said Albert's uncle. 'My heroine is now hesitating on the verge of an act which, for good or ill, must influence her whole subsequent career. You wouldn't like her to decide in the middle of such a row that she can't hear herself think?'

We said, 'No, we wouldn't.'

Then he said, 'If any outdoor amusement should commend itself to you this bright mid-summer day.'

So we all went out.

Then Daisy whispered to Dora – they always hang together. Daisy is not nearly so white-micey as she was at first, but she still seems to fear the deadly ordeal of public speaking. Dora said –

'Daisy's idea is a game that'll take us all day. She thinks keeping out of the way when he's making his heroine decide right would be a noble act, and fit to write in the Golden Book; and we might as well be playing something at the same time.'

We all said 'Yes, but what?'

There was a silent interval.

'Speak up, Daisy, my child.' Oswald said; 'fear not to lay bare the utmost thoughts of that faithful heart.'

Daisy giggled. Our own girls never giggle; they laugh right out or hold their tongues. Their kind brothers have taught them this. Then Daisy said –

'If we could have a sort of play to keep us out of the way. I once read a story about an animal race. Everybody had an animal, and they had to go how they liked, and the one that got in first got the prize. There was a tortoise in it, and a rabbit, and a peacock, and sheep, and dogs, and a kitten.'

This proposal left us cold, as Albert's uncle says, because we knew there could not be any prize worth bothering about. And though you may be ever ready and willing to do anything for nothing, yet if there's going to be a prize there must *be* a prize and there's an end of it.

Thus the idea was not followed up. Dicky yawned and said, 'Let's go into the barn and make a fort.'

So we did, with straw. It does not hurt straw to be messed about with like it does hay.

The downstairs – I mean down-ladder – part of the barn was fun too, especially for Pincher. There was as good ratting there as you could wish to see. Martha tried it, but she could not help running kindly beside the rat, as if she was in double harness with it. This is the noble bull-dog's gentle and affectionate nature coming out. We all enjoyed the ratting that day, but it ended, as usual, in the girls crying because of the poor rats. Girls cannot help this; we must not be waxy with them on account of it, they have their nature, the same as bull-dogs have, and it is this that makes them so useful in smoothing the pillows of the sick-bed and tending wounded heroes.

However, the forts, and Pincher, and the girls crying, and having to be thumped on the back, passed the time very agreeably till dinner. There was roast mutton with onion sauce, and a roly-poly pudding.

Albert's uncle said we had certainly effaced ourselves effectually, which means we hadn't bothered.

So we determined to do the same during the afternoon, for he told us his heroine was by no means out of the wood yet.

And at first it was easy. Jam roly gives you a peaceful feeling and you do not at first care if you never play any runabout game ever any more. But after a while the torpor begins to pass away. Oswald was the first to recover from his.

He had been lying on his front part in the orchard, but now he turned over on his back and kicked his legs up, and said –

'I say, look here; let's do something.'*

Daisy looked thoughtful. She was chewing the soft yellow parts of grass, but I could see she was still thinking about that animal race. So I explained to her that it would be very poor fun without a tortoise and a peacock, and she saw this, though not willingly.

It was H. O. who said –

'Doing anything with animals is prime! if they only will. Let's have a circus!'

At the word the last thought of the pudding faded from Oswald's memory, and he stretched himself, sat up, and said –

'Bully for H. O. Let's!'

The others also threw off the heavy weight of memory, and sat up and said 'Let's!' too.

Never, never in all our lives had we had such a gay galaxy of animals at our command. The rabbits and the

* See p. 128 for short story.

guinea-pigs, and even all the bright, glass-eyed, stuffed denizens of our late-lamented Jungle paled into insignificance before the number of live things on the farm.

(I hope you do not think that the words I use are getting too long. I know they are the right words. And Albert's uncle says your style is always altered a bit by what you read. And I have been reading the Vicomte de Bragelonne. Nearly all my new words come out of those.)

'The worst of a circus is,' Dora said, 'that you've got to teach the animals things. A circus where the performing creatures hadn't learned performing would be a bit silly. Let's give up a week to teaching them and then have the circus.'

Some people have no idea of the value of time. And Dora is one of those who do not understand that when you want to do a thing you *do* want to, and not to do something else, and perhaps your own thing, a week later.

Oswald said the first thing was to collect the performing animals.

'Then perhaps,' he said, 'we may find that they have hidden talents hitherto unsuspected by their harsh masters.'

So Denny took a pencil and wrote a list of the animals required.

This is it:

LIST OF ANIMALS REQUISITE FOR THE CIRCUS WE ARE GOING TO HAVE

1 Bull for bull-fight.
1 Horse for ditto (if possible).
1 Goat to do Alpine feats of daring.
1 Donkey to play see-saw.

2 White pigs – one to be Learned, and the other to play with the clown.

Turkeys, as many as possible, because they can make a noise that sounds like an audience applauding.

The dogs, for any odd parts.

1 Large black pig – to be the Elephant in the procession.

Calves (several) to be camels, and to stand on tubs.

Daisy ought to have been captain because it was partly her idea, but she let Oswald be, because she is of a retiring character. Oswald said –

'The first thing is to get all the creatures together; the paddock at the side of the orchard is the very place, because the hedge is good all round. When we've got the performers all there we'll make a programme, and then dress for our parts. It's a pity there won't be any audience but the turkeys.'

We took the animals in their right order, according to Denny's list. The bull was the first. He is black. He does not live in the cowhouse with the other horned people; he has a house all to himself two fields away. Oswald and Alice went to fetch him. They took a halter to lead the bull by, and a whip, not to hurt the bull with, but just to make him mind.

The others were to try to get one of the horses while we were gone.

Oswald as usual was full of bright ideas.

'I daresay,' he said, 'the bull will be shy at first, and he'll have to be goaded into the arena.'

'But goads hurt,' Alice said.

'They don't hurt the bull,' Oswald said; 'his power-ful hide is too thick.'

'Then why does he attend to it,' Alice asked, 'if it doesn't hurt?'

'Properly-brought-up bulls attend because they know they ought,' Oswald said. 'I think I shall ride the bull,' the brave boy went on. 'A bull-fight, where an intrepid rider appears on the bull, sharing its joys and sorrows. It would be something quite new.'

'You can't ride bulls,' Alice said; 'at least, not if their backs are sharp like cows.'

But Oswald thought he could. The bull lives in a house made of wood and prickly furze bushes, and he has a yard to his house. You cannot climb on the roof of his house at all comfortably.

When we got there he was half in his house and half out in his yard, and he was swinging his tail because of the flies which bothered. It was a very hot day.

'You'll see,' Alice said, 'he won't want a goad. He'll be so glad to get out for a walk he'll drop his head in my hand like a tame fawn, and follow me lovingly all the way.'

Oswald called to him. He said, 'Bull! Bull! Bull! Bull!' because we did not know the animal's real name. The bull took no notice; then Oswald picked up a stone and threw it at the bull, not angrily, but just to make it pay attention. But the bull did not pay a farthing's worth of it. So then Oswald leaned over the iron gate of the bull's yard and just flicked the bull with the whip-lash. And then the bull *did* pay attention. He started when the lash struck him, then suddenly he faced round, uttering a roar like that of the wounded King of Beasts, and putting his head down close to his feet he ran straight at the iron gate where we were standing.

Alice and Oswald mechanically turned away; they did not wish to annoy the bull any more, and they ran as fast as they could across the field so as not to keep the others waiting.

As they ran across the field Oswald had a dream-like fancy that perhaps the bull had rooted up the gate with one paralysing blow, and was now tearing across the field after him and Alice, with the broken gate balanced on its horns. We climbed the stile quickly and looked back; the bull was still on the right side of the gate.

Oswald said, 'I think we'll do without the bull. He did not seem to want to come. We must be kind to dumb animals.'

Alice said, between laughing and crying –

'Oh, Oswald, how can you!' But we did do without the bull, and we did not tell the others how we had hurried to get back. We just said, 'The bull didn't seem to care about coming.'

The others had not been idle. They had got old Clover, the cart-horse, but she would do nothing but graze, so we decided not to use her in the bull-fight, but to let her be the Elephant. The Elephant's is a nice quiet part, and she was quite big enough for a young one. Then the black pig could be Learned, and the other two could be something else. They had also got the goat; he was tethered to a young tree.

The donkey was there. Denny was leading him in the halter.

The dogs were there, of course – they always are.

So now we only had to get the turkeys for the applause and the calves and pigs.

The calves were easy to get, because they were in their own house. There were five. And the pigs were in their houses too. We got them out after long and patient toil, and persuaded them that they wanted to go into the paddock, where the circus was to be. This is done by pretending to drive them the other way. A pig only knows two ways – the way you want him to go, and the other. But the turkeys knew thousands of different ways, and tried them all. They made such an awful row, we had to drop all ideas of ever hearing applause from their lips, so we came away and left them.

'Never mind,' H. O. said, 'they'll be sorry enough afterwards, nasty, unobliging things, because now they won't see the circus. I hope the other animals will tell them about it.'

While the turkeys were engaged in baffling the rest of us, Dicky had found three sheep who seemed to wish to join the glad throng, so we let them.

Then we shut the gate of the paddock, and left the dumb circus performers to make friends with each other while we dressed.

Oswald and H. O. were to be clowns. It is quite easy with Albert's uncle's pyjamas, and flour on your hair and face, and the red they do the brick-floors with.

Alice had very short pink and white skirts, and roses in her hair and round her dress. Her dress was the pink calico and white muslin stuff off the dressing-table in the girls' room fastened with pins and tied round the waist with a small bath towel. She was to be the Dauntless Equestrienne, and to give her enhancing act a bare-backed daring, riding either a pig or a sheep, whichever we found was freshest and most skittish. Dora was dressed for the *Haute École*, which means a riding-habit and a high hat. She took Dick's topper that he wears with his Etons, and a skirt of Mrs Pettigrew's. Daisy, dressed the same as Alice, taking the muslin from Mrs Pettigrew's dressing-table without saying anything beforehand. None of us would have advised this, and indeed we were thinking of trying to put it back, when Denny and Noël, who were wishing to look like high-waymen, with brown-paper top-boots and slouch hats and Turkish towel cloaks, suddenly stopped dressing and gazed out of the window.

'Krikey!' said Dick, 'come on, Oswald!' and he bounded like an antelope from the room.

Oswald and the rest followed, casting a hasty glance

through the window. Noël had got brown-paper boots too, and a Turkish towel cloak. H. O. had been waiting for Dora to dress him up for the other clown. He had only his shirt and knickerbockers and his braces on. He came down as he was – as indeed we all did. And no wonder, for in the paddock, where the circus was to be, a blood-thrilling thing had transpired. The dogs were chasing the sheep. And we had now lived long enough in the country to know the fell nature of our dogs' improper conduct.

We all rushed into the paddock, calling to Pincher, and Martha, and Lady. Pincher came almost at once. He is a well-brought-up dog – Oswald trained him. Martha did not seem to hear. She is awfully deaf, but she did not matter so much, because the sheep could walk away from her easily. She has no pace and no wind. But Lady is a deer-hound. She is used to pursuing that fleet and antlered pride of the forest – the stag – and she can go like billyo. She was now far away in a distant region of the paddock, with a fat sheep just before her in full flight. I am sure if ever anybody's eyes did start out of their heads with horror, like in narratives of adventure, ours did then.

There was a moment's pause of speechless horror. We expected to see Lady pull down her quarry, and we know what a lot of money a sheep costs, to say nothing of its own personal feelings.

Then we started to run for all we were worth. It is hard to run swiftly as the arrow from the bow when you happen to be wearing pyjamas belonging to a grown-up person – as I was – but even so I beat Dicky. He said afterwards it was because his brown-paper boots came undone and tripped him up. Alice came in third. She held on the dressing-table muslin and ran jolly well. But ere we reached the fatal spot all was very nearly up with the sheep. We heard a plop; Lady stopped and looked round. She must have heard us bellowing to her as we ran. Then she came towards us, prancing with happiness, but we said 'Down!' and 'Bad dog!' and ran sternly on.

When we came to the brook which forms the northern boundary of the paddock we saw the sheep struggling in the water. It is not very deep, and I believe the sheep could have stood up, and been well in its depth, if it had liked, but it would not try.

It was a steepish bank. Alice and I got down and stuck our legs into the water, and then Dicky came down, and the three of us hauled that sheep up by its shoulders till it could rest on Alice and me as we sat on the bank. It kicked all the time we were hauling. It gave one extra kick at last, that raised it up, and I tell you that sopping wet, heavy, panting, silly donkey of a sheep sat there on our laps like a pet dog; and Dicky got his shoulder under it at the back and heaved constantly to keep it from flumping off into the water again, while the others fetched the shepherd.

When the shepherd came he called us every name you can think of, and then he said –

'Good thing master didn't come along. He would ha' called you some tidy names.'

He got the sheep out, and took it and the others away. And the calves too. He did not seem to care about the other performing animals.

Alice, Oswald and Dick had had almost enough circus for just then, so we sat in the sun and dried ourselves and wrote the programme of the circus. This was it:

PROGRAMME

1. Startling leap from the lofty precipice by the performing sheep. Real water, and real precipice. The

gallant rescue. O. A. and D. Bastable. (We thought we
might as well put that in though it was over and had
happened accidentally.)

2. Graceful bare-backed equestrienne act on the trained
pig, Eliza. A. Bastable.

3. Amusing clown interlude, introducing trained dog,
Pincher, and the other white pig. H. O. and O. Bastable.

4. The See-Saw. Trained donkeys. (H. O. said we had
only one donkey, so Dicky said H. O. could be the other.
When peace was restored we went on to 5.)

5. Elegant equestrian act by D. Bastable. *Haute École*,
on Clover, the incomparative trained elephant from the
plains of Venezuela.

6. Alpine feat of daring. The climbing of the Andes, by
Billy, the well-known acrobatic goat. (We thought we
could make the Andes out of hurdles and things, and so
we could have but for what always happens. (This is the
unexpected. (This is a saying Father told me – but I see I
am three deep in brackets so I will close them before I get
into any more).).).

7. The Black but Learned Pig. ('I daresay he knows
something,' Alice said, 'if we can only find out what.' We
did find out all too soon.)

We could not think of anything else, and our things
were nearly dry – all except Dick's brown-paper top-
boots, which were mingled with the gurgling waters of
the brook.

We went back to the seat of action – which was the
iron trough where the sheep have their salt put – and
began to dress up the creatures. We had just tied the
Union Jack we made out of Daisy's flannel petticoat
and cetera, when we gave the soldiers the baccy, round
the waist of the Black and Learned Pig, when we
heard screams from the back part of the house; and
suddenly we saw that Billy, the acrobatic goat, had got
loose from the tree we had tied him to. (He had eaten

all the parts of its bark that he could get at, but we did not notice it until next day, when led to the spot by a grown-up.)

The gate of the paddock was open. The gate leading to the bridge that goes over the moat to the back door was open too. We hastily proceeded in the direction of the screams, and, guided by the sound, threaded our way into the kitchen. As we went, Noël, ever fertile in melancholy ideas, said he wondered whether Mrs Pettigrew was being robbed, or only murdered.

In the kitchen we saw that Noël was wrong as usual. It was neither. Mrs Pettigrew, screaming like a steam-siren and waving a broom, occupied the foreground. In the distance the maid was shrieking in a hoarse and monotonous way, and trying to shut herself up inside a clothes-horse on which washing was being aired. On the dresser – which he had ascended by a chair – was Billy, the acrobatic goat, doing his Alpine daring act. He had found out his Andes for himself, and even as we gazed he turned and tossed his head in a way that showed us some mysterious purpose was hidden beneath his calm exterior. The next moment he put his off-horn neatly behind the end plate of the next to the bottom row, and ran it along against the wall. The plates fell crashing on to the soup tureen and vegetable dishes which adorned the lower range of the Andes.

Mrs Pettigrew's screams were almost drowned in the discording crash and crackle of the falling avalanche of crockery.

Oswald, though stricken with horror and polite regret, preserved the most dauntless coolness.

Disregarding the mop which Mrs Pettigrew kept on poking at the goat in a timid yet cross way, he sprang forward, crying out to his trusty followers, 'Stand by to catch him!'

*He put his horn neatly behind the end plate and
ran it along against the wall*

But Dick had thought of the same thing, and ere
Oswald could carry out his long-cherished and general-
like design, Dicky had caught the goat's legs and tripped
it up. The goat fell against another row of plates, righted
itself hastily in the gloomy ruins of the soup tureen and
the sauce-boats, and then fell again, this time towards
Dicky. The two fell heavily on the ground together.
The trusty followers had been so struck by the daring of
Dicky and his lion-hearted brother, that they had not
stood by to catch anything. The goat was not hurt, but
Dicky had a sprained thumb and a lump on his head
like a black marble door-knob. He had to go to bed.

I will draw a veil and asterisks over what Mrs Pettigrew said. Also Albert's uncle, who was brought to the
scene of ruin by her screams. Few words escaped our
lips. There are times when it is not wise to argue; however, little what has occurred is really our fault.

When they had said what they deemed enough and
we were let go, we all went out. Then Alice said dis-
tractedly, in a voice which she vainly strove to render
firm –

'Let's give up the circus. Let's put the toys back in
the boxes – no, I don't mean that – the creatures in
their places – and drop the whole thing. I want to go
and read to Dicky.'

Oswald has a spirit that no reverses can depreciate.
He hates to be beaten. But he gave in to Alice, as the
others said so too, and we went out to collect the performing troop and sort it out into its proper places.

Alas! we came too late. In the interest we had felt
about whether Mrs Pettigrew was the abject victim of
burglars or not, we had left both gates open again. The
old horse – I mean the trained elephant from Venezuela –
was there all right enough. The dogs we had beaten and
tied up after the first act, when the intrepid sheep
bounded, as it says in the programme. The two white
pigs were there, but the donkey was gone. We heard
his hoofs down the road, growing fainter and fainter, in
the direction of the 'Rose and Crown'. And just round
the gatepost we saw a flash of red and white and blue
and black that told us, with dumb signification, that the
pig was off in exactly the opposite direction. Why
couldn't they have gone the same way? But no, one was
a pig and the other was a donkey, as Denny said afterwards.

Daisy and H. O. started after the donkey; the rest of
us, with one accord, pursued the pig – I don't know

why. It trotted quietly down the road; it looked very
black against the white road, and the ends on the top,
where the Union Jack was tied, bobbed brightly as it
trotted. At first we thought it would be easy to catch up
to it. This was an error.

When we ran faster it ran faster; when we stopped it
stopped and looked round at us, and nodded. (I daresay you won't swallow this, but you may safely. It's as
true as true, and so's all that about the goat. I give you
my sacred word of honour.) I tell you the pig nodded
as much as to say –

'Oh, yes. You think you will, but you won't!' and
then as soon as we moved again off it went. That pig
led us on and on, o'er miles and miles of strange country.
One thing, it did keep to the roads. When we met
people, which wasn't often, we called out to them to help
us, but they only waved their arms and roared with
laughter. One chap on a bicycle almost tumbled off his
machine, and then he got off it and propped it against a
gate and sat down in the hedge to laugh properly. You
remember Alice was still dressed up as the gay
equestrienne in the dressing-table pink and white, with
rosy garlands, now very droopy, and she had no stockings on, only white sand-shoes, because she thought they
would be easier than boots for balancing on the pig in
the graceful bare-backed act.

Oswald was attired in red paint and flour and
pyjamas, for a clown. It is really *impossible* to run speed-
fully in another man's pyjamas, so Oswald had taken
them off, and wore his own brown knickerbockers
belonging to his Norfolks. He had tied the pyjamas
round his neck, to carry them easily. He was afraid to
leave them in a ditch, as Alice suggested, because he
did not know the roads, and for aught he recked they
might have been infested with footpads. If it had been

his own pyjamas it would have been different. (I'm going to ask for pyjamas next winter, they are so useful in many ways.)

Noël was a highwayman in brown-paper gaiters and bath towels and a cocked hat of newspaper. I don't know how he kept it on. And the pig was encircled by the dauntless banner of our country. All the same, I think if I had seen a band of youthful travellers in bitter distress about a pig I should have tried to lend a helping hand and not sat roaring in the hedge, no matter how the travellers and the pig might have been dressed.

It was hotter than anyone would believe who has never had occasion to hunt the pig when dressed for quite another part. The flour got out of Oswald's hair into his eyes and his mouth. His brow was wet with what the village blacksmith's was wet with, and not his fair brow alone. It ran down his face and washed the red off in streaks, and when he rubbed his eyes he only made it worse. Alice had to run holding the equestrienne skirts on with both hands, and I think the brown-paper boots bothered Noël from the first. Dora had her skirt over her arm and carried the topper in her hand. It was no use to tell ourselves it was a wild boar hunt – we were long past that.

At last we met a man who took pity on us. He was a kind-hearted man. I think, perhaps, he had a pig of his own – or, perhaps, children, Honour to his name!

He stood in the middle of the road and waved his arms. The pig right-wheeled through a gate into a private garden and cantered up the drive. We followed. What else were we to do, I should like to know?

The Learned Black Pig seemed to know its way. It turned first to the right and then to the left, and emerged on a lawn.

'Now, all together!' cried Oswald, mustering his failing voice to give the word of command. 'Surround him! – cut off his retreat!'

We almost surrounded him. He edged off towards the house.

'Now we've got him!' cried the crafty Oswald, as the pig got on to a bed of yellow pansies close against the red house wall.

All would even then have been well, but Denny, at the last, shrank from meeting the pig face to face in a manly way. He let the pig pass him, and the next moment, with a squeak that said 'There now!' as plain as words, the pig bolted into a French window. The pursuers halted not. This was no time for trivial ceremony. In another moment the pig was a captive. Alice and Oswald had their arms round him under the ruins of a table that had had teacups on it, and around the hunters and their prey stood the startled members of a parish society for making clothes for the poor heathen, that that pig had led us into the very midst of. They were reading a missionary report or something when we ran our quarry to earth under their table. Even as he crossed the threshold I heard something about 'black brothers being already white to the harvest'. All the ladies had been sewing flannel things for the poor blacks while the curate read aloud to them. You think they screamed when they saw the Pig and Us? You are right.

On the whole, I cannot say that the missionary people behaved badly. Oswald explained that it was entirely the pig's doing, and asked pardon quite properly for any alarm the ladies had felt; and Alice said how sorry we were but really it was *not* our fault this time. The curate looked a bit nasty, but the presence of ladies made him keep his hot blood to himself.

When we had explained, we said, 'Might we go?'

The curate said, 'The sooner the better.' But the Lady of the House asked for our names and addresses, and said she should write to our Father. (She did, and we heard of it too.) They did not do anything to us, as Oswald at one time believed to be the curate's idea. They let us go.

And we went, after we had asked for a piece of rope to lead the pig by.

'In case it should come back into your nice room,' Alice said. 'And that would be such a pity, wouldn't it?'

A little girl in a starched pinafore was sent for the rope. And as soon as the pig had agreed to let us tie it round his neck we came away. The scene in the drawing-room had not been long.

The pig went slowly,

> *'Like the meandering brook,'*

Denny said. Just by the gate the shrubs rustled and opened, and the little girl came out. Her pinafore was full of cake.

'Here,' she said. 'You must be hungry if you've come all that way. I think they might have given you some tea after all the trouble you've had.'

We took the cake with correct thanks.

'I wish *I* could play at circuses,' she said. 'Tell me about it.'

We told her while we ate the cake; and when we had done she said perhaps it was better to hear about than do, especially the goat's part and Dicky's.

'But I do wish auntie had given you tea,' she said.

We told her not to be too hard on her aunt, because you have to make allowances for grown-up people.

When we parted she said she would never forget us,

and Oswald gave her his pocket button-hook and cork-screw combined for a keepsake.

Dicky's act with the goat (which is true, and no kid) was the only thing out of that day that was put in the Golden Deed book, and he put that in himself while we were hunting the pig.

Alice and me capturing the pig was never put in. We would scorn to write our own good actions, but I suppose Dicky was dull with us all away; and you must pity the dull, and not blame them.

I will not seek to unfold to you how we got the pig home, or how the donkey was caught (that was poor sport compared to the pig). Nor will I tell you a word of all that was said and done to the intrepid hunters of the Black and Learned. I have told you all the interesting part. Seek not to know the rest. It is better buried in obliquity.

CHAPTER 7

BEING BEAVERS; OR, THE YOUNG EXPLORERS (ARCTIC OR OTHERWISE)

You read in books about the pleasures of London, and about how people who live in the country long for the gay whirl of fashion in town because the country is so dull. I do not agree with this at all. In London, or at any rate Lewisham, nothing happens unless you make it happen; or if it happens it doesn't happen to you, and you don't know the people it does happen to. But in the country the most interesting events occur quite freely, and they seem to happen to you as much as to anyone else. Very often quite without your doing anything to help.

The natural and right ways of earning your living in the country are much jollier than town ones, too; sowing and reaping, and doing things with animals, are much better sport than fishmongering or bakering or oil-shopping, and those sort of things, except, of course, a plumber's and gasfitter's, and he is the same in town or country – most interesting and like an engineer.

I remember what a nice man it was that came to cut the gas off once at our old house in Lewisham, when my father's business was feeling so poorly. He was a true gentleman, and gave Oswald and Dicky over two yards and a quarter of good lead piping, and a brass tap that only wanted a washer, and a whole handful of screws to do what we liked with. We screwed the back door up with the screws, I remember, one night when Eliza was out without leave. There was an awful row. We did not mean to get her into trouble. We only thought it would be amusing for her to find the door screwed up when she came down to take in the milk in the morning. But I must not say any more about the Lewisham house. It is only the pleasures of memory, and nothing to do with being beavers, or any sort of exploring.

I think Dora and Daisy are the kind of girls who will grow up very good, and perhaps marry missionaries. I am glad Oswald's destiny looks at present as if it might be different.

We made two expeditions to discover the source of the Nile (or the North Pole), and owing to their habit of sticking together and doing dull and praiseable things, like sewing, and helping with the cooking, and taking invalid delicacies to the poor and indignant, Daisy and Dora were wholly out of it both times, though Dora's foot was now quite well enough to have gone to the North Pole or the Equator either. They said they did not mind the first time, because they like to keep themselves clean; it is another of their queer ways. And they said they had had a better time than us. (It was only a clergyman and his wife who called, and hot cakes for tea.) The second time they said they were lucky not to have been in it. And perhaps they were right. But let me to my narrating. I hope you will like it. I am going to try to write it a different way, like the books they give you for a prize at a girls' school – I mean a 'young ladies' school', of course – not a high school. High schools are not nearly so silly as some other kinds. Here goes:

'"Ah, me!" sighed a slender maiden of twelve summers, removing her elegant hat and passing her tapery fingers lightly through her fair tresses, "how sad it is – is it not? – to see able-bodied youths and young ladies wasting the precious summer hours in idleness and luxury."

'The maiden frowned reproachingly, but yet with earnest gentleness, at the group of youths and maidens who sat beneath an umbragipeaous beech tree and ate black currants.

' "Dear brothers and sisters," the blushing girl went on, "could we not, even now, at the eleventh hour, turn to account these wasted lives of ours, and seek some occupation at once improving and agreeable?"

' 'I do not quite follow your meaning, dear sister," replied the cleverest of her brothers, on whose brow – '

It's no use. I can't write like these books. I wonder how the books' authors can keep it up.

What really happened was that we were all eating black currants in the orchard, out of a cabbage leaf, and Alice said –

'I say, look here, let's do something. It's simply silly to waste a day like this. It's just on eleven. Come on!'

And Oswald said, 'Where to?'

This was the beginning of it.

The moat that is all round our house is fed by streams. One of them is a sort of open overflow pipe from a good-sized stream that flows at the other side of the orchard.

It was this stream that Alice meant when she said –

'Why not go and discover the source of the Nile?'

Of course Oswald knows quite well that the source of the real live Egyptian Nile is no longer buried in that mysteriousness where it lurked undisturbed for such a long time. But he was not going to say so. It is a great thing to know when not to say things.

'Why not have it an Arctic expedition?' said Dicky;

'then we could take an ice-axe, and live on blubber and things. Besides, it sounds cooler.'

'Vote! vote!' cried Oswald. So we did.

Oswald, Alice, Noël, and Denny voted for the river of the ibis and the crocodile. Dicky, H. O., and the other girls for the region of perennial winter and rich blubber.

So Alice said, 'We can decide as we go. Let's start anyway.'

The question of supplies had now to be gone into. Everybody wanted to take something different, and nobody thought the other people's things would be the slightest use. It is sometimes thus even with grown-up expeditions. So then Oswald, who is equal to the hardest emergency that ever emerged yet, said –

'Let's each get what we like. The secret storehouse can be the shed in the corner of the stableyard where we got the door for the raft. Then the captain can decide who's to take what.'

This was done. You may think it but the work of a moment to fit out an expedition, but this is not so, especially when you know not whether your exploring party is speeding to Central Africa or merely to the world of icebergs and the Polar bear.

Dicky wished to take the wood-axe, the coal hammer, a blanket, and a mackintosh.

H. O. brought a large faggot in case we had to light fires, and a pair of old skates he had happened to notice in the box-room, in case the expedition turned out icy.

Noël had nicked a dozen boxes of matches, a spade, and a trowel, and had also obtained – I know not by what means – a jar of pickled onions.

Denny had a walking-stick – we can't break him of walking with it – a book to read in case he got tired of being a discoverer, a butterfly net and a box with a cork in it, a tennis ball, if we happened to want to play rounders in the pauses of exploring, two towels and an umbrella in the event of camping or if the river got big enough to bathe in or to be fallen into.

Alice had a comforter for Noël in case we got late, a pair of scissors and needle and cotton, two whole candles in case of caves. And she had thoughtfully brought the tablecloth off the small table in the dining-room, so that we could make all the things up into one bundle and take it in turns to carry it.

Oswald had fastened his master mind entirely on grub. Nor had the others neglected this.

All the stores for the expedition were put down on the tablecloth and the corners tied up. Then it was more than even Oswald's muscley arms could raise from the ground, so we decided not to take it, but only the best-selected grub. The rest we hid in the straw loft, for there are many ups and downs in life, and grub *is* grub at any time, and so are stores of all kinds. The pickled onions we had to leave, but not for ever.

Then Dora and Daisy came along with their arms round each other's necks as usual, like a picture on a grocer's almanac, and said they weren't coming.

It was, as I have said, a blazing hot day, and there were differences of opinion among the explorers about what eatables we ought to have taken, and H. O. had lost one of his garters and wouldn't let Alice tie it up with her handkerchief, which the gentle sister was quite willing to do. So it was a rather gloomy expedition that set off that bright sunny day to seek the source of the river where Cleopatra sailed in Shakespeare (or the frozen plains Mr Nansen wrote that big book about).

But the balmy calm of peaceful Nature soon made the others less cross – Oswald had not been cross exactly but only disinclined to do anything the others wanted – and by the time we had followed the stream a little way, and had seen a water-rat and shied a stone or two at him, harmony was restored. We did not hit the rat.

You will understand that we were not the sort of people to have lived so long near a stream without plumbing its depths. Indeed it was the same stream the sheep took its daring jump into the day we had the circus. And of course we had often paddled in it – in the shallower parts. But now our hearts were set on exploring. At least they ought to have been, but when we got to the place where the stream goes under a wooden sheep-bridge, Dicky cried, 'A camp! a camp!' and we were all glad to sit down at once. Not at all like real explorers, who know no rest, day or night, till they have got there (whether it's the North Pole, or the central point of the part marked 'Desert of Sahara' on old-fashioned maps).

The food supplies obtained by various members were good and plenty of it. Cake, hard eggs, sausage-rolls, currants, lemon cheese-cakes, raisins, and cold apple dumplings. It was all very decent, but Oswald could not help feeling that the source of the Nile (or North Pole) was a long way off, and perhaps nothing much when you got there.

So he was not wholly displeased when Denny said, as he lay kicking into the bank when the things to eat were all gone –

'I believe this is clay: did you ever make huge platters and bowls out of clay and dry them in the sun? Some people did in a book called Foul Play, and I believe they baked turtles, or oysters, or something, at the same time.'

He took up a bit of clay and began to mess it about, like you do putty when you get hold of a bit. And at once the heavy gloom that had hung over the explorers became expelled, and we all got under the shadow of the bridge and messed about with clay.

'It will be jolly!' Alice said, 'and we can give the huge platters to poor cottagers who are short of the usual sorts of crockery. That would really be a very golden deed.'

It is harder than you would think when you read about it, to make huge platters with clay. It flops about as soon as you get it any size, unless you keep it much too thick, and then when you turn up the edges they crack. Yet we did not mind the trouble. And we had all got our shoes and stockings off. It is impossible to go on being cross when your feet are in cold water; and there is something in the smooth messiness of clay, and not minding how dirty you get, that would soothe the savagest breast that ever beat.

After a bit, though, we gave up the idea of the huge platter and tried little things. We made some platters – they were like flower-pot saucers; and Alice made a bowl by doubling up her fists and getting Noël to slab the clay on outside. Then they smoothed the thing inside and out with wet fingers, and it was a bowl – at least they said it was. When we'd made a lot of things we set them in the sun to dry, and then it seemed a pity not to do the thing thoroughly. So we made a bonfire, and when it had burnt down we put our pots on the soft, white, hot ashes among the little red sparks, and kicked the ashes over them and heaped more fuel over the top. It was a fine fire.

Then tea-time seemed as if it ought to be near, and we decided to come back next day and get our pots.

As we went home across the fields Dicky looked back and said –

'The bonfire's going pretty strong.'

We looked. It was. Great flames were rising to heaven against the evening sky. And we had left it a smouldering flat heap.

There is something in the smoothness of clay . . .

'The clay must have caught alight.' H. O. said. 'Perhaps it's the kind that burns. I know I've heard of fireclay. And there's another sort you can eat.'

'Oh, shut up!' Dicky said with anxious scorn.

With one accord we turned back. We all felt *the* feeling – the one that means something fatal being up and it being your fault.

'Perhaps,' Alice said, 'a beautiful young lady in a muslin dress was passing by, and a spark flew on to her, and now she is rolling in agony enveloped in flames.'

We could not see the fire now, because of the corner of the wood, but we hoped Alice was mistaken.

But when we got in sight of the scene of our pottering industry we saw it was as bad nearly as Alice's wild dream. For the wooden fence leading up to the bridge had caught fire, and it was burning like billy oh.

Oswald started to run; so did the others. As he ran he said to himself, 'This is no time to think about your clothes. Oswald, be bold!'

And he was.

Arrived at the site of the conflagration, he saw that caps or straw hats full of water, however quickly and perseveringly given, would never put the bridge out, and his eventful past life made him know exactly the sort of wigging you get for an accident like this.

So he said, 'Dicky, soak your jacket and mine in the stream and chuck them along. Alice, stand clear, or your silly girl's clothes'll catch as sure as fate.'

Dicky and Oswald tore off their jackets, so did Denny, but we would not let him and H. O. wet theirs. Then the brave Oswald advanced warily to the end of the burning rails and put his wet jacket over the end bit, like a linseed poultice on the throat of a suffering invalid who has got bronchitis. The burning wood hissed and smouldered, and Oswald fell back, almost choked with the smoke.

But at once he caught up the other wet jacket and put it on another place, and of course it did the trick as he had known it would do. But it was a long job, and the smoke in his eyes made the young hero obliged to let Dicky and Denny take a turn as they had bothered to do from the first. At last all was safe; the devouring element was conquered. We covered up the beastly bonfire with clay to keep it from getting into mischief again, and then Alice said –

'Now we must go and tell.'

'Of course,' Oswald said shortly. He had meant to tell all the time.

So we went to the farmer who has the Moat House Farm, and we went at once, because if you have any news like that to tell it only makes it worse if you wait about. When we had told him he said –

'You little – .' I shall not say what he said besides that, because I am sure he must have been sorry for it next Sunday when he went to church, if not before.

We did not take any notice of what he said, but just kept on saying how sorry we were; and he did not take our apology like a man, but only said he daresayed, just like a woman does. Then he went to look at his bridge, and we went in to our tea. The jackets were never quite the same again.

Really great explorers would never be discouraged by the daresaying of a farmer, still less by his calling them names he ought not to. Albert's uncle was away so we got no double slating; and next day we started again to discover the source of the river of cataracts (or the region of mountain-like icebergs).

We set out, heavily provisioned with a large cake Daisy and Dora had made themselves, and six bottles of ginger-beer. I think real explorers most likely have their ginger-beer in something lighter to carry than stone bottles. Perhaps they have it by the cask, which would come cheaper; and you could make the girls carry it on their back, like in pictures of the daughters of regiments.

We passed the scene of the devouring conflagration, and the thought of the fire made us so thirsty we decided to drink the ginger-beer and leave the bottles in a place of concealment. Then we went on, determined to reach our destination, Tropic or Polar, that day.

Denny and H. O. wanted to stop and try to make a fashionable watering-place at that part where the stream spreads out like a small-sized sea, but Noël said, 'No.' We did not like fashionableness.

'*You* ought to, at any rate,' Denny said. 'A Mr Collins wrote an Ode to the Fashions, and he was a great poet.'

'The poet Milton wrote a long book about Satan,' Noël said, 'but I'm not bound to like *him*.' I think it was smart of Noël.

'People aren't obliged to like everything they write about even, let alone read,' Alice said. 'Look at "Ruin seize thee, ruthless king!" and all the pieces of poetry about war, and tyrants, and slaughtered saints – and the one you made yourself about the black beetle, Noël.'

By this time we had got by the pondy place and the danger of delay was past; but the others went on talking about poetry for quite a field and a half, as we walked along by the banks of the stream. The stream was broad and shallow at this part, and you could see the stones and gravel at the bottom, and millions of baby fishes, and a sort of skating-spiders walking about on the top of the water. Denny said the water must be ice for them to be able to walk on it, and this showed we were getting near the North Pole. But Oswald had seen a kingfisher by the wood, and he said it was an ibis, so this was even.

When Oswald had had as much poetry as he could bear he said, 'Let's be beavers and make a dam.'

And everybody was so hot they agreed joyously, and soon our clothes were tucked up as far as they could go and our legs looked green through the water, though they were pink out of it.

Making a dam is jolly good fun, though laborious, as books about beavers take care to let you know.

Dicky said it must be Canada if we were beavers, and so it was on the way to the Polar system, but Oswald pointed to his heated brow, and Dicky owned it was warm for Polar regions. He had brought the ice-axe (it is called the wood chopper sometimes), and Oswald, ever ready and able to command, set him and Denny to cut turfs from the bank while we heaped stones across the stream. It was clayey here, or of course dam making would have been vain, even for the best-trained beaver.

When we had made a ridge of stones we laid turfs against them – nearly across the stream, leaving about two feet for the water to go through – then more stones, and then lumps of clay stamped down as hard as we could. The industrious beavers spent hours over it, with only one easy to eat cake in. And at last the dam rose to the level of the bank. Then the beavers collected a great heap of clay, and four of them lifted it and dumped it down in the opening where the water was running. It did splash a little, but a true-hearted beaver knows better than to mind a bit of a wetting, as Oswald told Alice at the time. Then with more clay the work was completed. We must have used tons of clay; there was quite a big long hole in the bank above the dam where we had taken it out.

When our beaver task was performed we went on, and Dicky was so hot he had to take his jacket off and shut up about icebergs.

I cannot tell you about all the windings of the stream; it went through fields and woods and meadows, and at last the banks got steeper and higher, and the trees overhead darkly arched their mysterious branches, and we felt like the princes in a fairy tale who go out to seek their fortunes.

And then we saw a thing that was well worth coming all that way for; the stream suddenly disappeared under a dark stone archway, and however much you stood in the water and stuck your head down between your knees you could not see any light at the other end.

The stream was much smaller than where we had been beavers.

Gentle reader, you will guess in a moment who it was that said –

'Alice, you've got a candle. Let's explore.'

This gallant proposal met but a cold response.

The others said they didn't care much about it, and what about tea?

I often think the way people try to hide their cowardliness behind their teas is simply beastly.

Oswald took no notice. He just said, with that dignified manner, not at all like sulking, which he knows so well how to put on –

'All right. *I'm* going. If you funk it you'd better cut along home and ask your nurses to put you to bed.'

So then, of course, they agreed to go. Oswald went first with the candle. It was not comfortable; the architect of that dark subterranean passage had not imagined anyone would ever be brave enough to lead a band of beavers into its inky recesses, or he would have built it high enough to stand upright in. As it was, we were bent almost at a right angle, and this is very awkward if for long.

But the leader pressed dauntlessly on, and paid no attention to the groans of his faithful followers, nor to what they said about their backs.

It really was a very long tunnel, though, and even Oswald was not sorry to say, 'I see daylight.' The followers cheered as well as they could as they splashed after him. The floor was stone as well as the roof, so it was easy to walk on. I think the followers would have turned back if it had been sharp stones or gravel.

And now the spot of daylight at the end of the tunnel grew larger and larger, and presently the intrepid leader found himself blinking in the full sun, and the candle he carried looked simply silly. He emerged, and the others too, and they stretched their backs and the word 'krikey' fell from more than one lip. It had indeed been a cramping adventure. Bushes grew close to the mouth of the tunnel, so we could not see much landscape, and when we had stretched our backs we went on up-stream and nobody said they'd had jolly well enough of it, though in more than one young heart this was thought.

It was jolly to be in the sunshine again. I never knew before how cold it was underground. The stream was getting smaller and smaller.

Dicky said, 'This can't be the way. I expect there was a turning to the North Pole inside the tunnel, only we missed it. It was cold enough there.'

But here a twist in the stream brought us out from the bushes, and Oswald said –

'Here is strange, wild, tropical vegetation in the richest profusion. Such blossoms as these never opened in a frigid what's-its-name.'

It was indeed true. We had come out into a sort of marshy, swampy place like I think, a jungle is, that the stream ran through, and it was simply crammed with queer plants, and flowers we never saw before or since. And the stream was quite thin. It was torridly hot, and softish to walk on. There were rushes and reeds and small willows, and it was all tangled over with different sorts of grasses – and pools here and there. We saw no wild beasts, but there were more different kinds of wild flies and beetles than you could believe anybody could bear, and dragon-flies and gnats. The girls picked a lot of flowers. I know the names of some of them, but I will not tell you them because this is not meant to be instructing. So I will only name meadow-sweet, yarrow, loose-strife, lady's bed-straw and willow herb – both the larger and the lesser.

Everyone now wished to go home. It was much hotter there than in natural fields. It made you want to tear all your clothes off and play at savages, instead of keeping respectable in your boots.

But we had to bear the boots because it was so brambly.

It was Oswald who showed the others how flat it would be to go home the same way we came; and he pointed out the telegraph wires in the distance and said –

'There must be a road there, let's make for it,' which was quite a simple and ordinary thing to say, and he does not ask for any credit for it.

So we sloshed along, scratching our legs with the brambles, and the water squelched in our boots, and Alice's blue muslin frock was torn all over in those criss-cross tears which are considered so hard to darn.

We did not follow the stream any more. It was only a trickle now, so we knew we had tracked it to its source. And we got hotter and hotter and hotter, and the dews of agony stood in beads on our brows and rolled down our noses and off our chins. And the flies buzzed, and the gnats stung, and Oswald bravely sought to keep up Dicky's courage, when he tripped on a snag and came down on a bramble bush, by saying –

'*You* see it *is* the source of the Nile we've discovered. What price North Poles now?'

Alice said, 'Ah, but think of ices! I expect Oswald wishes it *had* been the Pole, anyway – '

Oswald is naturally the leader, especially when following up what is his own idea, but he knows that leaders have other duties besides just leading. One is to assist weak or wounded members of the expedition, whether Polar or Equatorish.

So the others had got a bit ahead through Oswald lending the tottering Denny a hand over the rough places. Denny's feet hurt him, because when he was a beaver his stockings had dropped out of his pocket, and boots without stockings are not a bed of luxuriousness. And he is often unlucky with his feet.

Presently we came to a pond, and Denny said –

'Let's paddle.'

Oswald likes Denny to have ideas; he knows it is healthy for the boy, and generally he backs him up, but just now it was getting late and the others were ahead, so he said –

'Oh, rot! come on.'

Generally the Dentist would have; but even worms will turn if they are hot enough, and if their feet are hurting them.

'I don't care, I shall!' he said.

Oswald overlooked the mutiny and did not say who was leader. He just said –

'Well don't be all day about it,' for he is a kind-hearted boy and can make allowances.

So Denny took off his boots and went into the pool.

'Oh, it's ripping!' he said. 'You ought to come in.'

'It looks beastly muddy,' said his tolerating leader.

'It is a bit,' Denny said, 'but the mud's just as cool as the water, and so soft, it squeezes between your toes quite different to boots.'

And so he splashed about, and kept asking Oswald to come along in.

But some unseen influence prevented Oswald doing this; or it may have been because both his bootlaces were in hard knots.

Oswald had cause to bless the unseen influence, or the bootlaces, or whatever it was.

Denny had got to the middle of the pool, and he was splashing about, and getting his clothes very wet indeed, and altogether you would have thought his was a most envious and happy state. But alas! the brightest cloud had a waterproof lining. He was just saying –

'You *are* a silly, Oswald. You'd much better – ' when he gave a blood-piercing scream, and began to kick about.

'What's up?' cried the ready Oswald; he feared the worst from the way Denny screamed, but he knew it could not be an old meat tin in this quiet and jungular spot, like it was in the moat when the shark bit Dora.

'I don't know, it's biting me. Oh, it's biting me all over my legs! Oh, what shall I do? Oh, it does hurt! Oh! oh! oh!' remarked Denny, among his screams, and he splashed towards the bank. Oswald went into the water and caught hold of him and helped him out. It is true that Oswald had his boots on, but I trust he would not have funked the unknown terrors of the deep, even without his boots, I am almost sure he would not have.

When Denny had scrambled and been hauled ashore, we saw with horror and amaze that his legs were stuck all over with large black, slug-looking things. Denny

turned green in the face – and even Oswald felt a bit
queer, for he knew in a moment what the black dread-
fulnesses were. He had read about them in a book called
Magnet Stories, where there was a girl called Theodosia,
and she could play brilliant trebles on the piano in
duets, but the other girl knew all about leeches which is
much more useful and golden deedy. Oswald tried to
pull the leeches off, but they wouldn't, and Denny
howled so he had to stop trying. He remembered from
the *Magnet Stories* how to make the leeches begin biting
– the girl did it with cream – but he could not remember
how to stop them, and they had not wanted any showing
how to begin.

'Oh, what shall I do? What shall I do? Oh, it does
hurt! Oh, oh!' Denny observed, and Oswald said –

'Be a man! Buck up! If you won't let me take them
off you'll just have to walk home in them.'

At this thought the unfortunate youth's tears fell fast.
But Oswald gave him an arm, and carried his boots for
him, and he consented to buck up, and the two struggled
on towards the others, who were coming back, attracted
by Denny's yells. He did not stop howling for a moment,
except to breathe. No one ought to blame him till they
have had eleven leeches on their right leg and six on
their left, making seventeen in all, as Dicky said, at
once.

It was lucky he did yell, as it turned out, because a
man on the road – where the telegraph wires were –
was interested by his howls, and came across the marsh
to us as hard as he could.

When he saw Denny's legs he said –

'Blest if I didn't think so,' and he picked Denny up
and carried him under one arm, where Denny went on
saying 'Oh!' and 'It does hurt' as hard as ever.

Our rescuer, who proved to be a fine big young man

in the bloom of youth, and a farm-labourer by trade, in
corduroys, carried the wretched sufferer to the cottage
where he lived with his aged mother; and then Oswald
found that what he had forgotten about the leeches was
salt. The young man in the bloom of youth's mother put
salt on the leeches, and they squirmed off, and fell with
sickening, slug-like flops on the brick floor.

Then the young man in corduroys and the bloom,
etc., carried Denny home on his back, after his legs had
been bandaged up, so that he looked like 'wounded
warriors returning'.

It was not far by the road, though such a long distance
by the way the young explorers had come.

He was a good young man, and though, of course,
acts of goodness are their own reward, still I was glad
he had the two half-crowns Albert's uncle gave him, as
well as his own good act. But I am not sure Alice ought
to have put him in the Golden Deed book which was
supposed to be reserved for Us.

Perhaps you will think this was the end of the source
of the Nile (or North Pole). If you do, it only shows
how mistaken the gentlest reader may be.

The wounded explorer was lying with his wounds
and bandages on the sofa, and we were all having our
tea, with raspberries and white currants, which we
richly needed after our torrid adventures, when Mrs
Pettigrew, the housekeeper, put her head in at the door
and said –

'Please could I speak to you half a moment, sir?' to
Albert's uncle. And her voice was the kind that makes
you look at each other when the grown-up has gone out,
and you are silent, with your bread-and-butter half-
way to the next bite, or your teacup in mid flight to
your lips.

It was as we suppose. Albert's uncle did not come back

for a long while. We did not keep the bread-and-butter on the wing all that time, of course, and we thought we might as well finish the raspberries and white currants. We kept some for Albert's uncle, of course, and they were the best ones too; but when he came back he did not notice our thoughtful unselfishness.

He came in, and his face wore the look that means bed, and very likely no supper.

He spoke, and it was the calmness of white-hot iron, which is something like the calmness of despair. He said –

'You have done it again. What on earth possessed you to make a dam?'

'We were being beavers,' said H. O., in proud tones He did not see as we did where Albert's uncle's tone pointed to.

'No doubt,' said Albert's uncle, rubbing his hands through his hair. 'No doubt! no doubt! Well, my beavers, you may go and build dams with your bolsters. Your dam stopped the stream; the clay you took for it left a channel through which it has run down and ruined about seven pounds' worth of freshly-reaped barley. Luckily the farmer found it out in time or you might have spoiled seventy 'pounds' worth. And you burned a bridge yesterday.'

We said we were sorry. There was nothing else to say, only Alice added, 'We didn't *mean* to be naughty.'

'Of course not,' said Albert's uncle, 'you never do. Oh, yes, I'll kiss you – but it's bed and it's two hundred lines to-morrow, and the line is – "Beware of Being Beavers and Burning Bridges. Dread Dams." It will be a capital exercise in capital B's and D's.'

We knew by that that, though annoyed, he was not furious; we went to bed.

I got jolly sick of capital B's and D's before sunset on

the morrow. That night, just as the others were falling asleep, Oswald said –

'I say.'

'Well,' retorted his brother.

'There is one thing about it,' Oswald went on, 'it does show it was a rattling good dam anyhow.'

And filled with this agreeable thought, the weary beavers (or explorers, Polar or otherwise) fell asleep.

CHAPTER 8

THE HIGH-BORN BABE

IT really was not such a bad baby – for a baby. Its face was round and quite clean, which babies' faces are not always, as I daresay you know by your own youthful relatives; and Dora said its cape was trimmed with real lace, whatever that may be – I don't see myself how one kind of lace can be realler than another. It was in a very swagger sort of perambulator when we saw it; and the perambulator was standing quite by itself in the lane that leads to the mill.

'I wonder whose baby it is,' Dora said. 'Isn't it a darling, Alice?'

Alice agreed to its being one, and said she thought it was most likely the child of noble parents stolen by gipsies.

'These two, as likely as not,' Noël said. 'Can't you see something crime-like in the very way they're lying?'

They were two tramps, and they were lying on the grass at the edge of the lane on the shady side fast asleep, only a very little further on than where the Baby was. They were very ragged, and their snores did have a sinister sound.

'I expect they stole the titled heir at dead of night, and they've been travelling hot-foot ever since, so now they're sleeping the sleep of exhaustedness,' Alice said. 'What a heart-rending scene when the patrician mother wakes in the morning and finds the infant aristocrat isn't in bed with his mamma.'

The Baby was fast asleep or else the girls would have kissed it. They are strangely fond of kissing. The author never could see anything in it himself.

'If the gipsies *did* steal it,' Dora said 'perhaps they'd sell it to us. I wonder what they'd take for it.'

'What could you do with it if you'd got it?' H. O. asked.

'Why, adopt it, of course,' Dora said. 'I've often thought I should enjoy adopting a baby. It would be a golden deed, too. We've hardly got any in the book yet.'

'I should have thought there were enough of us,' Dicky said.

'Ah, but you're none of you babies,' said Dora.

'Unless you count H. O. as a baby: he behaves jolly like one sometimes.'

This was because of what had happened that morning when Dicky found H. O. going fishing with a box of worms, and the box was the one Dicky keeps his silver studs in, and the medal he got at school, and what is left of his watch and chain. The box is lined with red velvet and it was not nice afterwards. And then H. O. said Dicky had hurt him, and he was a beastly bully, and he cried. We thought all this had been made up, and were sorry to see it threaten to break out again. So Oswald said –

'Oh, bother the Baby! Come along, do!'

And the others came.

We were going to the miller's with a message about some flour that hadn't come, and about a sack of sharps for the pigs.

After you go down the lane you come to a cloverfield, and then a cornfield, and then another lane, and then it is the mill. It is a jolly fine mill: in fact it is two – water and wind ones – one of each kind – with a house and farm buildings as well. I never saw a mill like it, and I don't believe you have either.

If we had been in a story-book the miller's wife would have taken us into the neat sanded kitchen where the old oak settle was black with time and rubbing, and dusted chairs for us – old brown Windsor chairs – and given us each a glass of sweet-scented cowslip wine and a thick slice of rich home-made cake. And there would have been fresh roses in an old china bowl on the table. As it was, she asked us all into the parlour and gave us Eiffel Tower lemonade and Marie biscuits. The chairs in her parlour were 'bent wood', and no flowers, except some wax ones under a glass shade, but she was very kind, and we were very much obliged to her. We got out to the miller, though, as soon as we could; only Dora and Daisy stayed with her, and she talked to them about her lodgers and about her relations in London.

The miller is a MAN. He showed us all over the mills – both kinds – and let us go right up into the very top of the wind-mill, and showed us how the top moved round so that the sails could catch the wind, and the great heaps of corn, some red and some yellow (the red is English wheat), and the heaps slice down a little bit at a time into a square hole and go down to the mill-stones. The corn makes a rustling soft noise that is very jolly – something like the noise of the sea – and you can hear it through all the other mill noises.

Then the miller let us go all over the water-mill. It is fairy palaces inside a mill. Everything is powdered over white, like sugar on pancakes when you are allowed to help yourself. And he opened a door and showed us the great water-wheel working on slow and sure, like some great, round, dripping giant, Noël said, and then he asked us if we fished.

'Yes,' was our immediate reply.

'Then why not try the mill-pool?' he said, and we replied politely; and when he was gone to tell his man something we owned to each other that he was a trump.

He did the thing thoroughly. He took us out and cut us ash saplings for rods; he found us in lines and hooks, and several different sorts of bait, including a handsome handful of meal-worms, which Oswald put loose in his pocket.

When it came to bait, Alice said she was going home with Dora and Daisy. Girls are strange, mysterious, silly things. Alice always enjoys a rat hunt until the rat is caught, but she hates fishing from beginning to end. We boys have got to like it. We don't feel now as we did when we turned off the water and stopped the competition of the competing anglers. We had a grand day's fishing that day. I can't think what made the miller so kind to us. Perhaps he felt a thrill of fellow-feeling in his manly breast for his fellow-sportsmen, for he was a noble fisherman himself.

We had glorious sport – eight roach, six dace, three eels, seven perch, and a young pike, but he was so very young the miller asked us to put him back, and of course we did.

'He'll live to bite another day,' said the miller.

The miller's wife gave us bread and cheese and more Eiffel Tower lemonade, and we went home at last, a little damp, but full of successful ambition, with our fish on a string.

It had been a strikingly good time – one of those times that happen in the country quite by themselves. Country people are much more friendly than town people. I suppose they don't have to spread their friendly feelings out over so many persons, so it's thicker, like a pound of butter on one loaf is thicker than on a dozen. Friendliness in the country is not scrape, like it is in London. Even Dicky and H. O. forgot the affair of honour that had taken place in the morning. H. O. changed rods with Dicky because H. O.'s was the best rod, and Dicky baited H. O.'s hook for him, just like loving, unselfish brothers in Sunday School magazines.

We were talking fishlikely as we went along down the lane and through the cornfield and the cloverfield, and then we came to the other lane where we had seen the Baby. The tramps were gone, and the perambulator was gone, and, of course, the Baby was gone too.

'I wonder if those gipsies *had* stolen the Baby?' Noël said dreamily. He had not fished much, but he had made a piece of poetry. It was this:

> *'How I wish*
> *I was a fish.*
> *I would not look*
> *At your hook,*
> *But lie still and be cool*
> *At the bottom of the pool*
> *And when you went to look*
> *At your cruel hook,*
> *You would not find me there,*
> *So there!'*

'If they did steal the Baby,' Noël went on, 'they will be tracked by the lordly perambulator. You can disguise a baby in rags and walnut juice, but there isn't any disguise dark enough to conceal a perambulator's person.'

'You might disguise it as a wheel-barrow,' said Dicky.

'Or cover it with leaves,' said H. O., 'like the robins.'

We told him to shut up and not gibber, but afterwards we had to own that even a young brother may sometimes talk sense by accident.

For we took the short cut home from the lane – it begins with a large gap in the hedge and the grass and weeds trodden down by the hasty feet of persons who were late for church and in too great a hurry to go round by the road. Our house is next to the church, as I think I have said before, some time.

The short cut leads to a stile at the edge of a bit of wood (the Parson's Shave, they call it, because it belongs to him). The wood has not been shaved for some time, and it has grown out beyond the stile; and here, among the hazels and chestnuts and young dog-wood bushes, we saw something white. We felt it was our duty to investigate, even if the white was only the under side of the tail of a dead rabbit caught in a trap. It was not – it was part of the perambulator. I forget whether I said that the perambulator was enamelled white – not the kind of enamelling you do at home with Aspinall's and the hairs of the brush come out and it is gritty-looking, but smooth, like the handles of ladies' very best lace parasols. And whoever had abandoned the helpless perambulator in that lonely spot had done exactly as H. O. said, and covered it with leaves, only they were green and some of them had dropped off.

The others were wild with excitement. Now or never, they thought, was a chance to be real detectives. Oswald alone retained a calm exterior. It was he who would not go straight to the police station.

He said: 'Let's try and ferret out something for ourselves before we tell the police. They always have a clue directly they hear about the finding of the body. And besides, we might as well let Alice be in anything there is going. And besides, we haven't had our dinners yet.'

This argument of Oswald's was so strong and powerful – his arguments are often that, as I daresay you have

'The clue is always left exactly as it is found till the police have seen it'

noticed – that the others agreed. It was Oswald, too, who showed his artless brothers why they had much better not take the deserted prambulator home with them.

'The dead body, or whatever the clue is, is always left exactly as it is found,' he said, 'till the police have seen it, and the coroner, and the inquest, and the doctor, and the sorrowing relations. Besides, suppose someone saw us with the beastly thing, and thought we had stolen it; then they would say, "*What have you done with the Baby?*" and then where should we be?'

Oswald's brothers could not answer this question, but once more Oswald's native eloquence and far-seeing discerningness conquered.

'Anyway,' Dicky said, 'let's shove the derelict a little further under cover.'

So we did.

Then we went on home. Dinner was ready and so were Alice and Daisy, but Dora was not there.

'She's got a – well, she's not coming to dinner anyway,' Alice said when we asked. 'She can tell you herself afterwards what it is she's got.'

Oswald thought it was headache, or pain in the temper, or in the pinafore, so he said no more, but as soon as Mrs Pettigrew had helped us and left the room he began the thrilling tale of the forsaken perambulator. He told it with the greatest thrillingness anyone could have, but Daisy and Alice seemed almost unmoved. Alice said –

'Yes, very strange,' and things like that, but both the girls seemed to be thinking of something else. They kept looking at each other and trying not to laugh, so Oswald saw they had got some silly secret and he said –

'Oh, all right! I don't care about telling you.' I only

thought you'd like to be in it. It's going to be a really big thing, with policemen in it, and perhaps a judge.'

'In what?' H. O. said; 'the perambulator?'

Daisy choked and then tried to drink, and spluttered and got purple, and had to be thumped on the back. But Oswald was not appeased. When Alice said, 'Do go on, Oswald. I'm sure we all like it very much,' he said –

'Oh, no, thank you,' very politely. 'As it happens,' he went on, 'I'd just as soon go through with this thing without having any girls in it.'

'In the perambulator?' said H. O. again.

'It's a man's job,' Oswald went on, without taking any notice of H. O.

'Do you really think so,' said Alice, 'when there's a baby in it?'

'But there isn't,' said H. O., 'if you mean in the perambulator.'

'Blow you and your perambulator,' said Oswald, with gloomy forbearance.

Alice kicked Oswald under the table and said –

'Don't be waxy, Oswald. Really and truly Daisy and I *have* got a secret, only it's Dora's secret, and she wants to tell you herself. If it was mine or Daisy's we'd tell you this minute, wouldn't we, Mouse?'

'This very second,' said the White Mouse.

And Oswald consented to take their apologies.

Then the pudding came in, and no more was said except asking for things to be passed – sugar and water, and bread and things.

Then when the pudding was all gone, Alice said –

'Come on.'

And we came on. We did not want to be disagreeable, though really we were keen on being detectives and sifting that perambulator to the very dregs. But boys have to try to take an interest in their sisters' secrets, however silly. This is part of being a good brother.

Alice led us across the field where the sheep once fell into the brook, and across the brook by the plank. At the other end of the next field there was a sort of wooden house on wheels, that the shepherd sleeps in at the time of year when lambs are being born, so that he can see that they are not stolen by gipsies before the owners have counted them.

To this hut Alice now led her kind brothers and Daisy's kind brother.

'Dora is inside,' she said, 'with the Secret. We were afraid to have it in the house in case it made a noise.'

The next moment the Secret was a secret no longer, for we all beheld Dora, sitting on a sack on the floor of the hut, with the Secret in her lap.

It was the High-born Babe!

Oswald was so overcome that he sat down suddenly, just like Betsy Trotwood did in *David Copperfield*, which just shows what a true author Dickens is.

'You've done it this time,' he said. 'I suppose you know you're a baby-stealer?'

'I'm not,' Dora said. 'I've adopted him.'

'Then it was you,' Dicky said, 'who scuttled the perambulator in the wood?'

'Yes,' Alice said; 'we couldn't get it over the stile unless Dora put down the Baby, and we were afraid of the nettles for his legs. His name is to be Lord Edward.'

'But, Dora – really, don't you think – '

'If you'd been there you'd have done the same,' said Dora firmly. 'The gipsies had gone. Of course something had frightened them and they fled from justice. And the little darling was awake and held out his arms to me. No, he hasn't cried a bit, and I know all about babies;

I've often nursed Mrs Simpkins's daughter's baby when she brings it up on Sundays. They have bread and milk to eat. You take him, Alice, and I'll go and get some bread and milk for him.'

Alice took the noble brat. It was horribly lively, and squirmed about in her arms, and wanted to crawl on the floor. She could only keep it quiet by saying things to it a boy would be ashamed even to think of saying, such as 'Goo goo', and 'Did ums was', and 'Ickle ducksums, then'.

When Alice used these expressions the Baby laughed and chuckled and replied –

'Daddadda', 'Bababa', or 'Glueglue'.

But if Alice stopped her remarks for an instant the thing screwed its face up as if it was going to cry, but she never gave it time to begin.

It was a rummy little animal.

Then Dora came back with the bread and milk, and they fed the noble infant. It was greedy and slobbery, but all three girls seemed unable to keep their eyes and hands off it. They looked at it exactly as if it was pretty.

We boys stayed watching them. There was no amusement left for us now, for Oswald saw that Dora's Secret knocked the bottom out of the perambulator.

When the infant aristocrat had eaten a hearty meal it sat on Alice's lap and played with the amber heart she wears that Albert's uncle brought her from Hastings after the business of the bad sixpence and the nobleness of Oswald.

'Now,' said Dora, 'this is a council, so I want to be business-like. The Duckums Darling has been stolen away; its wicked stealers have deserted the Precious. We've got it. Perhaps its ancestral halls are miles and miles away. I vote we keep the little Lovey Duck till it's advertised for.'

'If Albert's uncle lets you,' said Dicky darkly.

'Oh, don't say "you" like that,' Dora said; 'I want it to be all of our baby. It will have five fathers and three mothers, and a grandfather and a great Albert's uncle, and a great grand-uncle. I'm sure Albert's uncle will let us keep it – at any rate till it's advertised for.'

'And suppose it never is,' Noël said.

'Then so much the better,' said Dora, 'the little Duckywux.'

She began kissing the baby again. Oswald, ever thoughtful, said –

'Well, what about your dinner?'

'Bother dinner!' Dora said – so like a girl. 'Will you all agree to be his fathers and mothers?'

'Anything for a quiet life,' said Dicky, and Oswald said –

'Oh, yes, if you like. But you'll see we shan't be allowed to keep it.'

'You talk as if he was rabbits or white rats,' said Dora, 'and he's not – he's a little man, he is.'

'All right, he's no rabbit, but a man. Come on and get some grub, Dora.' rejoined the kind-hearted Oswald, and Dora did, with Oswald and the other boys. Only Noël stayed with Alice. He really seemed to like the baby. When I looked back he was standing on his head to amuse it, but the baby did not seem to like him any better whichever end of him was up.

Dora went back to the shepherd's house on wheels directly she had had her dinner. Mrs Pettigrew was very cross about her not being in to it, but she had kept her some mutton hot all the same. She is a decent sort. And there were stewed prunes. We had some to keep Dora company. Then we boys went fishing again in the moat, but we caught nothing.

Just before tea-time we all went back to the hut,

and before we got half across the last field we could hear the howling of the Secret.

'Poor little beggar,' said Oswald, with manly tenderness. 'They must be sticking pins in it.'

We found the girls and Noël looking quite pale and breathless. Daisy was walking up and down with the Secret in her arms. It looked like Alice in Wonderland nursing the baby that turned into a pig. Oswald said so, and added that its screams were like it too.

'What on earth is the matter with it?' he said.

'I don't know,' said Alice. 'Daisy's tired, and Dora and I are quite worn out. He's been crying for hours and hours. *You* take him a bit.'

'Not me,' replied Oswald, firmly, withdrawing a pace from the Secret.

Dora was fumbling with her waistband in the furthest corner of the hut.

'I think he's cold,' she said. 'I thought I'd take off my flannelette petticoat, only the horrid strings got into a hard knot. Here, Oswald, let's have your knife.'

With the word she plunged her hand into Oswald's jacket pocket, and next moment she was rubbing her hand like mad on her dress, and screaming almost as loud as the Baby. Then she began to laugh and to cry at the same time. This is called hysterics.

Oswald was sorry, but he was annoyed too. He had forgotten that his pocket was half full of the meal-worms the miller had kindly given him. And, anyway, Dora ought to have known that a man always carries his knife in his trousers pocket and not in his jacket one.

Alice and Daisy rushed to Dora. She had thrown herself down on the pile of sacks in the corner. The titled infant delayed its screams for a moment to listen to Dora's, but almost at once it went on again.

'Oh, get some water!' said Alice. 'Daisy, run!'

The White Mouse, ever docile and obedient, shoved the baby into the arms of the nearest person, who had to take it or it would have fallen a wreck to the ground. This nearest person was Oswald. He tried to pass it on to the others, but they wouldn't. Noël would have, but he was busy kissing Dora and begging her not to.

So our hero, for such I may perhaps term him, found himself the degraded nursemaid of a small but furious kid.

He was afraid to lay it down, for fear in its rage it should beat its brains out against the hard earth, and he did not wish, however innocently, to be the cause of its hurting itself at all. So he walked earnestly up and down with it, thumping it unceasingly on the back, while the others attended to Dora, who presently ceased to yell.

Suddenly it struck Oswald that the High-born also had ceased to yell. He looked at it, and could hardly believe the glad tidings of his faithful eyes. With bated breath he hastened back to the sheep-house.

The others turned on him, full of reproaches about the meal-worms and Dora, but he answered without anger.

'Shut up,' he said in a whisper of imperial command. 'Can't you see it's *gone to sleep?*'

As exhausted as if they had all taken part in all the events of a very long Athletic Sports, the youthful Bastables and their friends dragged their weary limbs back across the fields. Oswald was compelled to go on holding the titled infant, for fear it should wake up if it changed hands, and begin to yell again. Dora's flannelette petticoat had been got off somehow – how I do not seek to inquire – and the Secret was covered with it. The others surrounded Oswald as much as possible, with a view to concealment if we met Mrs

Pettigrew. But the coast was clear. Oswald took the
Secret up into his bedroom. Mrs Pettigrew doesn't
come there much, it's too many stairs.

With breathless precaution Oswald laid it down on
his bed. It sighed, but did not wake. Then we took it in
turns to sit by it and see that it did not get up and fling
itself out of bed, which, in one of its furious fits, it would
just as soon have done as not.

We expected Albert's uncle every minute.

At last we heard the gate, but he did not come in, so
we looked out and saw that there he was talking to a
distracted-looking man on a piebald horse – one of the
miller's horses.

A shiver of doubt coursed through our veins. We
could not remember having done anything wrong at
the miller's. But you never know. And it seemed strange
his sending a man up on his own horse. But when we
had looked a bit longer our fears went down and our
curiosity got up. For we saw that the distracted one was
a gentleman.

Presently he rode off, and Albert's uncle came in.
A deputation met him at the door – all the boys and
Dora, because the baby was her idea.

'We've found something,' Dora said, 'and we want
to know whether we may keep it.'

The rest of us said nothing. We were not so very
extra anxious to keep it after we had heard how much
and how long it could howl. Even Noël had said he had
no idea a baby could yell like it. Dora said it only cried
because it was sleepy, but we reflected that it would
certainly be sleepy once a day, if not oftener.

'What is it?' said Albert's uncle. 'Let's see this
treasure-trove. Is it a wild beast?'

'Come and see,' said Dora, and we led him to our
room.

Alice turned down the pink flannelette petticoat with silly pride, and showed the youthful heir fatly and pinkly sleeping.

'A baby!' said Albert's uncle. '*The* Baby! Oh, my cat's alive!'

That is an expression which he uses to express despair unmixed with anger.

'Where did you? – but that doesn't matter. We'll talk of this later.'

He rushed from the room, and in a moment or two we saw him mount his bicycle and ride off.

Quite shortly he returned with the distracted horseman.

It was *his* baby, and not titled at all. The horseman and his wife were the lodgers at the mill. The nursemaid was a girl from the village.

She *said* she only left the Baby five minutes while she went to speak to her sweetheart who was gardener at the Red House. But *we* knew she left it over an hour, and nearly two.

I never saw anyone so pleased as the distracted horseman.

When we were asked we explained about having thought the Baby was the prey of gipsies, and the distracted horseman stood hugging the Baby, and actually thanked us.

But when he had gone we had a brief lecture on minding our own business. But Dora still thinks she was right. As for Oswald and most of the others, they agreed that they would rather mind their own business all their lives than mind a baby for a single hour.

If you have never had to do with a baby in the frenzied throes of sleepiness you can have no idea what its screams are like.

If you have been through such a scene you will

understand how we managed to bear up under having no baby to adopt.

Oswald insisted on having the whole thing written in the Golden Deed book. Of course his share could not be put in without telling about Dora's generous adopting of the forlorn infant outcast, and Oswald could not and cannot forget that he was the one who did get that baby to sleep.

What a time Mr and Mrs Distracted Horseman must have of it, though – especially now they've sacked the nursemaid.

If Oswald is ever married – I suppose he must be some day – he will have ten nurses to each baby. Eight is not enough. We know that because we tried, and the whole eight of us were not enough for the needs of that deserted infant who was not so extra high-born after all.

CHAPTER 9

HUNTING THE FOX

IT is idle to expect everyone to know everything in the world without being told. If we had been brought up in the country we should have known that it is not done – to hunt the fox in August. But in the Lewisham Road the most observing boy does not notice the dates when it is proper to hunt foxes.

And there are some things you cannot bear to think that anybody would think you would do; that is why I wish to say plainly at the very beginning that none of us would have shot a fox on purpose even to save our skins. Of course, if a man were at bay in a cave, and had to defend girls from the simultaneous attack of a herd of savage foxes it would be different. A man is bound to protect girls and take care of them – they can jolly well take care of themselves really it seems to me – still, this is what Albert's uncle calls one of the 'rules of the game', so we are bound to defend them and fight for them to the death, if needful.

Denny knows a quotation which says –

> '*What dire offence from harmless causes springs,*
> *What mighty contests rise from trefoil things.*'

He says this means that all great events come from three things – threefold, like the clover or trefoil, and the causes are always harmless. Trefoil is short for threefold.

There were certainly three things that led up to the adventure which is now going to be told you. The first was our Indian uncle coming down to the country to see us. The second was Denny's tooth. The third was only our wanting to go hunting; but if you count it in it makes the thing about the trefoil come right. And all these causes were harmless.

It is a flattering thing to say, and it was not Oswald who said it, but Dora. She said she was certain our uncle missed us, and that he felt he could no longer live without seeing his dear ones (that was us).

Anyway, he came down, without warning, which is one of the few bad habits that excellent Indian man has, and this habit has ended in unpleasantness more than once, as when we played Jungles.

However, this time it was all right. He came on rather a dull kind of day, when no one had thought of anything particularly amusing to do. So that, as it happened to be dinner-time and we had just washed our hands and faces, we were all spotlessly clean (compared with what we are sometimes, I mean, of course).

We were just sitting down to dinner, and Albert's uncle was just plunging the knife into the hot heart of the steak pudding, when there was the rumble of wheels, and the station fly stopped at the garden gate. And in the fly, sitting very upright, with his hands on his knees, was our Indian relative so much beloved. He looked very smart, with a rose in his buttonhole. How different from what he looked in other days when he helped us to pretend that our currant pudding was a wild boar we were killing with our forks. Yet, though tidier, his heart still beat kind and true. You should not judge people harshly because their clothes are tidy. He had dinner with us, and then we showed him round the place, and told him everything we thought he would like to hear, and about the Tower of Mystery, and he said –

'It makes my blood boil to think of it.'

Noël said he was sorry for that, because everyone else we had told it to had owned, when we asked them, that it froze their blood.

'Ah,' said the Uncle, 'but in India we learn how to freeze our blood and boil it at the same time.'

In those hot longitudes, perhaps, the blood is always near boiling-point, which accounts for Indian tempers, though not for the curry and pepper they eat. But I must not wander; there is no curry at all in this story. About temper I will not say.

Then Uncle let us all go with him to the station when the fly came back for him; and when we said good-bye he tipped us all half a quid, without any insidious distinctions about age or considering whether you were a boy or a girl. Our Indian uncle is a true-born Briton, with no nonsense about him.

We cheered him like one man as the train went off, and then we offered the fly-driver a shilling to take us back to the four cross-roads, and the grateful creature did it for nothing because, he said, the gent had tipped him something like. How scarce is true gratitude! So we cheered the driver too for this rare virtue, and then went home to talk about what we should do with our money.

I cannot tell you all that we did with it, because money melts away 'like snow-wreaths in thaw-jean', as Denny says, and somehow the more you have the more quickly it melts. We all went into Maidstone, and came back with the most beautiful lot of brown-paper parcels, with things inside that supplied long-felt wants. But none of them belongs to this narration, except what Oswald and Denny clubbed to buy.

This was a pistol, and it took all the money they both had, but when Oswald felt the uncomfortable inside sensation that reminds you who it is and his money that are soon parted he said to himself –

'I don't care. We ought to have a pistol in the house, and one that will go off, too – not those rotten flint-locks. Suppose there should be burglars and us totally unarmed?'

We took it in turns to have the pistol, and we decided always to practise with it far from the house, so as not to frighten the grown-ups, who are always much nervouser about firearms than we are.

It was Denny's idea getting it; and Oswald owns it surprised him, but the boy was much changed in his character. We got it while the others were grubbing at the pastry-cook's in the High Street, and we said nothing till after tea, though it was hard not to fire at the birds on the telegraph wires as we came home in the train.

After tea we called a council in the straw-loft, and Oswald said –

'Denny and I have got a secret.'

'I know what it is,' Dicky said contemptibly. 'You've found out that shop in Maidstone where peppermint rock is four ounces a penny. H. O. and I found it out before you did.'

Oswald said, 'You shut up. If you don't want to hear the secret you'd better bunk. I'm going to administer the secret oath.'

This is a very solemn oath, and only used about real things, and never for pretending ones, so Dicky said –

'Oh, all right; go ahead! I thought you were only rotting.'

So they all took the secret oath. Noël made it up long before, when he had found the first thrush's nest we ever saw in the Blackheath garden:

'I will not tell, I will not reveal,
I will not touch, or try to steal;
And may I be called a beastly sneak,
If this great secret I ever repeat.'

It is a little wrong about the poetry, but it is a very binding promise. They all repeated it, down to H. O.

'Now then,' Dicky said, 'what's up?'

Oswald, in proud silence, drew the pistol from his breast and held it out, and there was a murmur of awful amazement and respect from every one of the council. The pistol was not loaded, so we let even the girls have it to look at.

And then Dicky said, 'Let's go hunting.'

And we decided that we would. H. O. wanted to go down to the village and get penny horns at the shop for the huntsmen to wind, like in the song, but we thought it would be more modest not to wind horns or anything noisy, at anyrate not until we had run down our prey. But his talking of the song made us decide that it was the fox we wanted to hunt. We had not been particular which animal we hunted before that.

Oswald let Denny have· first go with the pistol, and when we went to bed he slept with it under his pillow, but not loaded, for fear he should have a nightmare and draw his fell weapon before he was properly awake.

Oswald let Denny have it, because Denny had toothache, and a pistol is consoling though it does not actually stop the pain of the tooth. The toothache got worse, and Albert's uncle looked at it, and said it was very loose, and Denny owned he had tried to crack a peach-stone with it. Which accounts. He had creosote and camphor, and went to bed early, with his tooth tied up in red flannel.

Oswald knows it is right to be very kind when people

are ill, and he forbore to wake the sufferer next morning by buzzing a pillow at him, as he generally does. He got up and went over to shake the invalid, but the bird had flown and the nest was cold. The pistol was not in the nest either, but Oswald found it afterwards under the looking-glass on the dressing-table. He had just awakened the others (with a hair-brush because they had not got anything the matter with their teeth), when he heard wheels, and, looking out, beheld Denny and Albert's uncle being driven from the door in the farmer's high cart with the red wheels.

We dressed extra quick, so as to get downstairs to the bottom of the mystery. And we found a note from Albert's uncle. It was addressed to Dora, and said –

'Denny's toothache got him up in the small hours. He's off to the dentist to have it out with him, man to man. Home to dinner.'

Dora said, 'Denny's gone to the dentist.'

'I expect it's a relation,' H. O. said. 'Denny must be short for Dentist.'

I suppose he was trying to be funny – he really does try very hard. He wants to be a clown when he grows up. The others laughed.

'I wonder,' said Dicky, 'whether he'll get a shilling or half-a-crown for it.'

Oswald had been meditating in gloomy silence, now he cheered up and said –

'Of course! I'd forgotten that. He'll get his tooth money, and the drive too. So it's quite fair for us to have the fox-hunt while he's gone. I was thinking we should have to put it off.'

The others agreed that it would not be unfair.

'We can have another one another time if he wants to,' Oswald said.

We know foxes are hunted in red coats and on horseback – but we could not do this – but H. O. had the old red football jersey that was Albert's uncle's when he was at Loretto. He was pleased.

'But I do wish we'd had horns,' he said grievingly. 'I should have liked to wind the horn.'

'We can pretend horns,' Dora said; but he answered, 'I didn't want to pretend. I wanted to wind something.'

'Wind your watch,' Dicky said. And that was unkind, because we all know H. O.'s watch is broken, and when you wind it, it only rattles inside without going in the least.

We did not bother to dress up much for the hunting expedition – just cocked hats and lath swords; and we tied a card on to H. O.'s chest with 'Moat House Fox-Hunters' on it; and we tied red flannel round all the dogs' necks to show they were fox-hounds. Yet it did not seem to show it plainly; somehow it made them look as if they were not fox-hounds, but their own natural breeds – only with sore throats.

Oswald slipped the pistol and a few cartridges into his pocket. He knew, of course, that foxes are not shot; but as he said –

'Who knows whether we may not meet a bear or a crocodile.'

We set off gaily. Across the orchard and through two cornfields, and along the hedge of another field, and so we got into the wood, through a gap we had happened to make a day or two before, playing 'follow my leader'.

The wood was very quiet and green; the dogs were happy and most busy. Once Pincher started a rabbit. We said, 'View Halloo!' and immediately started in pursuit; but the rabbit went and hid, so that even Pincher could not find him, and we went on. But we saw no foxes.

So at last we made Dicky be a fox, and chased him down the green rides. A wide walk in a wood is called a ride, even if people never do anything but walk in it.

We had only three hounds – Lady, Pincher and Martha – so we joined the glad throng and were being hounds as hard as we could, when we suddenly came barking round a corner in full chase and stopped short, for we saw that our fox had stayed his hasty flight. The fox was stooping over something reddish that lay beside the path, and he cried –

'I say, look here!' in tones that thrilled us throughout.

Our fox – whom we must now call Dicky, so as not to muddle the narration – pointed to the reddy thing that the dogs were sniffing at.

'It's a real live fox,' he said. And so it was. At least it was real – only it was quite dead – and when Oswald lifted it up its head was bleeding. It had evidently been shot through the brain and expired instantly. Oswald explained this to the girls when they began to cry at the sight of the poor beast; I do not say he did not feel a bit sorry himself.

The fox was cold, but its fur was so pretty, and its tail and its little feet. Dicky strung the dogs on the leash; they were so much interested we thought it was better.

'It does seem horrid to think it'll never see again out of its poor little eyes,' Dora said, blowing her nose.

'And never run about through the wood again, lend me your hanky, Dora,' said Alice.

'And never be hunted or get into a hen-roost or a trap or anything exciting, poor little thing,' said Dicky.

The girls began to pick green chestnut leaves to cover up the poor fox's fatal wound, and Noël began to walk up and down making faces, the way he always does when he's making poetry. He cannot make one without the other. It works both ways, which is a comfort.

'What are we going to do now?' H. O. said; 'the huntsman ought to cut off its tail, I'm quite certain. Only, I've broken the big blade of my knife, and the other never was any good.'

The girls gave H. O. a shove, and even Oswald said, 'Shut up', for somehow we all felt we did not want to play fox-hunting any more that day. When his deadly wound was covered the fox hardly looked dead at all.

'Oh, I wish it wasn't true!' Alice said.

Daisy had been crying all the time, and now she said, 'I should like to pray God to make it not true.'

But Dora kissed her, and told her that was no good – only she might pray God to take care of the fox's poor little babies, if it had had any, which I believe she has done ever since.

'If only we could wake up and find it was a horrid dream,' Alice said. It seems silly that we should have cared so much when we had really set out to hunt foxes with dogs, but it is true. The fox's feet looked so helpless. And there was a dusty mark on its side that I know would not have been there if it had been alive and able to wash itself.

Noël now said, 'This is the piece of poetry':

> *'Here lies poor Reynard who is slain,*
> *He will not come to life again.*
> *I never will the huntsman's horn*
> *Wind since the day that I was born*
> *Until the day I die.*
> *For I don't like hunting, and this is why.'*

'Let's have a funeral,' said H. O. This pleased everybody, and we got Dora to take off her petticoat to wrap the fox in, so that we could carry it to our garden and bury it without bloodying our jackets. Girls' clothes are silly in one way, but I think they are useful too. A boy cannot take off more than his jacket and waistcoat in any emergency, or he is at once entirely undressed. But I have known Dora take off two petticoats for useful purposes and look just the same outside afterwards.

We boys took it in turns to carry the fox. It was very heavy. When we got near the edge of the wood Noël said –

'It would be better to bury it here, where the leaves can talk funeral songs over its grave for ever, and the other foxes can come and cry if they want to.' He dumped the fox down on the moss under a young oak tree as he spoke.

'If Dicky fetched the spade and fork we could bury it here, and then he could tie up the dogs at the same time.'

'You're sick of carrying it,' Dicky remarked, 'that's what it is.' But he went on condition the rest of us boys went too.

While we were gone the girls dragged the fox to the edge of the wood; it was a different edge to the one we went in by – close to a lane – and while they waited for the digging or fatigue party to come back, they collected a lot of moss and green things to make the fox's long home soft for it to lie in. There are no flowers in the woods in August, which is a pity.

When we got back with the spade and fork we dug a hole to bury the fox in. We did not bring the dogs back, because they were too interested in the funeral to behave with real, respectable calmness.

The ground was loose and soft and easy to dig when we had scraped away the broken bits of sticks and the dead leaves and the wild honeysuckle; Oswald used the

fork and Dicky had the spade. Noël made faces and
poetry – he was struck so that morning – and the girls
sat stroking the clean parts of the fox's fur till the grave
was deep enough. At last it was; then Daisy threw in the
leaves and grass, and Alice and Dora took the poor dead
fox by his two ends and we helped to put him in the
grave. We could not lower him slowly – he was dropped
in, really. Then we covered the furry body with leaves,
and Noël said the Burial Ode he had made up. He says
this was it, but it sounds better now than it did then,
so I think he must have done something to it since:

THE FOX'S BURIAL ODE

'Dear Fox, sleep here, and do not wake,
We picked these leaves for your sake.
You must not try to rise or move,
We give you this with our love.
Close by the wood where once you grew
Your mourning friends have buried you.
If you had lived you'd not have been
(Been proper friends with us, I mean),
But now you're laid upon the shelf,
Poor fox, you cannot help yourself,
So, as I say, we are your loving friends
And here your Burial Ode, dear Foxy, ends.
P.S. – When in the moonlight bright
The foxes wander of a night,
They'll pass your grave and fondly think of you,
Exactly like we mean to always do.
So now, dear fox, adieu!
Your friends are few
But true
To you.
Adieu!'

When this had been said we filled in the grave and
covered the top if it with dry leaves and sticks to make

it look like the rest of the wood. People might think
it was a treasure, and dig it up, if they thought there
was anything buried there, and we wished the poor fox
to sleep sound and not to be disturbed.

The interring was over. We folded up Dora's blood-
stained pink cotton petticoat, and turned to leave the
sad spot.

We had not gone a dozen yards down the lane when
we heard footsteps and a whistle behind us, and a
scrabbling and whining, and a gentleman with two fox-
terriers had called a halt just by the place where we had
laid low the 'little red rover'.

The gentleman stood in the lane, but the dogs were
digging – we could see their tails wagging and see the
dust fly. And we *saw where*. We ran back.

'Oh, please, do stop your dogs digging there!' Alice
said.

The gentleman said 'Why?'

'Because we've just had a funeral, and that's the
grave.'

The gentleman whistled, but the fox-terriers were not
trained like Pincher, who was brought up by Oswald.
The gentleman took a stride through the hedge gap.

'What have you been burying – pet dicky bird, eh?'
said the gentleman, kindly. He had riding breeches and
white whiskers.

We did not answer, because now, for the first time, it
came over all of us, in a rush of blushes and uncomfort-
ableness, that burying a fox is a suspicious act. I don't
know why we felt this, but we did.

Noël said dreamily –

> '*We found his murdered body in the wood,*
> *And dug a grave by which the mourners stood.*'

But no one heard him except Oswald, because Alice

and Dora and Daisy were all jumping about with the jumps of unrestrained anguish, and saying, 'Oh, call them off! Do! do! – oh, don't, don't! Don't let them dig.'

Alas! Oswald was, as usual, right. The ground of the grave had not been trampled down hard enough, and he had said so plainly at the time, but his prudent counsels had been overruled. Now these busy-bodying, meddling, mischief-making fox-terriers (how different from Pincher, who minds his own business unless told otherwise) had scratched away the earth and laid bare the reddish tip of the poor corpse's tail.

We all turned to go without a word, it seemed to be no use staying any longer.

But in a moment the gentleman with the whiskers had got Noël and Dicky each by an ear – they were nearest him. H. O. hid in the hedge. Oswald, to whose noble breast sneakishness is, I am thankful to say, a stranger, would have scorned to escape, but he ordered his sisters to bunk in a tone of command which made refusal impossible.

'And bunk sharp, too,' he added sternly. 'Cut along home.'

So they cut.

The white-whiskered gentleman now encouraged his mangy fox-terriers, by every means at his command, to continue their vile and degrading occupation; holding on all the time to the ears of Dicky and Noël, who scorned to ask for mercy. Dicky got purple and Noël got white. It was Oswald who said –

'Don't hang on to them, sir. We won't cut. I give you my word of honour.'

'*Your* word of honour,' said the gentleman, in tones for which, in happier days, when people drew their bright blades and fought duels, I would have had his heart's dearest blood. But now Oswald remained calm and polite as ever.

'Yes, on my honour,' he said, and the gentleman dropped the ears of Oswald's brothers at the sound of his firm, unswerving tones. He dropped the ears and pulled out the body of the fox and held it up. The dogs jumped up and yelled.

'Now,' he said, 'you talk very big about words of honour. Can you speak the truth?'

Dickie said, 'If you think we shot it, you're wrong. We know better than that.'

The white-whiskered one turned suddenly to H. O. and pulled him out of the hedge.

'And what does that mean?' he said, and he was pink with fury to the ends of his large ears, as he pointed to the card on H. O.'s breast, which said, 'Moat House Fox-Hunters'.

Then Oswald said, 'We *were* playing at fox-hunting, but we couldn't find anything but a rabbit that hid, so my brother was being the fox; and then we found the fox shot dead, and I don't know who did it; and we were sorry for it and we buried it – and that's all.'

'Not quite,' said the riding-breeches gentleman, with what I think you call a bitter smile, 'not quite. This is my land and I'll have you up for trespass and damage. Come along now, no nonsense! I'm a magistrate and I'm Master of the Hounds. A vixen, too! What did you shoot her with? You're too young to have a gun. Sneaked your Father's revolver, I suppose?'

Oswald thought it was better to be goldenly silent. But it was vain. The Master of the Hounds made him empty his pockets, and there was the pistol and the cartridges.

The magistrate laughed a harsh laugh of successful disagreeableness.

'All right,' said he, 'where's your licence? You come with me. A week or two in prison.'

I don't believe now he could have done it, but we all thought then he could and would, what's more.

So H. O. began to cry, but Noël spoke up. His teeth were chattering yet he spoke up like a man.

He said, 'You don't know us. You've no right not to believe us till you've found us out in a lie. We don't tell lies. You ask Albert's uncle if we do.'

'Hold your tongue,' said the White-Whiskered.

But Noël's blood was up.

'If you do put us in prison without being sure,' he said, trembling more and more, 'you are a horrible tyrant like Caligula, and Herod, or Nero, and the Spanish Inquisition, and I will write a poem about it in prison, and people will curse you for ever.'

'Upon my word,' said White Whiskers. 'We'll see about that,' and he turned up the lane with the fox hanging from one hand and Noël's ear once more reposing in the other.

I thought Noël would cry or faint. But he bore up nobly – exactly like an early Christian martyr.

The rest of us came along too. I carried the spade and Dicky had the fork. H. O. had the card, and Noël had the magistrate. At the end of the lane there was Alice. She had bunked home, obeying the orders of her thoughtful brother, but she had bottled back again like a shot, so as not to be out of the scrape. She is almost worthy to be a boy for some things.

She spoke to Mr Magistrate and said –

'Where are you taking him?'

The outraged majesty of the magistrate said, 'To prison, you naughty little girl.'

Alice said, 'Noël will faint. Somebody once tried to take him to prison before – about a dog. Do please come to our house and see our uncle – at least he's not – but it's the same thing. We didn't kill the fox, if that's what you think – indeed we didn't. Oh, dear, I do wish you'd think of your own little boys and girls if you've got any, or else about when you were little. You wouldn't be so horrid if you did.'

I don't know which, if either, of these objects the fox-hound master thought of, but he said –

'Well, lead on,' and he let go Noël's ear and Alice snuggled up to Noël and put her arm round him.

It was a frightened procession, whose cheeks were pale with alarm – except those between white whiskers, and they were red – that wound in at our gate and into the hall among the old oak furniture, and black and white marble floor and things.

Dora and Daisy were at the door. The pink petticoat lay on the table, all stained with the gore of the departed. Dora looked at us all, and she saw that it was serious. She pulled out the big oak chair and said, 'Won't you sit down?' very kindly to the white-whiskered magistrate.

He grunted, but did as she said.

Then he looked about him in a silence that was not comforting, and so did we.

At last he said –

'Come, you didn't try to bolt. Speak the truth, and I'll say no more.'

We said we had.

Then he laid the fox on the table, spreading out the petticoat under it, and he took out a knife and the girls hid their faces. Even Oswald did not care to look. Wounds in battle are all very well, but it's different to see a dead fox cut into with a knife.

Next moment the magistrate wiped something on his handkerchief and then laid it on the table, and put one of my cartridges besides it. It was the bullet that had killed the fox.

'Look here!' he said. And it was too true. The bullets were the same.

A thrill of despair ran through Oswald. He knows now how a hero feels when he is innocently accused of a crime and the judge is putting on the black cap, and the evidence is convulsive and all human aid is despaired of.

'I can't help it,' he said, 'we didn't kill it, and that's all there is to it.'

The white-whiskered magistrate may have been master of the fox-hounds, but he was not master of his temper, which is more important, I should think, than a lot of beastly dogs.

He said several words which Oswald would never repeat, much less in his own conversing, and besides that he called us 'obstinate little beggars'.

Then suddenly Albert's uncle entered in the midst of a silence freighted with despairing reflections. The M.F.H. got up and told his tale: it was mainly lies, or, to be more polite, it was hardly any of it true, though I supposed he believed it.

'I am very sorry, sir,' said Albert's uncle, looking at the bullets. 'You'll excuse my asking for the children's version?'

'Oh, certainly, sir, certainly,' fuming, the fox-hound magistrate replied.

Then Albert's uncle said, 'Now Oswald, I know I can trust you to speak the exact truth.'

So Oswald did.

Then the white-whiskered fox-master laid the bullets before Albert's uncle, and I felt this would be a trial to his faith far worse than the rack or the thumbscrew in the days of the Armada.

And then Denny came in. He looked at the fox on the table.

'You found it, then?' he said.

The M.F.H. would have spoken but Albert's uncle said, 'One moment, Denny; you've seen this fox before?'

'Rather,' said Denny; 'I – '

But Albert's uncle said, 'Take time. Think before you speak and say the exact truth. No, don't whisper to Oswald. This boy,' he said to the injured fox-master, 'has been with me since seven this morning. His tale, whatever it is, will be independent evidence.'

But Denny would not speak, though again and again Albert's uncle told him to.

'I can't till I've asked Oswald something,' he said at last.

White Whiskers said, 'That looks bad – eh?'

But Oswald said, 'Don't whisper, old chap. Ask me whatever you like, but speak up.'

So Denny said, 'I can't without breaking the secret oath.'

So then Oswald began to see, and he said, 'Break away for all you're worth, it's all right.' And Denny said, drawing relief's deepest breath, 'Well then, Oswald and I have got a pistol – shares – and I had it last night. And when I couldn't sleep last night because of the toothache I got up and went out early this morning. And I took the pistol. And I loaded it just for fun. And down in the wood I heard a whining like a dog, and I went, and there was the poor fox caught in an iron trap with teeth. And I went to let it out and it bit me – look, here's the place – and the pistol went off and the fox died, and I am so sorry.'

'But why didn't you tell the others?'

'They weren't awake when I went to the dentist's.'

'But why didn't you tell your uncle if you've been with him all the morning?'

'It was the oath,' H. O. said –

> *'May I be called a beastly sneak*
> *If this great secret I ever repeat.'*

White Whiskers actually grinned.

'Well,' he said, 'I see it was an accident, my boy.' Then he turned to us and said –

'I owe you an apology for doubting your word – all of you. I hope it's accepted.'

We said it was all right and he was to never mind.

But all the same we hated him for it. He tried to make up for his unbelievingness afterwards by asking Albert's uncle to shoot rabbits; but we did not really forgive him till the day when he sent the fox's brush to Alice, mounted in silver with a note about her plucky conduct in standing by her brothers.

We got a lecture about not playing with firearms, but no punishment, because our conduct had not been exactly sinful, Albert's uncle said, but merely silly.

The pistol and the cartridges were confiscated.

I hope the house will never be attacked by burglars. When it is, Albert's uncle will only have himself to thank if we are rapidly overpowered, because it will be his fault that we shall have to meet them totally unarmed, and be their almost unresisting prey.

CHAPTER 10

THE SALE OF ANTIQUITIES

IT began one morning at breakfast. It was the fifteenth of August – the birthday of Napoleon the Great, Oswald Bastable, and another very nice writer. Oswald was to keep his birthday on the Saturday, so that his Father could be there. A birthday when there are only many happy returns is a little like Sunday or Christmas Eve. Oswald had a birthday-card or two – that was all; but he did not repine, because he knew they always make it up to you for putting off keeping your birthday, and he looked forward to Saturday.

Albert's uncle had a whole stack of letters as usual, and presently he tossed one over to Dora, and said, 'What do you say, little lady? Shall we let them come?'

But Dora, butter-fingered as ever, missed the catch, and Dick and Noël both had a try for it, so that the letter went into the place where the bacon had been, and where now only a frozen-looking lake of bacon fat was slowly hardening, and then somehow it got into the marmalade, and then H. O. got it, and Dora said –

'I don't want the nasty thing now – all grease and stickiness.' So H. O. read it aloud –

'MAIDSTONE SOCIETY OF ANTIQUITIES AND
FIELD CLUB

Aug. 14, 1900

'DEAR SIR, – At a meeting of the – '

H. O. stuck fast here, and the writing was really very
bad, like a spider that has been in the ink-pot crawling
in a hurry over the paper without stopping to rub its
feet properly on the mat. So Oswald took the letter.
He is above minding a little marmalade or bacon. He
began to read. It ran thus:

'It's not Antiquities, you little silly,' he said; 'it's
Antiquaries.'

'The other's a very good word,' said Albert's uncle,
'and I never call names at breakfast myself – it upsets
the digestion, my egregious Oswald.'

'That's a name though,' said Alice, 'and you got it
out of "Stalky", too. Go on, Oswald.'

So Oswald went on where he had been interrupted:

'MAIDSTONE SOCIETY OF "ANTIQUARIES"
AND FIELD CLUB

Aug. 14, 1900.

'DEAR SIR, – At a meeting of the Committee of this
Society it was agreed that a field day should be held on
Aug. 20, when the Society proposes to visit the interesting
church of Ivybridge and also the Roman remains in the
vicinity. Our president, Mr Longchamps, F.R.S., has obtained permission to open a barrow in the Three Trees
pasture. We venture to ask whether you would allow the
members of the Society to walk through your grounds and
to inspect – from without, of course – your beautiful house,
which is, as you are doubtless aware, of great historic
interest, having been for some years the residence of the
celebrated Sir Thomas Wyatt. – I am, dear Sir, yours
faithfully,

EDWARD K. TURNBULL (*Hon. Sec.*).'

'Just so,' said Albert's uncle; 'well, shall we permit
the eye of the Maidstone Antiquities to profane these

sacred solitudes, and the foot of the Field Club to kick up a dust on our gravel?'

'Our gravel is all grass,' H. O. said. And the girls said, 'Oh, do let them come!' It was Alice who said –

'Why not ask them to tea? They'll be very tired coming all the way from Maidstone.'

'Would you really like it?' Albert's uncle asked. 'I'm afraid they'll be but dull dogs, the Antiquities, stuffy old gentlemen with amphorae in their buttonholes instead of orchids, and pedigrees poking out of all their pockets.'

We laughed – because we knew what an amphorae is. If you don't you might look it up in the dicker. It's not a flower, though it sounds like one out of the gardening book, the kind you never hear of anyone growing.

Dora said she thought it would be splendid.

'And we could have out the best china,' she said, 'and decorate the table with flowers. We could have tea in the garden. We've never had a party since we've been here.'

'I warn you that your guests may be boresome; however, have it your own way,' Albert's uncle said; and he went off to write the invitation to tea to the Maidstone Antiquities. I know that is the wrong word – but somehow we all used it whenever we spoke of them, which was often.

In a day or two Albert's uncle came in to tea with a lightly-clouded brow.

'You've let me in for a nice thing,' he said. 'I asked the Antiquities to tea, and I asked casually how many we might expect. I thought we might need at least the full dozen of the best teacups. Now the secretary writes accepting my kind invitation – '

'Oh, good!' we cried. 'And how many are coming?'

'Oh, only about sixty,' was the groaning rejoinder. 'Perhaps more, should the weather be exceptionally favourable.'

Though stunned at first, we presently decided that we were pleased. We had never, never given such a big party.

The girls were allowed to help in the kitchen, where Mrs Pettigrew made cakes all day long without stopping. They did not let us boys be there, though I cannot see any harm in putting your finger in a cake before it is baked, and then licking your finger, if you are careful to put a different finger in the cake next time. Cake before it is baked is delicious – like a sort of cream.

Albert's uncle said he was the prey of despair. He drove in to Maidstone one day. When we asked him where he was going, he said –

'To get my hair cut: if I keep it this length I shall certainly tear it out by double handfuls in the extremity of my anguish every time I think of those innumerable Antiquities.'

But we found out afterwards that he really went to borrow china and things to give the Antiquities their tea out of; though he did have his hair cut too, because he is the soul of truth and honour.

Oswald had a very good sort of birthday, with bows and arrows as well as other presents. I think these were meant to make up for the pistol that was taken away after the adventure of the fox-hunting. These gave us boys something to do between the birthday-keeping, which was on the Saturday, and the Wednesday when the Antiquities were to come.

We did not allow the girls to play with the bows and arrows, because they had the cakes that we were cut off from: there was little or no unpleasantness over this.

On the Tuesday we went down to look at the Roman

place where the Antiquities were going to dig. We sat on the Roman wall and ate nuts. And as we sat there, we saw coming through the beet-field two labourers with picks and shovels, and a very young man with thin legs and a bicycle. It turned out afterwards to be a free-wheel, the first we had ever seen.

They stopped at a mound inside the Roman wall, and the men took their coats off and spat on their hands.

We went down at once, of course. The thin-legged bicyclist explained his machine to us very fully and carefully when we asked him, and then we saw the men were cutting turfs and turning them over and rolling them up and putting them in a heap. So we asked the gentleman with the thin legs what they were doing. He said –

'They are beginning the preliminary excavation in readiness for to-morrow.'

'What's up to-morrow?' H. O. asked.

'To-morrow we propose to open this barrow and examine it.'

'Then *you're* the Antiquities?' said H. O.

'I'm the secretary,' said the gentleman, smiling, but narrowly.

'Oh, you're all coming to tea with us,' Dora said, and added anxiously, 'how many of you do you think there'll be?'

'Oh, not more than eighty or ninety, I should think,' replied the gentleman.

This took our breath away and we went home. As we went, Oswald, who notices many things that would pass unobserved by the light and careless, saw Denny frowning hard.

So he said, 'What's up?'

'I've got an idea,' the Dentist said. 'Let's call a council.' The Dentist had grown quite used to our ways now. We had called him Dentist ever since the fox-hunt day. He called a council as if he had been used to calling such things all his life, and having them come, too; whereas we all know that his former existing was that of a white mouse in a trap, with that cat of a Murdstone aunt watching him through the bars.

(That is what is called a figure of speech. Albert's uncle told me.)

Councils are held in the straw-loft. As soon as we were all there, and the straw had stopped rustling after our sitting down, Dicky said – 'I hope it's nothing to do with the Wouldbegoods?'

'No,' said Denny in a hurry: 'quite the opposite.'

'I hope it's nothing wrong,' said Dora and Daisy together.

'It's – it's "Hail to thee, blithe spirit – bird thou never wert",' said Denny. 'I mean, I think it's what is called a lark.'

'You never know your luck. Go on, Dentist,' said Dicky.

'Well, then, do you know a book called *The Daisy Chain*?'

We didn't.

'It's by Miss Charlotte M. Yonge,' Daisy interrupted, 'and it's about a family of poor motherless children who tried so hard to be good, and they were confirmed, and had a bazaar, and went to church at the Minster, and one of them got married and wore black watered silk and silver ornaments. So her baby died, and then she was sorry she had not been a good mother to it. And – '

Here Dicky got up and said he'd got some snares to attend to, and he'd receive a report of the Council after it was over. But he only got as far as the trap-door, and then Oswald, the fleet of foot, closed with him, and they rolled together on the floor, while all the others called out 'Come back! Come back!' like guinea-hens on a fence.

Through the rustle and bustle and hustle of the struggle with Dicky, Oswald heard the voice of Denny murmuring one of his everlasting quotations –

> '"Come back, come back!" he cried in Greek,
> "Across the stormy water,
> And I'll forgive your Highland cheek,
> My daughter, O my daughter!"'

When quiet was restored and Dicky had agreed to go through with the Council, Denny said –

'*The Daisy Chain* is not a bit like that really. It's a ripping book. One of the boys dresses up like a lady and comes to call, and another tries to hit his little sister with a hoe. It's jolly fine, I tell you.'

Denny is learning to say what he thinks, just like other boys. He would never have learnt such words as 'ripping' and 'jolly fine' while under the auntal tyranny.

Since then I have read *The Daisy Chain*. It is a first-rate book for girls and little boys.

But we did not want to talk about *The Daisy Chain* just then, so Oswald said –

'But what's your lark?'

Denny got pale pink and said –

'Don't hurry me. I'll tell you directly. Let me think a minute.'

Then he shut his pale pink eyelids a moment in thought, and then opened them and stood up on the straw and said very fast –

'Friends, Romans, countrymen, lend me your ears, or if not ears, pots. You know Albert's uncle said they were going to open the barrow, to look for Roman remains to-morrow. Don't you think it seems a pity they shouldn't find any?'

'Perhaps they will,' Dora said. But Oswald *saw*, and he said 'Primus! Go ahead, old man.'

The Dentist went ahead.

'In *The Daisy Chain*,' he said, 'they dug in a Roman encampment and the children went first and put some pottery there they'd made themselves, and Harry's old medal of the Duke of Wellington. The doctor helped them to some stuff to partly efface the inscription, and all the grown-ups were sold. I thought we might –

> '*You may break, you may shatter*
> *The vase if you will;*
> *But the scent of the Romans*
> *Will cling round it still.*'

Denny sat down amid applause. It really was a great idea, at least for *him*. It seemed to add just what was wanted to the visit of the Maidstone Antiquities. To sell the Antiquities thoroughly would be indeed splendiferous. Of course Dora made haste to point out that we had not got an old medal of the Duke of Wellington, and that we hadn't any doctor who would 'help us to stuff to efface', and etcetera; but we sternly bade her stow it. We weren't going to do *exactly* like those *Daisy Chain* kids.

The pottery was easy. We had made a lot of it by the stream – which was the Nile when we discovered its source – and dried it in the sun, and then baked it under a bonfire, like in *Foul Play*. And most of the things were such queer shapes that they should have done for almost anything – Roman or Greek, or even Egyptian or antediluvian, or household milk-jugs of the cavemen, Albert's uncle said. The pots were, fortunately, quite ready and dirty, because we had already buried them in mixed sand and river mud to improve the colour, and not remembered to wash it off.

So the Council at once collected it all – and some rusty hinges and some brass buttons and a file without a handle; and the girl Councillors carried it all concealed in their pinafores, while the men members carried digging tools. H. O. and Daisy were sent on ahead as scouts to see if the coast was clear. We have learned the true usefulness of scouts from reading about the Transvaal War. But all was still in the hush of evening sunset on the Roman ruin.

We posted sentries, who were to lie on their stomachs on the walls and give a long, low, signifying whistle if aught approached.

Then we dug a tunnel, like the one we once did after treasure, when we happened to bury a boy. It took some time; but never shall it be said that a Bastable grudged time or trouble when a lark was at stake. We put the things in as naturally as we could, and shoved the dirt back, till everything looked just as before. Then we went home, late for tea. But it was in a good cause; and there was no hot toast, only bread-and-butter, which does not get cold with waiting.

That night Alice whispered to Oswald on the stairs, as we went up to bed –

'Meet me outside your door when the others are asleep. Hist! Not a word.'

Oswald said, 'No kid?'

And she replied in the affirmation.

So he kept awake by biting his tongue and pulling his hair – for he shrinks from no pain if it is needful and right.

And when the others all slept the sleep of innocent youth, he got up and went out, and there was Alice dressed.

She said, 'I've found some broken things that look

ever so much more Roman – they were on top of the cupboard in the library. If you'll come with me, we'll bury them – just to see how surprised the others will be.'

It was a wild and daring act, but Oswald did not mind.

He said –

'Wait half a shake.' And he put on his knickerbockers and jacket, and slipped a few peppermints into his pocket in case of catching cold. It is these thoughtful expedients which mark the born explorer and adventurer.

It *was* a little cold; but the white moonlight was very fair to see, and we decided we'd do some other daring moonlight act some other day. We got out of the front door, which is never locked till Albert's uncle goes to bed at twelve or one, and we ran swiftly and silently across the bridge and through the fields to the Roman ruin.

Alice told me afterwards she should have been afraid if it had been dark. But the moonlight made it as bright as day is in your dreams.

Oswald had taken the spade and a sheet of newspaper.

We did not take all the pots Alice had found – but just the two that weren't broken – two crooked jugs, made of stuff like flower-pots are made of. We made two long cuts with the spade and lifted the turf up and scratched the earth under, and took it out very carefully in handfuls on to the newspaper, till the hole was deepish. Then we put in the jugs, and filled it up with earth and flattened the turf over. Turf stretches like elastic. This we did a couple of yards from the place where the mound was dug into by the men, and we had been so careful with the newspaper that there was no loose earth about.

Then we went home in the wet moonlight – at least,

It was a wild and daring act

the grass was very wet – chuckling through the peppermint, and got up to bed without anyone knowing a
single thing about it.

The next day the Antiquities came. It was a jolly hot day, and the tables were spread under the trees on the lawn, like a large and very grand Sunday-school treat. There were dozens of different kinds of cake, and bread-and-butter, both white and brown, and goose-berries and plums and jam sandwiches. And the girls decorated the tables with flowers – blue larkspur and white canterbury bells. And at about three there was a noise of people walking in the road, and presently the Antiquities began to come in at the front gate, and stood about on the lawn by twos and threes and sixes and sevens, looking shy and uncomfy, exactly like a Sunday-school treat. Presently some gentlemen came, who looked like the teachers; they were not shy, and they came right up to the door. So Albert's uncle, who had not been too proud to be up in our room with us watch-ing the people on the lawn through the netting of our short blinds, said –

'I suppose that's the Committee. Come on!'

So we all went down – we were in our Sunday things – and Albert's uncle received the Committee like a feudal system baron, and we were his retainers.

He talked about dates, and king posts and gables, and mullions, and foundations, and records, and Sir Thomas Wyatt, and poetry, and Julius Caesar, and Roman remains, and lych gates and churches, and dog's-tooth moulding till the brain of Oswald reeled. I suppose that Albert's uncle remarked that all our mouths were open, which is a sign of reels in the brain, for he whispered –

'Go hence, and mingle unsuspected with the crowd!'

So we went out on to the lawn, which was now crowded with men and women and one child. This was a girl; she was fat, and we tried to talk to her, though we did not like her. (She was covered in red velvet like an arm-chair.) But she wouldn't. We thought at first she was from a deaf-and-dumb asylum, where her kind teachers had only managed to teach the afflicted to say 'Yes' and 'No'. But afterwards we knew better, for Noël heard her say to her mother, 'I wish you hadn't brought me, mamma. I didn't have a pretty teacup, and I haven't enjoyed my tea one bit.' And she had had five pieces of cake, besides little cakes and nearly a whole plate of plums, and there were only twelve pretty teacups altogether.

Several grown-ups talked to us in a most uninterested way, and then the President read a paper about the Moat House, which we couldn't understand, and other people made speeches we couldn't understand either, except the part about kind hospitality, which made us not know where to look.

Then Dora and Alice and Daisy and Mrs Pettigrew poured out the tea, and we handed cups and plates.

Albert's uncle took me behind a bush to see him tear what was left of his hair when he found there were one hundred and twenty-three Antiquities present, and I heard the President say to the Secretary that 'tea always fetched them'.

Then it was time for the Roman ruin, and our hearts beat high as we took our hats – it was exactly like Sunday – and joined the crowded procession of eager Antiquities. Many of them had umbrellas and overcoats, though the weather was fiery and without a cloud. That is the sort of people they were. The ladies all wore stiff bonnets, and no one took their gloves off, though, of course, it was quite in the country, and it is not wrong to take your gloves off there.

We had planned to be quite close when the digging went on; but Albert's uncle made us a mystic sign and drew us apart.

Then he said: 'The stalls and dress circle are for the guests. The hosts and hostesses retire to the gallery, whence, I am credibly informed, an excellent view may be obtained.'

So we all went up on the Roman walls, and thus missed the cream of the lark; for we could not exactly see what was happening. But we saw that things were being taken from the ground as the men dug, and passed round for the Antiquities to look at. And we knew they must be our Roman remains; but the Antiquities did not seem to care for them much, though we heard sounds of pleased laughter. And at last Alice and I exchanged meaning glances when the spot was reached where we had put in the extras. Then the crowd closed up thick, and we heard excited talk and we knew we really *had* sold the Antiquities this time.

Presently the bonnets and coats began to spread out and trickle towards the house and we were aware that all would soon be over. So we cut home the back way, just in time to hear the President saying to Albert's uncle –

'A genuine find – most interesting. Oh, really, you ought to have *one*. Well, if you insist – '

And so, by slow and dull degrees, the thick sprinkling of Antiquities melted off the lawn; the party was over, and only the dirty teacups and plates, and the trampled grass and the pleasures of memory were left.

We had a very beautiful supper – out of doors, too – with jam sandwiches and cakes and things that were over; and as we watched the setting monarch of the skies – I mean the sun – Alice said –

'Let's tell.'

We let the Dentist tell, because it was he who hatched the lark, but we helped him a little in the narrating of the fell plot, because he has yet to learn how to tell a story straight from the beginning.

When he had done, and we had done, Albert's uncle said, 'Well, it amused you; and you'll be glad to learn that it amused your friends the Antiquities.'

'Didn't they think they were Roman?' Daisy said; 'they did in *The Daisy Chain*.'

'Not in the least,' said Albert's uncle; 'but the Treasurer and Secretary were charmed by your ingenious preparations for their reception.'

'We didn't want them to be disappointed,' said Dora.

'They weren't,' said Albert's uncle. 'Steady on with those plums, H.O. A little way beyond the treasure you had prepared for them they found two specimens of *real* Roman pottery which sent every man-jack of them home thanking his stars he had been born a happy little Antiquary child.'

'Those were *our* jugs,' said Alice, 'and we really *have* sold the Antiquities. She unfolded the tale about our getting the jugs and burying them in the moonlight, and the mound; and the others listened with deeply respectful interest. 'We really have done it this time, haven't we?' she added in tones of well-deserved triumph.

But Oswald had noticed a queer look about Albert's uncle from almost the beginning of Alice's recital; and he now had the sensation of something being up, which has on other occasions frozen his noble blood. The silence of Albert's uncle now froze it yet more Arcticly.

'Haven't we?' repeated Alice, unconscious of what her sensitive's brother's delicate feelings had already got hold of. 'We have done it this time, haven't we?'

'Since you ask me thus pointedly,' answered Albert's uncle at last, 'I cannot but confess that I think you have indeed done it. Those pots on the top of the

library cupboard *are* Roman pottery. The amphorae
which you hid in the mound are probably – I can't say
for certain, mind – priceless. They are the property of
the owner of this house. You have taken them out and
buried them. The President of the Maidstone Anti-
quarian Society has taken them away in his bag. Now
what are you going to do?'

Alice and I did not know what to say, or where to
look. The others added to our pained position by some
ungenerous murmurs about our not being so jolly
clever as we thought ourselves.

There was a very far from pleasing silence. Then
Oswald got up. He said –

'Alice, come here a sec., I want to speak to you.'

As Albert's uncle had offered no advice, Oswald
disdained to ask him for any.

Alice got up too, and she and Oswald went into the
garden, and sat down on the bench under the quince
tree, and wished they had never tried to have a private
lark of their very own with the Antiquities – 'A Private
Sale', Albert's uncle called it afterwards. But regrets,
as nearly always happens, were vain. Something had
to be done.

But what?

Oswald and Alice sat in silent desperateness, and the
voices of the gay and careless others came to them
from the lawn, where, heartless in their youngness, they
were playing tag. I don't know how they could. Oswald
would not like to play tag when his brother and sister
were in a hole, but Oswald is an exception to some
boys. But Dicky told me afterwards he thought it was
only a joke of Albert's uncle's.

The dusk grew dusker, till you could hardly tell the
quinces from the leaves, and Alice and Oswald still sat
exhausted with hard thinking, but they could not think

of anything. And it grew so dark that the moonlight began to show.

Then Alice jumped up – just as Oswald was opening his mouth to say the same thing – and said, 'Of course – how silly! I know. Come on in, Oswald.'

And they went on in.

Oswald was still far too proud to consult anyone else. But he just asked carelessly if Alice and he might go into Maidstone the next day to buy some wire-netting for a rabbit-hutch, and to see after one or two things.

Albert's uncle said certainly. And they went by train with the bailiff from the farm, who was going in about some sheep-dip and to buy pigs. At any other time Oswald would not have been able to bear to leave the bailiff without seeing the pigs bought. But now it was different. For he and Alice had the weight on their bosoms of being thieves without having meant it – and nothing, not even pigs, had power to charm the young but honourable Oswald till that stain had been wiped away.

So he took Alice to the Secretary of the Maidstone Antiquities' house, and Mr Turnbull was out, but the maid-servant kindly told us where the President lived, and ere long the trembling feet of the unfortunate brother and sister vibrated on the spotless gravel of Camperdown Villa.

When they asked, they were told that Mr Longchamps was at home. Then they waited, paralysed with un-described emotions, in a large room with books and swords and glass bookcases with rotten-looking odds and ends in them. Mr Longchamps was a collector. That means he stuck to anything, no matter how ugly and silly, if only it was old.

He came in rubbing his hands, and very kind. He

remembered us very well, he said, and asked what he could do for us.

Oswald for once was dumb. He could not find words in which to own himself the ass he had been. But Alice was less delicately moulded. She said –

'Oh, if you please, we are most awfully sorry, and we hope you'll forgive us, but we thought it would be such a pity for you and all the other poor dear Antiquities to come all that way and then find nothing Roman – so we put some pots and things in the barrow for you to find.'

'So I perceived,' said the President, stroking his white beard and smiling most agreeably at us; 'a harmless joke, my dear! Youth's the season for jesting. There's no harm done – pray think no more about it. It's very honourable of you to come and apologize, I'm sure.'

His brow began to wear the furrowed, anxious look of one who would fain be rid of his guests and get back to what he was doing before they interrupted him.

Alice said, 'We didn't come for that. It's *much* worse. Those were two *real* true Roman jugs you took away; we put them there; they aren't ours. We didn't know they were real Roman. We wanted to sell the Antiquities – I mean Antiquaries – and we were sold ourselves.'

'This is serious,' said the gentleman. 'I suppose you'd know the – the "jugs" if you saw them again?'

'Anywhere,' said Oswald, with the confidential rashness of one who does not know what he is talking about.

Mr Longchamps opened the door of a little room leading out of the one we were in, and beckoned us to follow. We found ourselves amid shelves and shelves of pottery of all sorts; and two whole shelves – small ones – were filled with the sort of jug we wanted.

'Well,' said the President, with a veiled menacing sort of smile, like a wicked cardinal, 'which is it?'

Oswald said, 'I don't know.'

Alice said, 'I should know if I had it in my hand.'

The President patiently took the jugs down one after another, and Alice tried to look inside them. And one after another she shook her head and gave them back.

At last she said, 'You didn't *wash* them?'

Mr Longchamps shuddered and said 'No'.

'Then,' said Alice, 'there is something written with lead-pencil inside both the jugs. I wish I hadn't. I would rather you didn't read it. I didn't know it would be a nice old gentleman like you would find it. I thought it would be the younger gentleman with the thin legs and the narrow smile.'

'Mr Turnbull.' The President seemed to recognize the description unerringly. 'Well, well – boys will be boys – girls, I mean. I won't be angry. Look at all the "jugs" and see if you can find yours.'

Alice did – and the next one she looked at she said, 'This is one' – and two jugs further on she said, 'This is the other.'

'Well,' the President said, 'these are certainly the specimens which I obtained yesterday. If your uncle will call on me I will return them to him. But it's a disappointment. Yes, I think you must let me look inside.'

He did. And at the first one he said nothing. At the second he laughed.

'Well, well,' he said, 'we can't expect old heads on young shoulders. You're not the first who went forth to shear and returned shorn. Nor, it appears, am I. Next time you have a Sale of Antiquities, take care that you yourself are not "sold". Good-day to you, my dear. Don't let the incident prey on your mind,' he said to

Alice. 'Bless your heart, I was a boy once myself, unlikely as you may think it. Good-bye.'

We were in time to see the pigs bought after all.

I asked Alice what on earth it was she'd scribbled inside the beastly jugs, and she owned that just to make the lark complete she had written 'Sucks' in one of the jugs, and 'Sold again, silly', in the other.

But we know well enough who it was that was sold. And if ever we have any Antiquities to tea again, they shan't find so much as a Greek waistcoat button if we can help it.

Unless it's the President, for he did not behave at all badly. For a man of his age I think he behaved exceedingly well. Oswald can picture a very different scene having been enacted over those rotten pots if the President had been an otherwise sort of man.

But that picture is not pleasing, so Oswald will not distress you by drawing it for you. You can most likely do it easily for yourself.

THE BENEVOLENT BAR

THE tramp was very dusty about the feet and legs, and his clothes were very ragged and dirty, but he had cheerful twinkly grey eyes, and he touched his cap to the girls when he spoke to us, though a little as though he would rather not.

We were on the top of the big wall of the Roman ruin in the Three Tree pasture. We had just concluded a severe siege with bows and arrows – the ones that were given us to make up for the pistol that was confiscated after the sad but not sinful occasion when it shot a fox.

To avoid accidents that you would be sorry for afterwards, Oswald, in his thoughtfulness, had decreed that everyone was to wear wire masks.

Luckily there were plenty of these, because a man who lived in the Moat House once went to Rome, where they throw hundreds and thousands at each other in play, and call it a Comfit Battle or Battaglia di Confetti (that's real Italian). And he wanted to get up that sort of thing among the village people – but they were too beastly slack, so he chucked it.

And in the attic were the wire masks he brought home with him from Rome, which people wear to prevent the nasty comfits getting in their mouths and eyes.

So we were all armed to the teeth with masks and arrows, but in attacking or defending a fort your real strength is not in your equipment, but in your power of Shove. Oswald, Alice, Noël and Denny defended the fort. We were much the strongest side, but that was how Dicky and Oswald picked up.

The others got in, it is true, but that was only because an arrow hit Dicky on the nose, and it bled quarts as usual, though hit only through the wire mask. Then he put into dock for repairs, and while the defending party weren't looking he sneaked up the wall at the back and shoved Oswald off, and fell on top of him, so that the fort, now that it had lost its gallant young leader, the life and soul of the besieged party, was of course soon overpowered, and had to surrender.

Then we sat on the top and ate some peppermints Albert's uncle brought us a bag of from Maidstone when he went to fetch away the Roman pottery we tried to sell the Antiquities with.

The battle was over, and peace raged among us as we sat in the sun on the big wall and looked at the fields, all blue and swimming in the heat.

We saw the tramp coming through the beetfield. He made a dusty blot on the fair scene.

When he saw us he came close to the wall, and touched his cap, as I have said, and remarked –

'Excuse me interrupting of your sports, young gentlemen and ladies, but if you could so far oblige as to tell a labouring man the way to the nearest pub. It's a dry day and no error.'

'The "Rose and Crown" is the best pub,' said Dicky, 'and the landlady is a friend of ours. It's about a mile if you go by the field path.'

'Lor' love a duck!' said the tramp, 'a mile's a long way, and walking's a dry job this ere weather.'

We said we agreed with him.

'Upon my sacred,' said the tramp, 'if there was a pump handy I believe I'd take a turn at it – I would indeed, so help me if I wouldn't! Though water always upsets me and makes my 'and shaky.'

We had not cared much about tramps since the adventure of the villainous sailor-man and the Tower of Mystery, but we had the dogs on the wall with us (Lady was awfully difficult to get up, on account of her long deer-hound legs), and the position was a strong one, and easy to defend. Besides the tramp did not look like that bad sailor, nor talk like it. And we considerably outnumbered the tramp, anyway.

Alice nudged Oswald and said something about Sir Philip Sidney and the tramp's need being greater than his, so Oswald was obliged to go to the hole in the top of the wall where we store provisions during sieges and get out the bottle of ginger-beer which he had gone without when the others had theirs so as to drink it when he got really thirsty.

Meanwhile Alice said –

'We've got some ginger-beer; my brother's getting it. I hope you won't mind drinking out of our glass. We can't wash it, you know – unless we rinse it out with a little ginger-beer.'

'Don't ye do it, miss,' he said eagerly; 'never waste good liquor on washing.'

The glass was beside us on the wall. Oswald filled it with ginger-beer and handed down the foaming tankard to the tramp. He had to lie on his young stomach to do this.

The tramp was really quite polite – one of Nature's gentlemen, and a man as well, we found out afterwards. He said –

'Here's to you!' before he drank. Then he drained the glass till the rim rested on his nose.

'Swelp me, but I *was* dry,' he said. 'Don't seem to matter much what it is, this weather, do it? – so long as it's suthink wet. Well, here's thanking you.'

'You're very welcome,' said Dora; 'I'm glad you liked it.'

'Like it?' – said he. 'I don't suppose you know what it's like to have a thirst on you. Talk of free schools and free libraries, and free baths and wash-houses and such! Why don't someone start free *drinks*? He'd be a 'ero, he would. I'd vote for him any day of the week and one over. Ef yer don't objec I'll set down a bit and put on a pipe.'

He sat down on the grass and began to smoke. We asked him questions about himself, and he told us many of his secret sorrows – especially about there being no work nowadays for an honest man. At last he dropped asleep in the middle of a story about a vestry he worked for that hadn't acted fair and square by him like he had by them, or it (I don't know if vestry is singular or plural), and we went home. But before we went we held a hurried council and collected what money we could from the little we had with us (it was ninepence-halfpenny), and wrapped it in an old envelope Dicky had in his pocket and put it gently on the billowing middle of the poor tramp's sleeping waistcoat, so that he would find it when he woke. None of the dogs said a single syllable while we were doing this, so we knew they believed him to be poor but honest, and we always find it safe to take their word for things like that.

As we went home a brooding silence fell upon us; we found out afterwards that those words of the poor tramp's about free drinks had sunk deep in all our hearts, and rankled there.

After dinner we went out and sat with our feet in the stream. People tell you it makes your grub disagree with you to do this just after meals, but it never hurts us. There is a fallen willow across the stream that just seats the eight of us, only the ones at the end can't get their feet into the water properly because of the bushes, so we keep changing places. We had got some liquorice root to chew. This helps thought. Dora broke a peaceful silence with this speech –

'Free drinks.'

The words awoke a response in every breast.

'I wonder someone doesn't,' H. O. said, leaning back till he nearly toppled in, and was only saved by Oswald and Alice at their own deadly peril.

'Do for goodness sake sit still, H. O.,' observed Alice. 'It would be a glorious act! I wish *we* could.'

'What, sit still?' asked H. O.

'No, my child,' replied Oswald, 'most of us can do that when we try. Your angel sister was only wishing to set up free drinks for the poor and thirsty.'

'Not for all of them,' Alice said, 'just a few. Change places now, Dicky. My feet aren't properly wet at all.'

It is very difficult to change places safely on the willow. The changers have to crawl over the laps of the others, while the rest sit tight and hold on for all they're worth. But the hard task was accomplished and then Alice went on –

'And we couldn't do it for always, only a day or two – just while our money held out. Eiffel Tower lemonade's the best, and you get a jolly lot of it for your money too. There must be a great many sincerely thirsty persons go along the Dover Road every day.'

'It wouldn't be bad. We've got a little chink between us,' said Oswald.

'And then think how the poor grateful creatures would linger and tell us about their inmost sorrows. It would be most frightfully interesting. We could write all their agonied life histories down afterwards like *All the Year Round* Christmas numbers. Oh, do let's!'

Alice was wriggling so with earnestness that Dicky thumped her to make her calm.

'We might do it, just for one day,' Oswald said, 'but it wouldn't be much – only a drop in the ocean compared with the enormous dryness of all the people in the whole world. Still, every little helps, as the mermaid said when she cried into the sea.'

'I know a piece of poetry about that,' Denny said.

> *'Small things are best.*
> *Care and unrest*
> *To wealth and rank are given,*
> *But little things*
> *On little wings –*

do something or other, I forget what, but it means the same as Oswald was saying about the mermaid.'

'What are you going to call it?' asked Noël, coming out of a dream.

'Call what?'

'The Free Drinks game.'

> *'It's a horrid shame*
> *If the Free Drinks game*
> *Doesn't have a name.*
> *You would be to blame*
> *If anyone came*
> *And –'*

'Oh, shut up!' remarked Dicky. 'You've been making that rot up all the time we've been talking instead of listening properly.' Dicky hates poetry. I don't mind it so very much myself, especially Macaulay's and Kipling's and Noël's.

'There was a lot more – "lame" and "dame" and "name" and "game" and things – and now I've forgotten it,' Noël said in gloom.

'Never mind,' Alice answered, 'it'll come back to you in the silent watches of the night; you see if it doesn't. But really, Noël's right, it *ought* to have a name.'

'Free Drinks Company.'

'Thirsty Travellers' Rest.'

'The Travellers' Joy.'

These names were suggested, but not cared for extra. Then someone said – I think it was Oswald –

'Why not "The House Beautiful"?'

'It can't be a house, it must be in the road. It'll only be a stall.'

'The "Stall Beautiful" is simply silly,' Oswald said.

'The "Bar Beautiful" then,' said Dicky, who knows what the 'Rose and Crown' bar is like inside, which of course is hidden from girls.

'Oh, wait a minute,' cried the Dentist, snapping his fingers like he always does when he is trying to remember things. 'I thought of something, only Daisy tickled me and it's gone – I know – let's call it the Benevolent Bar!'

It was exactly right, and told the whole truth in two words. 'Benevolent' showed it was free and 'Bar' showed what was free; e.g. things to drink. The 'Benevolent Bar' it was.

We went home at once to prepare for the morrow, for of course we meant to do it the very next day. Procrastination is you know what – and delays are dangerous. If we had waited long we might have happened to spend our money on something else.

The utmost secrecy had to be observed, because Mrs Pettigrew hates tramps. Most people do who keep fowls. Albert's uncle was in London till the next evening, so we could not consult him, but we know he is always chock full of intelligent sympathy with the poor and needy.

Acting with the deepest disguise, we made an awning to cover the Benevolent Bar keepers from the searching rays of the monarch of the skies. We found some old striped sun-blinds in the attic, and the girls sewed them together. They were not very big when they were done, so we added the girls' striped petticoats. I am sorry their petticoats turn up so constantly in my narrative, but they really are very useful, especially when the band is cut off. The girls borrowed Mrs Pettigrew's sewing-machine; they could not ask her leave without explanations, which we did not wish to give just then, and she had lent it to them before. They took it into the cellar to work it, so that she should not hear the noise and ask bothering questions. They had to balance it on one end of the beer-stand. It was not easy. While they were doing the sewing we boys went out and got willow poles and chopped the twigs off, and got ready as well as we could to put up the awning.

When we returned a detachment of us went down to the shop in the village for Eiffel Tower lemonade. We bought seven-and-sixpence worth; then we made a great label to say what the bar was for. Then there was nothing else to do except to make rosettes out of a blue sash of Daisy's to show we belonged to the Benevolent Bar.

The next day was as hot as ever. We rose early from our innocent slumbers, and went out to the Dover Road to the spot we had marked down the day before. It was at a cross-roads, so as to be able to give drinks to as many people as possible.

We hid the awning and poles behind the hedge and went home to brekker.

After break we got the big zinc bath they wash clothes in, and after filling it with clean water we just had to empty it again because it was too heavy to lift. So we carried it vacant to the trysting-spot and left H. O. and Noël to guard it while we went and fetched separate pails of water; very heavy work, and no one who wasn't really benevolent would have bothered about it for an instant. Oswald alone carried three pails. So did Dicky and the Dentist. Then we rolled down some empty barrels and stood up three of them by the roadside, and put planks on them. This made a very first-class table, and we covered it with the best tablecloth we could find in the linen cupboard. We brought out several glasses and some teacups – not the best ones, Oswald was firm about that – and the kettle and spirit-lamp and the tea-pot, in case any weary tramp-woman fancied a cup of tea instead of Eiffel Tower. H. O. and Noël had to go down to the shop for tea; they need not have grumbled; they had not carried any of the water. And their having to go the second time was only because we forgot to tell them to get some real lemons to put on the bar to show what the drink would be like when you got it. The man at the shop kindly gave us tick for the lemons, and we cashed up out of our next week's pocket-money.

Two or three people passed while we were getting things ready, but no one said anything except the man who said, 'Bloomin' Sunday-school treat', and as it was too early in the day for anyone to be thirsty we did not stop the wayfarers to tell them their thirst could be slaked without cost at our Benevolent Bar.

But when everything was quite ready, and our blue rosettes fastened on our breasts over our benevolent hearts, we stuck up the great placard we had made with 'Benevolent Bar. Free Drinks to all Weary

Travellers', in white wadding on red calico, like Christmas decorations in church. We had meant to fasten this to the edge of the awning, but we had to pin it to the front of the tablecloth, because I am sorry to say the awning went wrong from the first. We could not drive the willow poles into the road; it was much too hard. And in the ditch it was too soft, besides being no use. So we had just to cover our benevolent heads with our hats, and take it in turns to go into the shadow of the tree on the other side of the road. For we had pitched our table on the sunny side of the way, of course, relying on our broken-reed-like awning, and wishing to give it a fair chance.

Everything looked very nice, and we longed to see somebody really miserable come along so as to be able to allieve their distress.

A man and woman were the first; they stopped and stared, but when Alice said, 'Free drinks! Free drinks! Aren't you thirsty?' they said, 'No thank you,' and went on. Then came a person from the village; he didn't even say 'Thank you' when we asked him, and Oswald began to fear it might be like the awful time when we wandered about on Christmas Day trying to find poor persons and persuade them to eat our Conscience pudding.

But a man in a blue jersey and a red bundle eased Oswald's fears by being willing to drink a glass of lemonade, and even to say, 'Thank you, I'm sure,' quite nicely.

After that it was better. As we had foreseen, there were plenty of thirsty people walking along the Dover Road, and even some from the cross-road.

We had had the pleasure of seeing nineteen tumblers drained to the dregs ere we tasted any ourselves. Nobody asked for tea.

More people went by than we gave lemonade to. Some wouldn't have it because they were too grand. One man told us he could pay for his own liquor when he was dry, which, praise be, he wasn't over and above, at present; and others asked if we hadn't any beer, and when we said 'No', they said it showed what sort we were – as if the sort was not a good one, which it is.

And another man said, 'Slops again! You never get nothing for nothing, not this side of heaven you don't. Look at the bloomin' blue ribbon on em! Oh, Lor'!' and went on quite sadly without having a drink.

Our Pig-man who helped us on the Tower of Mystery day went by and we hailed him, and explained it all to him and gave him a drink, and asked him to call as he came back. He liked it all, and said we were a real good sort. How different from the man who wanted the beer. Then he went on.

One thing I didn't like, and that was the way boys began to gather. Of course we could not refuse to give drinks to any traveller who was old enough to ask for it, but when one boy had had three glasses of lemonade and asked for another, Oswald said –

'I think you've had jolly well enough. You can't be really thirsty after all that lot.'

The boy said, 'Oh, can't I? You'll just see if I can't,' and went away. Presently he came back with four other boys, all bigger than Oswald; and they all asked for lemonade. Oswald gave it to the four new ones, but he was determined in his behaviour to the other one, and wouldn't give him a drop. Then the five of them went and sat on a gate a little way off and kept laughing in a nasty way, and whenever a boy went by they called out –

'I say, 'ere's a go,' and as often as not the new boy would hang about with them. It was disquieting, for though they had nearly all had lemonade we could see it had not made them friendly.

A great glorious glow of goodness gladdened (those go all together and are called alliteration) our hearts when we saw our own tramp coming down the road. The dogs did not growl at him as they had at the boys or the beer-man. (I did not say before that we had the dogs with us, but of course we had, because we had promised never to go out without them.)

Oswald said, 'Hullo,' and the tramp said, 'Hullo.'

Then Alice said, 'You see we've taken your advice; we're giving free drinks. Doesn't it all look nice?'

'It does that,' said the tramp. 'I don't mind if I do.'

So we gave him two glasses of lemonade succeedingly, and thanked him for giving us the idea. He said we were very welcome, and if we'd no objection he'd sit down a bit and put on a pipe. He did, and after talking a little more he fell asleep. Drinking anything seemed to end in sleep with him. I always thought it was only beer and things made people sleepy, but he was not so. When he was asleep he rolled into the ditch, but it did not wake him up.

The boys were getting very noisy, and they began to shout things, and to make silly noises with their mouths, and when Oswald and Dicky went over to them and told them to just chuck it, they were worse than ever. I think perhaps Oswald and Dicky might have fought and settled them – though there were eleven, yet back to back you can always do it against overwhelming numbers in a book – only Alice called out –

'Oswald, here's some more, come back!'

We went. Three big men were coming down the road, very red and hot, and not amiable-looking. They stopped in front of the Benevolent Bar and slowly read the wadding and red-stuff label.

Then one of them said he was blessed, or something like that, and another said he was too. The third one said, 'Blessed or not, a drink's a drink. Blue ribbon, though, by — ' (a word you ought not to say, though it is in the Bible and the catechism as well). 'Let's have a liquor, little missy.'

The dogs were growling, but Oswald thought it best not to take any notice of what the dogs said, but to give these men each a drink. So he did. They drank, but not as if they cared about it very much, and then they set their glasses down on the table, a liberty no one else had entered into, and began to try and chaff Oswald. Oswald said in an undervoice to H. O. –

'Just take charge. I want to speak to the girls a sec. Call if you want anything.' And then he drew the others away, to say he thought there'd been enough of it, and considering the boys and new three men, perhaps we'd better chuck it and go home. We'd been benevolent nearly four hours anyway.

While this conversation and the objections of the others were going on, H. O. perpetuated an act which nearly wrecked the Benevolent Bar.

Of course Oswald was not an eye or ear witness of what happened, but from what H. O. said in the calmer moments of later life, I think this was about what happened.

One of the big disagreeable men said to H. O. –

'Ain't got such a thing as a drop o' spirit, 'ave yer?'

H. O. said no, we hadn't, only lemonade and tea.

'Lemonade and tea! blank' (bad word I told you about) 'and blazes,' replied the bad character, for such he afterwards proved to be. 'What's *that* then?'

He pointed to a bottle labelled Dewar's whisky, which stood on the table near the spirit-kettle.

'Oh, is *that* what you want?' said H. O. kindly.

The man is understood to have said he should bloomin' well think so, but H. O. is not sure about the bloomin'.

He held out his glass with about half the lemonade in it, and H. O. generously filled up the tumbler out of the bottle, labelled Dewar's whisky. The man took a great drink, and then suddenly he spat out what happened to be left in his mouth just then, and began to swear. It was then that Oswald and Dicky rushed upon the scene. The man was shaking his fist in H. O.'s face, and H. O. was still holding on to the bottle we had brought out the methylated spirit in for the lamp, in case of anyone wanting tea, which they hadn't.

'If I was Jim,' said the second ruffian, for such indeed they were, when he had snatched the bottle from H. O. and smelt it, 'I'd chuck the whole show over the hedge, so I would, and you young gutter-snipes after it, so I wouldn't.'

Oswald saw in a moment that in point of strength, if not numbers, he and his party were out-matched, and the unfriendly boys were drawing gladly near. It is no shame to signal for help when in distress – the best ships do it every day. Oswald shouted 'Help, help!' Before the words were out of his brave yet trembling lips our own tramp leapt like an antelope from the ditch and said –

'Now then, what's up?'

The biggest of the three men immediately knocked him down. He lay still.

The biggest then said, 'Come on – any more of you? Come on!'

Oswald was so enraged at this cowardly attack that

he actually hit out at the big man – and he really got one in just above the belt. Then he shut his eyes, because he felt that now all was indeed up. There was a shout and a scuffle, and Oswald opened his eyes in astonishment at finding himself still whole and unimpaired. Our own tramp had artfully simulated insensibleness, to get the men off their guard, and then had suddenly got his arms round a leg each of two of the men, and pulled them to the ground, helped by Dicky, who saw his game and rushed in at the same time, exactly like Oswald would have done if he had not had his eyes shut ready to meet his doom.

The unpleasant boys shouted, and the third man tried to help his unrespectable friends, now on their backs involved in a desperate struggle with our own tramp, who was on top of them, accompanied by Dicky. It all happened in a minute, and it was all mixed up. The dogs were growling and barking – Martha had one of the men by the trouser leg and Pincher had another; the girls were screaming like mad and the strange boys shouted and laughed (little beasts!), and then suddenly our Pig-man came round the corner, and two friends of his with him. He had gone and fetched them to take care of us if anything unpleasant occurred. It was a very thoughtful, and just like him.

'Fetch the police!' cried the Pig-man in noble tones, and H. O. started running to do it. But the scoundrels struggled from under Dicky and our tramp, shook off the dogs and some bits of trouser, and fled heavily down the road.

Our Pig-man said, 'Get along home!' to the disagreeable boys, and 'Shoo'd' them as if they were hens, and they went. H. O. ran back when they began to go up the road, and there we were, all standing breathless

'*Fetch the police,*' *cried our Pig-man in noble tones*

and in tears on the scene of the late desperate engagement. Oswald gives you his word of honour that his and Dicky's tears were tears of pure rage. There are such things as tears of pure rage. Anyone who knows will tell you so.

We picked up our own tramp and bathed the lump on his forehead with lemonade. The water in the zinc bath had been upset in the struggle. Then he and the Pig-man and his kind friends helped us carry our things home.

The Pig-man advised us on the way not to try these sort of kind actions without getting a grown-up to help us. We've been advised this before, but now I really think we shall never try to be benevolent to the poor and needy again. At any rate not unless we know them very well first.

We have seen our own tramp often since. The Pig-man gave him a job. He has got work to do at last. The Pig-man says he is not such a very bad chap, only he will fall asleep after the least drop of drink. We know that is his failing. We saw it at once. But it was lucky for us he fell asleep that day near our benevolent bar.

I will not go into what my father said about it all. There was a good deal in it about minding your own business – there generally is in most of the talkings-to we get. But he gave our tramp a sovereign, and the Pig-man says he went to sleep on it for a solid week.

CHAPTER 12

THE CANTERBURY PILGRIMS

THE author of these few lines really does hope to goodness that no one will be such an owl as to think from the number of things we did when we were in the country, that we were wretched, neglected little children, whose grown-up relations sparkled in the bright haunts of pleasure, and whirled in the giddy what's-its-name of fashion, while we were left to weep forsaken at home. It was nothing of the kind, and I wish you to know that my father was with us a good deal – and Albert's uncle (who is really no uncle of ours, but only of Albert next door when we lived in Lewisham) gave up a good many of his valuable hours to us. And the father of Denny and Daisy came now and then, and other people, quite as many as we wished to see. And we had some very decent times with them; and enjoyed ourselves very much indeed, thank you. In some ways the good times you have with grown-ups are better than the ones you have by yourselves. At any rate they are safer. It is almost impossible, then, to do anything fatal without being pulled up short by a grown-up ere yet the deed is done. And, if you are careful, anything that goes wrong can be looked on as the grown-up's fault. But these secure pleasures are not so interesting to tell about as the things you do when there is no one to stop you on the edge of the rash act.

It is curious, too, that many of our most interesting

games happened when grown-ups were far away. For instance when we were pilgrims.

It was just after the business of the Benevolent Bar, and it was a wet day. It is not easy to amuse yourself indoors on a wet day as older people seem to think, especially when you are far removed from your own home, and haven't got all your own books and things. The girls were playing Halma – which is a beastly game – Noël was writing poetry, H. O. was singing 'I don't know what to do' to the tune of 'Canaan's happy shore'. It goes like this, and is very tiresome to listen to –

> *'I don't know what to do – oo – oo – oo!*
> *I don't know what to do – oo – oo!*
> *It is a beastly rainy day*
> *And I don't know what to do.'*

The rest of us were trying to make him shut up. We put a carpet bag over his head, but he went on inside it; and then we sat on him, but he sang under us; we held him upside down and made him crawl head first under the sofa, but when, even there, he kept it up, we saw that nothing short of violence would induce him to silence, so we let him go. And then he said we had hurt him, and we said we were only in fun, and he said if we were he wasn't, and ill feeling might have grown up even out of a playful brotherly act like ours had been, only Alice chucked the Halma and said –

'Let dogs delight. Come on – let's play something.'

Then Dora said, 'Yes, but look here. Now we're together I do want to say something. What about the Wouldbegoods Society?'

Many of us groaned, and one said, 'Hear! hear!' I will not say which one, but it was not Oswald.

'No, but really,' Dora said, 'I don't want to be

preachy – but you know we *did* say we'd try to be good. And it says in a book I was reading only yesterday that *not* being naughty is not enough. You must *be* good. And we've hardly done anything. The Golden Deed book's almost empty.'

'Couldn't we have a book of leaden deeds?' said Noël, coming out of his poetry, 'then there'd be plenty for Alice to write about if she wants to, or brass or zinc or aluminium deeds? We shan't ever fill the book with golden ones.'

H. O. had rolled himself in the red tablecloth and said Noël was only advising us to be naughty, and again peace waved in the balance. But Alice said, 'Oh, H. O., *don't* – he didn't mean that; but really and truly, I wish wrong things weren't so interesting. You begin to do a noble act, and then it gets so exciting, and before you know where you are you are doing something wrong as hard as you can lick.'

'And enjoying it too,' Dick said.

'It's very curious,' Denny said, 'but you don't seem to be able to be certain inside yourself whether what you're doing is right if you happen to like doing it, but if you don't like doing it you know quite well. I only thought of that just now. I wish Noël would make a poem about it.'

'I am,' Noël said; 'it began about a crocodile but it is finishing itself up quite different from what I meant it to at first. Just wait a minute.'

He wrote very hard while his kind brothers and sisters and his little friends waited the minute he had said, and then he read:

'*The crocodile is very wise,*
He lives in the Nile with little eyes,
He eats the hippopotamus too,
And if he could he would eat up you.

'The lovely woods and starry skies
He looks upon with glad surprise!
He sees the riches of the east,
And the tiger and lion, kings of beast.

'So let all be good and beware
Of saying shan't and won't and don't care;
For doing wrong is easier far
Than any of the right things I know about are.

And I couldn't make it king of beasts because of it not
rhyming with east, so I put the *s* off beasts on to king.
It comes even in the end.'

We all said it was a very nice piece of poetry. Noël
gets really ill if you don't like what he writes, and then
he said, 'If it's trying that's wanted, I don't care how
hard we *try* to be good, but we may as well do it some
nice way. Let's be Pilgrim's Progress, like I wanted to
at first.'

And we were all beginning to say we didn't want to,
when suddenly Dora said, 'Oh, look here! I know.
We'll be the Canterbury Pilgrims. People used to go
pilgrimages to make themselves good.'

'With peas in their shoes,' the Dentist said. 'It's in
a piece of poetry – only the man boiled his peas –
which is quite unfair.'

'Oh, yes,' said H. O., 'and cocked hats.'

'Not cocked – cockled' – it was Alice who said this.
'And they had staffs and scrips, and they told each
other tales. We might as well.'

Oswald and Dora had been reading about the
Canterbury Pilgrims in a book called *A Short History of
the English People*. It is not at all short really – three fat
volumes – but it has jolly good pictures. It was written
by a gentleman named Green. So Oswald said –

'All right. I'll be the Knight.'

'I'll be the wife of Bath,' Dora said. 'What will you be, Dicky?'

'Oh, I don't care, I'll be Mr Bath if you like.'

'We don't know much about the people,' Alice said. 'How many were there?'

'Thirty,' Oswald replied, 'but we needn't be all of them. There's a Nun-Priest.'

'Is that a man or a woman?'

Oswald said he could not be sure by the picture, but Alice and Noël could be it between them. So that was settled. Then we got the book and looked at the dresses to see if we could make up dresses for the parts. At first we thought we would, because it would be something to do, and it was a very wet day; but they looked difficult, especially the Miller's. Denny wanted to be the Miller, but in the end he was the Doctor, because it was next door to Dentist, which is what we call him for short. Daisy was to be the Prioress – because she is good, and has 'a soft little red mouth', and H. O. *would* be the Manciple (I don't know what that is), because the picture of him is bigger than most of the others, and he said Manciple was a nice portmanteau word – half mandarin and half disciple.

'Let's get the easiest parts of the dresses ready first,' Alice said – 'the pilgrims' staffs and hats and the cockles.'

So Oswald and Dicky braved the fury of the elements and went into the wood beyond the orchard to cut ash-sticks. We got eight jolly good long ones. Then we took them home, and the girls bothered till we changed our clothes, which were indeed sopping with the elements we had faced.

Then we peeled the sticks. They were nice and white at first, but they soon got dirty when we carried them. It is a curious thing: however often you wash your hands they always seem to come off on anything white. And we nailed paper rosettes to the tops of them. That was the nearest we could get to cockle-shells.

'And we may as well have them there as on our hats,' Alice said. 'And let's call each other by our right names to-day, just to get into it. Don't you think so, Knight?'

'Yea, Nun-Priest,' Oswald was replying, but Noël said she was only half the Nun-Priest, and again a threat of unpleasantness darkened the air. But Alice said –

'Don't be a piggy-wiggy, Noël, dear; you can have it all, I don't want it. I'll just be a plain pilgrim, or Henry who killed Becket.'

So she was called the Plain Pilgrim, and she did not mind.

We thought of cocked hats, but they are warm to wear, and the big garden hats that make you look like pictures on the covers of plantation songs did beautifully. We put cockle-shells on them. Sandals we did try, with pieces of oil-cloth cut the shape of soles and fastened with tape, but the dust gets into your toes so, and we decided boots were better for such a long walk. Some of the pilgrims who were very earnest decided to tie their boots with white tape crossed outside to pretend sandals. Denny was one of these earnest palmers. As for dresses, there was no time to make them properly, and at first we thought of nightgowns; but we decided not to, in case people in Canterbury were not used to that sort of pilgrim nowadays. We made up our minds to go as we were – or as we might happen to be next day.

You will be ready to believe we hoped next day would be fine. It was.

Fair was the morn when the pilgrims arose and went down to breakfast. Albert's uncle had had brekker early and was hard at work in his study. We heard his quill pen squeaking when we listened at the door. It is not wrong to listen at doors when there is only one person inside, because nobody would tell itself secrets aloud when it was alone.

We got lunch from the housekeeper, Mrs Pettigrew. She seems almost to *like* us all to go out and take our lunch with us. Though I should think it must be very dull for her all alone. I remember, though, that Eliza, our late general at Lewisham, was just the same. We took the dear dogs of course. Since the Tower of Mystery happened we are not allowed to go anywhere without the escort of these faithful friends of man. We did not take Martha, because bull-dogs do not like long walks. Remember this if you ever have one of those valuable animals.

When we were all ready, with our big hats and cockle-shells, and our staves and our tape sandals, the pilgrims looked very nice.

'Only we haven't any scrips,' Dora said.

'What is a scrip?'

'I think it's something to read. A roll of parchment or something.'

So we had old newspapers rolled up, and carried them in our hands. We took the *Globe* and the *Westminster Gazette* because they are pink and green. The Dentist wore his white sandshoes, sandalled with black tape, and bare legs. They really looked almost as good as bare feet.

'We *ought* to have peas in our shoes,' he said. But we did not think so. We knew what a very little stone in your boot will do, let alone peas.

Of course we knew the way to go to Canterbury, because the old Pilgrims' Road runs just above our house. It is a very pretty road, narrow, and often shady.

It is nice for walking, but carts do not like it because it is rough and rutty; so there is grass growing in patches on it.

I have said that it was a fine day, which means that it was not raining, but the sun did not shine all the time.

"'Tis well, O Knight,' said Alice, 'that the orb of day shines not in undi – what's-its-name? – splendour.'

'Thou sayest sooth, Plain Pilgrim,' replied Oswald. "'Tis jolly warm even as it is.'

'I wish I wasn't two people,' Noël said, 'it seems to make me hotter. I think I'll be a Reeve or something.'

But we would not let him, and we explained that if he hadn't been so beastly particular Alice would have been half of him, and he had only himself to thank if being all of a Nun-Priest made him hot.

But it *was* warm certainly, and it was some time since we'd gone so far in boots. Yet when H. O. complained we did our duty as pilgrims and made him shut up. He did as soon as Alice said that about whining and grizzling being below the dignity of a Manciple.

It was so warm that the Prioress and the wife of Bath gave up walking with their arms round each other in their usual silly way (Albert's uncle calls it Laura Matildaing), and the Doctor and Mr Bath had to take their jackets off and carry them.

I am sure if an artist or a photographer, or any person who liked pilgrims, had seen us he would have been very pleased. The paper cockle-shells were first-rate, but it was awkward having them on the top of the staffs, because they got in your way when you wanted the staff to use as a walking-stick.

We stepped out like a man all of us, and kept it up as well as we could in book-talk, and at first all was merry as a dinner-bell; but presently Oswald, who was the 'very perfect gentle knight', could not help noticing that one of us was growing very silent and rather pale, like people are when they have eaten something that disagrees with them before they are quite sure of the fell truth.

So he said, 'What's up, Dentist, old man?' quite kindly and like a perfect knight, though, of course, he was annoyed with Denny. It is sickening when people turn pale in the middle of a game and everything is spoiled, and you have to go home, and tell the spoiler how sorry you are that he is knocked up, and pretend not to mind about the game being spoiled.

Denny said, 'Nothing', but Oswald knew better.

Then Alice said, 'Let's rest a bit, Oswald, it *is* hot.'

'Sir Oswald, if you please, Plain Pilgrim,' returned her brother dignifiedly. 'Remember I'm a knight.'

So then we sat down and had lunch, and Denny looked better. We played adverbs, and twenty questions, and apprenticing your son, for a bit in the shade, and then Dicky said it was time to set sail if we meant to make the port of Canterbury that night. Of course, pilgrims reck not of ports, but Dicky never does play the game thoughtfully.

We went on. I believe we should have got to Canterbury all right and quite early, only Denny got paler and paler, and presently Oswald saw, beyond any doubt, that he was beginning to walk lame.

'Shoes hurt you, Dentist?' he said, still with kind striving cheerfulness.

'Not much – it's all right,' returned the other.

So on we went – but we were all a bit tired now – and the sun was hotter and hotter; the clouds had gone away. We had to begin to sing to keep up our spirits. We sang 'The British Grenadiers' and 'John Brown's

Body', which is grand to march to, and a lot of others. We were just starting on 'Tramp, tramp, tramp, the boys are marching', when Denny stopped short. He stood first on one foot and then on the other, and suddenly screwed up his face and put his knuckles in his eyes and sat down on a heap of stones by the roadside.

When we pulled his hands down he was actually crying. The author does not wish to say it is babyish to cry.

'Whatever is up?' we all asked, and Daisy and Dora petted him to get him to say, but he only went on howling, and said it was nothing, only would we go on and leave him, and call for him as we came back.

Oswald thought very likely something had given Denny the stomach-ache, and he did not like to say so before all of us, so he sent the others away and told them to walk on a bit.

Then he said, 'Now, Denny, don't be a young ass. What is it? *Is* it stomach-ache?'

And Denny stopped crying to say 'No!' as loud as he could.

'Well, then,' Oswald said, 'look here, you're spoiling the whole thing. Don't be a jackape, Denny. What is it?'

'You won't tell the others if I tell you?'

'Not if you say not,' Oswald answered in kindly tones.

'Well, it's my shoes.'

'Take them off, man.'

'You won't laugh?'

'NO!' cried Oswald, so impatiently that the others looked back to see why he was shouting. He waved them away, and with humble gentleness began to undo the black-tape sandals. Denny let him, crying hard all the time.

When Oswald had got off the first shoe the mystery was made plain to him.

'Well! Of all the – ' he said in proper indignation.

Denny quailed – though he said he did not – but then he doesn't know what quailing is, and if Denny did not quail then Oswald does not know what quailing is either.

For when Oswald took the shoe off he naturally chucked it down and gave it a kick, and a lot of little pinky yellow things rolled out. And Oswald look closer at the interesting sight. And the little things were *split peas*.

'Perhaps you'll tell me,' said the gentle knight, with the politeness of despair, 'why on earth you've played the goat like this?'

'Oh, don't be angry,' Denny said; and now his shoes were off, he curled and uncurled his toes and stopped crying. 'I *knew* pilgrims put peas in their shoes – and – oh, I wish you wouldn't laugh!'

'I'm not,' said Oswald, still with bitter politeness.

'I didn't want to tell you I was going to, because I wanted to be better than all of you, and I thought if you knew I was going to you'd want to too, and you wouldn't when I said it first. So I just put some peas in my pocket and dropped one or two at a time into my shoes when you weren't looking.'

In his secret heart Oswald said, 'Greedy young ass'. For it *is* greedy to want to have more of anything than other people, even goodness.

Outwardly Oswald said nothing.

'You see' – Denny went on – 'I do want to be good. And if pilgriming is to do you good, you ought to do it properly. I shouldn't mind being hurt in my feet if it would make me good for ever and ever. And besides, I wanted to play the game thoroughly. You always say I don't.'

The breast of the kind Oswald was touched by these last words.

'I think you're quite good enough,' he said. 'I'll fetch back the others – no, they won't laugh.'

And we all went back to Denny, and the girls made a fuss with him. But Oswald and Dicky were grave and stood aloof. They were old enough to see that being good was all very well, but after all you had to get the boy home somehow.

When they said this, as agreeably as they could, Denny said –

'It's all right – someone will give me a lift.'

'You think everything in the world can be put right with a lift,' Dicky said, and he did not speak lovingly.

'So it can,' said Denny, 'when it's your feet. I shall easily get a lift home.'

'Not here you won't,' said Alice. 'No one goes down this road; but the high road's just round the corner, where you see the telegraph wires.'

Dickie and Oswald made a sedan chair and carried Denny to the high road, and we sat down in a ditch to wait. For a long time nothing went by but a brewer's dray. We hailed it, of course, but the man was so sound asleep that our hails were vain, and none of us thought soon enough about springing like a flash to the horses' heads, though we all thought of it directly the dray was out of sight.

So we had to keep on sitting there by the dusty road, and more than one pilgrim was heard to say it wished we had never come. Oswald was not one of those who uttered this useless wish.

At last, just when despair was beginning to eat into the vital parts of even Oswald, there was a quick tap-tapping of horses' feet on the road, and a dog-cart came in sight with a lady in it all alone.

We hailed her like the desperate shipwrecked mariners in the long-boat hail the passing sail.

She pulled up. She was not a very old lady – twenty-five we found out afterwards her age was – and she looked jolly.

'Well,' she said, 'what's the matter?'

'It's this poor little boy,' Dora said, pointing to the Dentist, who had gone to sleep in the dry ditch, with his mouth open as usual. 'His feet hurt him so, and will you give him a lift?'

'But why are you all rigged out like this?' asked the lady, looking at our cockle-shells and sandals and things.

We told her.

'And how has he hurt his feet?' she asked.

And we told her that.

She looked very kind. 'Poor little chap,' she said. 'Where do you want to go?'

We told her that too. We had no concealments from this lady.

'Well,' she said, 'I have to go on to – what is its name?'

'Canterbury,' said H. O.

'Well, yes, Canterbury,' she said; 'it's only about half a mile. I'll take the poor little pilgrim – and, yes, the three girls. You boys must walk. Then we'll have tea and see the sights, and I'll drive you home – at least some of you. How will that do?'

We thanked her very much indeed, and said it would do very nicely.

Then we helped Denny into the cart, and the girls got up, and the red wheels of the cart spun away through the dust.

We hailed her like desperate,

'I wish it had been an omnibus the lady was driving,' said H. O., 'then we could all have had a ride.'

'Don't you be so discontented,' Dicky said.

And Noël said –

'You ought to be jolly thankful you haven't got to carry Denny all the way home on your back. You'd have had to if you'd been out alone with him.'

When we got to Canterbury it was much smaller than we expected, and the cathedral not much bigger than the Church that is next to the Moat House. There seemed to be only one big street, but we supposed the rest of the city was hidden away somewhere.

There was a large inn, with a green before it, and the red-wheeled dogcart was standing in the stable-

shipwrecked mariners

yard, and the lady, with Denny and the others, sitting on the benches in the porch, looking out for us. The inn was called the 'George and Dragon', and it made me think of the days when there were coaches and highwaymen and foot-pads and jolly landlords, and adventures at country inns, like you read about.

'We've ordered tea,' said the lady. 'Would you like to wash your hands?' We saw that she wished us to, so we said yes, we would. The girls and Denny were already much cleaner than when we parted from them.

There was a courtyard to the inn and a wooden staircase outside the house. We were taken up this, and washed our hands in a big room with a fourpost wooden bed and dark red hangings – just the sort of hangings that would not show the stains of gore in the dear old adventurous times.

Then we had tea in a great big room with wooden chairs and tables, very polished and old.

It was a very nice tea, with lettuces, and cold meat, and three kinds of jam, as well as cake, and new bread, which we are not allowed at home.

While tea was being had, the lady talked to us. She was very kind. There are two sorts of people in the world, besides others; one sort understand what you're driving at, and the other don't. This lady was the one sort.

After everyone had had as much to eat as they could possibly want, the lady said, 'What was it you particularly wanted to see at Canterbury?'

'The cathedral,' Alice said, 'and the place where Thomas à Becket was murdered.'

'And the Danejohn,' said Dicky.

Oswald wanted to see the walls, because he likes the Story of St Alphege and the Danes.

'Well, well,' said the lady, and she put on her hat; it was a really sensible one – not a blob of fluffy stuff and feathers put on sideways and stuck on with long pins, and no shade to your face, but almost as big as ours, with a big brim and red flowers, and black strings to tie under your chin to keep it from blowing off.

Then we went out all together to see Canterbury. Dicky and Oswald took it in turns to carry Denny on their backs. The lady called him 'The Wounded Comrade'.

We went first to the church. Oswald, whose quick brain was easily aroused to suspicions, was afraid the lady might begin talking in the church, but she did not. The church door was open. I remember mother telling us once it was right and good for churches to be left open all day, so that tired people could go in and be quiet, and say their prayers, if they wanted to. But it does not seem respectful to talk out loud in church. (*See* Note A.)

When we got outside the lady said, 'You can imagine how on the chancel steps began the mad struggle in which Becket, after hurling one of his assailants, armour and all, to the ground –'

'It would have been much cleverer,' H. O. interrupted, 'to hurl him without his armour, and leave that standing up.'

'Go on,' said Alice and Oswald, when they had given H. O. a withering glance. And the lady did go on. She told us all about Becket, and then about St Alphege, who had bones thrown at him till he died, because he wouldn't tax his poor people to please the beastly rotten Danes.

And Denny recited a piece of poetry he knows called 'The Ballad of Canterbury'.

It begins about Danish warships snake-shaped, and ends about doing as you'd be done by. It is long, but it has all the beef-bones in it, and all about St Alphege.

Then the lady showed us the Danejohn, and it was like an oast-house. And Canterbury walls that Alphege defied the Danes from looked down on a quite common farmyard. The hospital was like a barn, and other things were like other things, but we went all about and enjoyed it very much. The lady was quite amusing, besides sometimes talking like a real cathedral guide I met afterwards. (*See* Note B.) When at last we said we thought Canterbury was very small considering, the lady said –

'Well, it seemed a pity to come so far and not at least *hear* something about Canterbury.'

And then at once we knew the worst, and Alice said –

'What a horrid sell!'

But Oswald, with immediate courteousness, said –

'I don't care. You did it awfully well.'

And he did not say, though he owns he thought of it –

'I knew it all the time,' though it was a great tempta-
tion. Because really it was more than half true. He had
felt from the first that this was too small for Canterbury. (*See* Note C.)

The real name of the place was Hazelbridge, and
not Canterbury at all. We went to Canterbury another
time. (*See* Note D.)

We were not angry with the lady for selling us about
it being Canterbury, because she had really kept it up
first-rate. And she asked us if we minded, very hand-
somely, and we said we liked it. But now we did not
care how soon we got home. The lady saw this, and
said –

'Come, our chariots are ready, and our horses
caparisoned.'

That is a first-rate word out of a book. It cheered
Oswald up, and he liked her for using it, though he
wondered why she said chariots. When we got back
to the inn I saw her dogcart was there, and a grocer's
cart too, with B. Munn, grocer, Hazelbridge, on it.
She took the girls in her cart, and the boys went with
the grocer. His horse was a very good one to go, only
you had to hit it with the wrong end of the whip. But
the cart was very bumpety.

The evening dews were falling – at least, I suppose
so, but you do not feel dew in a grocer's cart – when we
reached home. We all thanked the lady very much, and
said we hoped we should see her again some day. She
said she hoped so.

The grocer drove off, and when we had all shaken
hands with the lady and kissed her, according as we

were boys or girls, or little boys, she touched up her horse and drove away.

She turned at the corner to wave to us, and just as we had done waving, and were turning into the house, Albert's uncle came into our midst like a whirling wind. He was in flannels, and his shirt had no stud in at the neck, and his hair was all rumpled up and his hands were inky, and we knew he had left off in the middle of a chapter by the wildness of his eye.

'Who was that lady?' he said. 'Where did you meet her?'

Mindful, as ever, of what he was told, Oswald began to tell the story from the beginning.

'The other day, protector of the poor,' he began, 'Dora and I were reading about the Canterbury pilgrims. . . .'

Oswald thought Albert's uncle would be pleased to find his instructions about beginning at the beginning had borne fruit, but instead he interrupted.

'Stow it, you young duffer! Where did you meet her?'

Oswald answered briefly, in wounded accents, 'Hazelbridge.'

Then Albert's uncle rushed upstairs three at a time, and as he went he called out to Oswald –

'Get out my bike, old man, and blow up the back tyre.'

I am sure Oswald was as quick as anyone could have been, but long ere the tyre was thoroughly blowed Albert's uncle appeared, with a collar-stud and tie and blazer, and his hair tidy, and wrenching the unoffending machine from Oswald's surprised fingers.

Albert's uncle finished pumping up the tyre, and then flinging himself into the saddle he set off, scorching down the road at a pace not surpassed by any highwayman, however black and high-mettled his steed.

We were left looking at each other.

'He must have recognized her,' Dicky said.

'Perhaps,' Noël said, 'she is the old nurse who alone knows the dark secret of his highborn birth.'

'Not old enough, by chalks,' Oswald said.

'I shouldn't wonder,' said Alice, 'if she holds the secret of the will that will make him rolling in long-lost wealth.'

'I wonder if he'll catch her,' Noël said. 'I'm quite certain all his future depends on it. Perhaps she's his long-lost sister, and the estate was left to them equally, only she couldn't be found, so it couldn't be shared up.'

'Perhaps he's only in love with her,' Dora said; 'parted by cruel Fate at an early age, he has ranged the wide world ever since trying to find her.'

'I hope to goodness he hasn't – anyway, he's not ranged since we knew him – never further than Hastings,' Oswald said. 'We don't want any of that rot.'

'What rot?' Daisy asked.

And Oswald said –

'Getting married, and all that sort of rubbish.'

And Daisy and Dora were the only ones that didn't agree with him. Even Alice owned that being bridesmaids must be fairly good fun. It's no good. You may treat girls as well as you like, and give them every comfort and luxury, and play fair just as if they were boys, but there is something unmanly about the best of girls. They go silly, like milk goes sour, without any warning.

When Albert's uncle returned he was very hot, with a beaded brow, but pale as the Dentist when the peas were at their worst.

'Did you catch her?' H. O. asked.

Albert's uncle's brow looked black as the cloud that thunder will presently break from.

'No,' he said.

'Is she your long-lost nurse?' H. O. went on, before we could stop him.

'Long-lost grandmother! I knew the lady long ago in India,' said Albert's uncle, as he left the room, slamming the door in a way we should be forbidden to.

And that was the end of the Canterbury Pilgrimage.

As for the lady, we did not then know whether she was his long-lost grandmother that he had known in India or not, though we thought she seemed youngish for the part. We found out afterwards whether she was or not, but that comes in another part. His manner was not the one that makes you go on asking questions.

The Canterbury Pilgriming did not exactly make us good, but then, as Dora said, we had not done anything wrong that day. So we were twenty-four hours to the good.

Note A. – Afterwards we went and saw real Canterbury. It is very large. A disagreeable man showed us round the cathedral, and jawed all the time quite loud as if it wasn't a church. I remember one thing he said. It was this:

'This is the Dean's Chapel; it was the Lady Chapel in the wicked days when people used to worship the Virgin Mary.'

And H. O. said, 'I suppose they worship the Dean now?'

Some strange people who were there laughed out loud. I think this is worse in church than not taking your cap off when you come in, as H. O. forgot to do, because the cathedral was so big he didn't think it was a church.

Note B. (See *Note C.*)
Note C. (See *Note D.*)
Note D. (See *Note E.*)
Note E. (See *Note A.*)

This ends the Canterbury Pilgrims.

CHAPTER 13

THE DRAGON'S TEETH; OR, ARMY-SEED

ALBERT's uncle was out on his bicycle as usual. After the day when we became Canterbury Pilgrims and were brought home in the dog-cart with red wheels by the lady he told us was his long-lost grandmother he had known years ago in India, he spent not nearly so much of his time in writing, and he used to shave every morning instead of only when requisite, as in earlier days. And he was always going out on his bicycle in his new Norfolk suit. We are not so unobserving as grown-up people make out. We knew well enough he was looking for the long-lost. And we jolly well wished he might find her. Oswald, always full of sympathy with misfortune, however undeserved, had himself tried several times to find the lady. So had the others. But all this is what they call a digression; it has nothing to do with the dragon's teeth I am now narrating.

It began with the pig dying – it was the one we had for the circus, but it having behaved so badly that day had nothing to do with its illness and death, though the girls said they felt remorse, and perhaps if we hadn't made it run so that day it might have been spared to us. But Oswald cannot pretend that people were right just because they happen to be dead, and as long as that pig was alive we all knew well enough that it was it that made us run – and not us it.

The pig was buried in the kitchen garden. Bill, that

we made the tombstone for, dug the grave, and while he was away at his dinner we took a turn at digging, because we like to be useful, and besides, when you dig you never know what you may turn up. I knew a man once that found a gold ring on the point of his fork when he was digging potatoes, and you know how we found two half-crowns ourselves once when we were digging for treasure.

Oswald was taking his turn with the spade, and the others were sitting on the gravel and telling him how to do it.

'Work with a will,' Dicky said, yawning.

Alice said, 'I wish we were in a book. People in books never dig without finding something. I think I'd rather it was a secret passage than anything.'

Oswald stopped to wipe his honest brow ere replying.

'A secret's nothing when you've found it out. Look at the secret staircase. It's no good, not even for hide-and-seek, because of its squeaking. I'd rather have the pot of gold we used to dig for when we were little.' It was really only last year, but you seem to grow old very quickly after you have once passed the prime of your youth, which is at ten, I believe.

'How would you like to find the mouldering bones of Royalist soldiers foully done to death by nasty Iron-sides?' Noël asked, with his mouth full of plum.

'If they were really dead it wouldn't matter,' Dora said. 'What I'm afraid of is a skeleton that can walk about and catch at your legs when you're going upstairs to bed.'

'Skeletons can't walk,' Alice said in a hurry; 'you know they can't, Dora.'

And she glared at Dora till she made her sorry she had said what she had. The things you are frightened of, or even those you would rather not meet in the dark, should never be mentioned before the little ones, or else they cry when it comes to bed-time, and say it was because of what you said.

'We shan't find anything. No jolly fear,' said Dicky.

And just then my spade I was digging with struck on something hard, and it felt hollow. I did really think for one joyful space that we had found that pot of gold. But the thing, whatever it was, seemed to be longish; longer, that is, than a pot of gold would naturally be. And as I uncovered it I saw that it was not at all pot-of-gold-colour, but like a bone Pincher has buried. So Oswald said –

'It *is* the skeleton.'

The girls all drew back, and Alice said, 'Oswald, I wish you wouldn't.'

A moment later the discovery was unearthed, and Oswald lifted it up, with both hands.

'It's a dragon's head,' Noël said, and it certainly looked like it. It was long and narrowish and bony, and with great yellow teeth sticking in the jaw.

Bill came back just then and said it was a horse's head, but H. O. and Noël would not believe it, and Oswald owns that no horse he has ever seen had a head at all that shape.

But Oswald did not stop to argue, because he saw a keeper who showed me how to set snares going by, and he wanted to talk to him about ferrets, so he went off and Dicky and Denny and Alice with him. Also Daisy and Dora went off to finish reading *Ministering Children*. So H. O. and Noël were left with the bony head. They took it away.

The incident had quite faded from the mind of Oswald next day. But just before breakfast Noël and H. O. came in, looking hot and anxious. They had got up early and had not washed at all – not even their hands and faces. Noël made Oswald a secret signal. All the others saw it, and with proper delicate feeling pretended not to have.

When Oswald had gone out with Noël and H. O. in obedience to the secret signal, Noël said –

'You know that dragon's head yesterday?'

'Well?' Oswald said quickly, but not crossly – the two things are quite different.

'Well, you know what happened in Greek history when some chap sowed dragon's teeth?'

'They came up armed men,' said H. O., but Noël sternly bade him shut up, and Oswald said 'Well,' again. If he spoke impatiently it was because he smelt the bacon being taken in to breakfast.

'Well,' Noël went on, 'what do you suppose would have come up if we'd sowed those dragon's teeth we found yesterday?'

'Why, nothing, you young duffer,' said Oswald, who could now smell the coffee. 'All that isn't History – it's Humbug. Come on in to brekker.'

'It's *not* humbug,' H. O. cried, 'it *is* history. We *did* sow – '

'Shut up,' said Noël again. 'Look here, Oswald. We did sow those dragon's teeth in Randall's ten-acre meadow, and what do you think has come up?'

'Toadstools I should think,' was Oswald's contemptible rejoinder.

'They have come up a camp of soldiers,' said Noël – '*armed men*. So you see it *was* history. We have sowed army-seed, just like Cadmus, and it has come up. It was a very wet night. I daresay that helped it along.'

Oswald could not decide which to disbelieve – his brother or his ears. So, disguising his doubtful emotions without a word, he led the way to the bacon and the banqueting hall.

He said nothing about the army-seed then, neither did Noël and H. O. But after the bacon we went into the garden, and then the good elder brother said –

'Why don't you tell the others your cock-and-bull story?'

So they did, and their story was received with warm expressions of doubt. It was Dicky who observed –

'Let's go and have a squint at Randall's ten-acre, anyhow. I saw a hare there the other day.'

We went. It is some little way, and as we went, disbelief reigned superb in every breast except Noël's and H. O.'s, so you will see that even the ready pen of the present author cannot be expected to describe to you his variable sensations when he got to the top of the hill and suddenly saw that his little brothers had spoken the truth. I do not mean that they generally tell lies, but people make mistakes sometimes, and the effect is the same as lies if you believe them.

There *was* a camp there with real tents and soldiers in grey and red tunics. I daresay the girls would have said coats. We stood in ambush, too astonished even to think of lying in it, though of course we know that this is customary. The ambush was the wood on top of the little hill, between Randall's ten-acre meadow and Sugden's Waste Wake pasture.

'There would be cover here for a couple of regiments,' whispered Oswald, who was, I think, gifted by Fate with the far-seeingness of a born general.

Alice merely said 'Hist', and we went down to mingle with the troops as though by accident, and seek for information.

The first man we came to at the edge of the camp was cleaning a sort of cauldron thing like witches brew bats in.

We went up to him and said, 'Who are you? Are you English, or are you the enemy?'

'We're the enemy,' he said, and he did not seem ashamed of being what he was. And he spoke English with quite a good accent for a foreigner.

'The enemy!' Oswald echoed in shocked tones. It is a terrible thing to a loyal and patriotic youth to see an enemy cleaning a pot in an English field, with English sand, and looking as much at home as if he was in his foreign fastnesses.

The enemy seemed to read Oswald's thoughts with deadly unerringness. He said –

'The English are somewhere over on the other side of the hill. They are trying to keep us out of Maidstone.'

After this our plan of mingling with the troops did not seem worth going on with. This soldier, in spite of his unerringness in reading Oswald's innermost heart, seemed not so very sharp in other things, or he would never have given away his secret plans like this, for he must have known from our accents that we were Britons to the backbone. Or perhaps (Oswald thought this, and it made his blood at once boil and freeze, which our uncle had told us was possible, but only in India), perhaps he thought that Maidstone was already as good as taken and it didn't matter what he said. While Oswald was debating within his intellect what to say next, and how to say it so as to discover as many as possible of the enemy's dark secrets, Noël said –

'How did you get here? You weren't here yesterday at tea-time.'

The soldier gave the pot another sandy rub, and said –

'I daresay it does seem quick work – the camp seems as if it had sprung up in the night, doesn't it? – like a mushroom.'

Alice and Oswald looked at each other, and then at

He spoke English with quite a good accent for a foreigner

the rest of us. The words '*sprung up in the night*' seemed to touch a string in every heart.

'You see,' whispered Noël, 'he won't tell us how he came here. *Now*, is it humbug or history?'

Oswald, after whisperedly requesting his young brother to dry up and not bother, remarked, 'Then you're an invading army?'

'Well,' said the soldier, 'we're a skeleton battalion, as a matter of fact, but we're invading all right enough.'

And now indeed the blood of the stupidest of us froze, just as the quick-witted Oswald's had done earlier in the interview. Even H. O. opened his mouth and went the colour of mottled soap; he is so fat that this is the nearest he can go to turning pale.

Denny said, 'But you don't look like skeletons.'

The soldier stared, then he laughed and said, 'Ah, that's the padding in our tunics. You should see us in the grey dawn taking our morning bath in a bucket.'

It was a dreadful picture for the imagination. A skeleton, with its bones all loose most likely, bathing anyhow in a pail. There was a silence while we thought it over.

Now, ever since the cleaning-cauldron soldier had said that about taking Maidstone, Alice had kept on pulling at Oswald's jacket behind, and he had kept on not taking any notice. But now he could not stand it any longer, so he said –

'Well, what is it?'

Alice drew him aside, or rather, she pulled at his jacket so that he nearly fell over backwards, and then she whispered, 'Come along, don't stay parleying with the foe. He's only talking to you to gain time.'

'What for?' said Oswald.

'Why, so that we shouldn't warn the other army, you silly,' Alice said, and Oswald was so upset by what she said, that he forgot to be properly angry with her for the wrong word she used.

'But we ought to warn them at home,' she said; 'suppose the Moat House was burned down, and all the supplies commandeered for the foe?'

Alice turned boldly to the soldier. '*Do* you burn down farms?' she asked.

'Well, not as a rule,' he said, and he had the cheek to wink at Oswald, but Oswald would not look at him. 'We've not burned a farm since – oh, not for years.'

'A farm in Greek history it was, I expect,' Denny murmured.

'Civilized warriors do not burn farms nowadays,' Alice said sternly, 'whatever they did in Greek times. You ought to know that.'

The soldier said things had changed a good deal since Greek times. So we said good morning as quickly as we could: it is proper to be polite even to your enemy, except just at the moments when it has really come to rifles and bayonets or other weapons.

The soldier said 'So long!' in quite a modern voice, and we retraced our footsteps in silence to the ambush – I mean the wood. Oswald did think of lying in the ambush then, but it was rather wet, because of the rain the night before, that H. O. said had brought the army-seed up. And Alice walked very fast, saying nothing but 'Hurry up, can't you!' and dragging H. O. by one hand and Noël by the other. So we got into the road.

Then Alice faced round and said, 'This is all our fault. If we hadn't sowed those dragon's teeth there wouldn't have been any invading army.'

I am sorry to say Daisy said, 'Never mind, Alice, dear. *We* didn't sow the nasty things, did we, Dora?'

But Denny told her it was just the same. It was *we* had done it, so long as it was any of us, especially if it got any of us into trouble. Oswald was very pleased to see that the Dentist was beginning to understand the meaning of true manliness, and about the honour of the house of Bastable, though of course he is only a Foulkes. Yet it is something to know he does his best to learn.

If you are very grown-up, or very clever, I daresay you will now have thought of a great many things. If you have you need not say anything, especially if you're reading this aloud to anybody. It's no good putting in what you think in this part, because none of us thought anything of the kind at the time.

We simply stood in the road without any of your clever thoughts, filled with shame and distress to think of what might happen owing to the dragon's teeth being sown. It was a lesson to us never to sow seed without being quite sure what sort it is. This is particularly true of the penny packets, which sometimes do not come up at all, quite unlike dragon's teeth.

Of course H. O. and Noël were more unhappy than the rest of us. This was only fair.

'How can we possibly prevent their getting to Maidstone?' Dickie said. 'Did you notice the red cuffs on their uniforms? Taken from the bodies of dead English soldiers, I shouldn't wonder.'

'If they're the old Greek kind of dragon's-teeth soldiers, they ought to fight each other to death,' Noël said; 'at least, if we had a helmet to throw among them.'

But none of us had, and it was decided that it would be of no use for H. O. to go back and throw his straw hat at them, though he wanted to.

Denny said suddenly –

'Couldn't we alter the sign-posts, so that they wouldn't know the way to Maidstone?'

Oswald saw that this was the time for true generalship to be shown. He said –

'Fetch all the tools out of your chest – Dicky go too, there's a good chap, and don't let him cut his legs with the saw.' He did once, tumbling over it. 'Meet us at the cross-roads, you know, where we had the Benevolent Bar. Courage and dispatch, and look sharp about it.'

When they had gone we hastened to the crossroads, and there a great idea occurred to Oswald. He used the forces at his command so ably that in a very short time the board in the field which says 'No thoroughfare. Trespassers will be prosecuted' was set up in the middle of the road to Maidstone. We put stones, from a heap by the road, behind it to make is stand up.

Then Dicky and Denny came back, and Dicky shinned up the sign-post and sawed off the two arms, and we nailed them up wrong, so that it said 'To Maidstone' on the Dover Road, and 'To Dover' on the road to Maidstone. We decided to leave the Trespassers board on the real Maidstone road, as an extra guard.

Then we settled to start at once to warn Maidstone.

Some of us did not want the girls to go, but it would have been unkind to say so. However, there was at least one breast that felt a pang of joy when Dora and Daisy gave out that they would rather stay where they were and tell anybody who came by which was the real road.

'Because it would be so dreadful if someone was going to buy pigs or fetch a doctor or anything in a hurry and then found they had got to Dover instead of where they wanted to go to,' Dora said. But when it came to dinner-time they went home, so that they were entirely out of it. This often happens to them by some strange fatalism.

We left Martha to take care of the two girls, and Lady and Pincher went with us. It was getting late in the day, but I am bound to remember no one said anything about their dinners, whatever they may have ʼght. We cannot always help our thoughts. We happened to know it was roast rabbits and currant jelly that day.

We walked two and two, and sang the 'British Grenadiers' and 'Soldiers of the Queen' so as to be as much part of the British Army as possible. The Cauldron-Man had said the English were the other side of the hill. But we could not see any scarlet anywhere, though we looked for it as carefully as if we had been fierce bulls.

But suddenly we went round a turn in the road and came plump into a lot of soldiers. Only they were not red-coats. They were dressed in grey and silver. And it was a sort of furzy-common place, and three roads branching out. The men were lying about, with some of their belts undone, smoking pipes and cigarettes.

'It's not British soldiers,' Alice said. 'Oh dear, oh dear, I'm afraid it's more enemy. You didn't sow the army-seed anywhere else, did you, H. O. dear?'

H. O. was positive he hadn't. 'But perhaps lots more came up where we did sow them,' he said; 'they're all over England by now very likely. *I* don't know how many men can grow out of one dragon's tooth.'

Then Noël said, 'It was my doing anyhow, and I'm not afraid,' and he walked straight up to the nearest soldier, who was cleaning his pipe with a piece of grass, and said –

'Please, are you the enemy?' The man said –

'No, young Commander-in-Chief, we're the English.'
Then Oswald took command.

'Where is the General?' he said.

'We're out of generals just now, Field-Marshal,' the man said, and his voice was a gentleman's voice. 'Not a single one in stock. We might suit you in majors now – and captains are quite cheap. Competent corporals going for a song. And we have a very nice colonel, too – quiet to ride or drive.'

Oswald does not mind chaff at proper times. But this was not one.

'You seem to be taking it very easy,' he said with disdainful expression.

'This *is* an easy,' said the grey soldier, sucking at his pipe to see if it would draw.

'I suppose *you* don't care if the enemy gets into Maidstone or not!' exclaimed Oswald bitterly. 'If I were a soldier I'd rather die than be beaten.'

The soldier saluted. 'Good old patriotic sentiment,' he said, smiling at the heart-felt boy. But Oswald could bear no more.

'Which is the Colonel?' he asked.

'Over there – near the grey horse.'

'The one lighting a cigarette?' H. O. asked.

'Yes – but I say, kiddie, he won't stand any jaw. There's not an ounce of vice about him, but he's peppery. He might kick out. You'd better bunk.'

'Better what?' asked H. O.

'Bunk, bottle, scoot, skip, vanish, exit,' said the soldier.

'That's what you'd do when the fighting begins,' said H. O. He is often rude like that – but it was what we all thought, all the same. The soldier only laughed.

A spirited but hasty altercation among ourselves in whispers ended in our allowing Alice to be the one to speak to the Colonel. It was she who wanted to. 'However peppery he is he won't kick a girl,' she said, and perhaps this was true.

But of course we all went with her. So there were six of us to stand in front of the Colonel. And as we went along we agreed that we would salute him on the word three. So when we got near, Dick said, 'One, two, three', and we all saluted very well – except H. O., who chose that minute to trip over a rifle a soldier had left lying about, and was only saved from falling by a man in a cocked hat who caught him deftly by the back of his jacket and stood him on his legs.

'Let go, can't you,' said H. O. 'Are you the General?'

Before the Cocked Hat had time to frame a reply, Alice spoke to the Colonel. I knew what she meant to say, because she had told me as we threaded our way among the resting soldiery. What she really said was –

'Oh, how *can* you!'

'How can I *what*?' said the Colonel, rather crossly.

'Why, *smoke*?' said Alice.

'My good children, if you're an infant Band of Hope, let me recommend you to play in some other back-yard,' said the Cock-Hatted Man.

H. O. said, 'Band of Hope yourself' – but no one noticed it.

'We're *not* a Band of Hope,' said Noël. 'We're British, and the man over there told us you are. And Maidstone's in danger, and the enemy not a mile off, and you stand *smoking*.' Noël was standing crying, himself, or something very like it.

'It's quite true,' Alice said.

The Colonel said, 'Fiddle-de-dee.'

But the Cocked-Hatted Man said, 'What was the enemy like?'

We told him exactly. And even the Colonel then owned there might be something in it.

'Can you show me the place where they are on the map?' he asked.

'Not on the map, we can't,' said Dicky; 'at least, I don't think so, but on the ground we could. We could take you there in a quarter of an hour.'

The Cocked-Hatted One looked at the Colonel, who returned his scrutiny, then he shrugged his shoulders.

'Well, we've got to do something,' he said, as if to himself. 'Lead on, Macduff!'

The Colonel roused his soldiery from their stupor of pipes by words of command which the present author is sorry he can't remember.

Then he bade us boys lead the way. I tell you it felt fine, marching at the head of a regiment. Alice got a lift on the Cocked-Hatted One's horse. It was a red-roan steed of might, exactly as if it had been in a ballad. They call a grey-roan a 'blue' in South Africa, the Cocked-Hatted One said.

We led the British Army by unfrequented lanes till we got to the gate of Sugden's Waste Wake pasture. Then the Colonel called a whispered halt, and choosing two of us to guide him, the dauntless and discerning commander went on, on foot, with an orderly. He chose Dicky and Oswald as guides. So we led him to the ambush, and we went through it as quietly as we could. But twigs do crackle and snap so when you are reconnoitring, or anxious to escape detection for whatever reason.

Our Colonel's orderly crackled most. If you're not near enough to tell a colonel by the crown and stars on his shoulder-strap, you can tell him by the orderly behind him, like 'follow my leader'.

'Look out!' said Oswald in a low but commanding

whisper, 'the camp's down in that field. You can see if you take a squint through this gap.'

The speaker took a squint himself as he spoke, and drew back, baffled beyond the power of speech. While he was struggling with his baffledness the British Colonel had his squint. He also drew back, and said a word that he must have known was not right – at least when he was a boy.

'I don't care,' said Oswald, 'they were there this morning. White tents like mushrooms, and an enemy cleaning a cauldron.'

'With sand,' said Dicky.

'That's most convincing,' said the Colonel, and I did not like the way he said it.

'I say,' Oswald said, 'let's get to the top corner of the ambush – the wood, I mean. You can see the cross-roads from there.'

We did, and quickly, for the crackling of branches no longer dismayed our almost despairing spirits.

We came to the edge of the wood, and Oswald's patriotic heart really did give a jump, and he cried, 'There they are, on the Dover Road.'

Our miscellaneous signboard had done its work.

'By Jove, young un, you're right! And in quarter column, too! We've got em on toast – on toast – egad!'

I never heard anyone not in a book say 'egad' before, so I saw something really out of the way was indeed up.

The Colonel was a man of prompt and decisive action. He sent the orderly to tell the Major to advance two companies on the left flank and take cover. Then we led him back through the wood the nearest way, because he said he must rejoin the main body at once. We found the main body very friendly with Noël and H. O. and the others, and Alice was talking to the Cocked-Hatted One as if she had known him all her life. 'I think he's a general in disguise,' Noël said. 'He's been giving us chocolate out of a pocket in his saddle.' Oswald thought about the roast rabbit then – and he is not ashamed to own it – yet he did not say a word. But Alice is really not a bad sort. She had saved two bars of chocolate for him and Dicky. Even in war girls can sometimes be useful in their humble way.

The Colonel fussed about and said, 'Take cover there!' and everybody hid in the ditch, and the horses and the Cocked Hat, with Alice, retreated down the road out of sight. We were in the ditch too. It was muddy – but nobody thought of their boots in that perilous moment. It seemed a long time we were crouching there. Oswald began to feel the water squelching in his boots, so we held our breath and listened. Oswald laid his ear to the road like a Red Indian. You would not do this in time of peace, but when your country is in danger you care but little about keeping your ears clean. His backwoods' strategy was successful. He rose and dusted himself and said –

'They're coming!'

It was true. The footsteps of the approaching foe were now to be heard quite audibly, even by ears in their natural position. The wicked enemy approached. They were marching with a careless swaggeringness that showed how little they suspected the horrible doom which was about to teach them England's might and supremeness. Just as the enemy turned the corner so that we could see them, the Colonel shouted –

'Right section, fire!' and there was a deafening banging.

The enemy's officer said something, and then the enemy got confused and tried to get into the fields through the hedges. But all was vain. There was firing now from our men, on the left as well as the right. And then our Colonel strode nobly up to the enemy's Colonel and demanded surrender. He told me so afterwards. His exact words are only known to himself and the other Colonel. But the enemy's Colonel said, 'I would rather die than surrender,' or words to that effect.

Our Colonel returned to his men and gave the order to fix bayonets, and even Oswald felt his manly cheek turn pale at the thought of the amount of blood to be shed. What would have happened can never now be revealed. For at this moment a man on a piebald horse came clattering over a hedge – as carelessly as if the air was not full of lead and steel at all. Another man rode behind him with a lance and a red pennon on it. I think he must have been the enemy's General coming to tell his men not to throw away their lives on a forlorn hope, for directly he said they were captured the enemy gave in and owned that they were. The enemy's Colonel saluted and ordered his men to form quarter column again. I should have thought he would have had about enough of that myself.

He had now given up all thought of sullen resistance to the bitter end. He rolled a cigarette for himself, and had the foreign cheek to say to our Colonel –

'By Jove, old man, you got me clean that time! Your scouts seem to have marked us down uncommonly neatly.'

It was a proud moment when our Colonel laid his military hand on Oswald's shoulder and said –

'This is my chief scout,' which were high words, but not undeserved, and Oswald owns he felt red with gratifying pride when he heard them.

'So you are the traitor, young man,' said the wicked Colonel, going on with his cheek.

Oswald bore it because our Colonel had, and you

should be generous to a fallen foe, but it is hard to be called a traitor when you haven't.

He did not treat the wicked Colonel with silent scorn as he might have done, but he said –

'We aren't traitors. We are the Bastables and one of us is a Foulkes. We only mingled unsuspected with the enemy's soldiery and learned the secrets of their acts, which is what Baden-Powell always does when the natives rebel in South Africa; and Denis Foulkes thought of altering the sign-posts to lead the foe astray. And if we did cause all this fighting, and get Maidstone threatened with capture and all that, it was only because we didn't believe Greek things could happen in Great Britain and Ireland, even if you sow dragon's teeth, and besides, some of us were not asked about sowing them.'

Then the Cocked-Hatted One led his horse and walked with us and made us tell him all about it, and so did the Colonel. The wicked Colonel listened too, which was only another proof of his cheek.

And Oswald told the tale in the modest yet manly way that some people think he has, and gave the others all the credit they deserved. His narration was interrupted no less than four times by shouts of 'Bravo!' in which the enemy's Colonel once more showed his cheek by joining. By the time the story was told we were in sight of another camp. It was the British one this time. The Colonel asked us to have tea in his tent, and it only shows the magnanimosity of English chivalry in the field of battle that he asked the enemy's Colonel too. With his usual cheek he accepted. We were jolly hungry.

When everyone had had as much tea as they possibly could, the Colonel shook hands with us all, and to Oswald he said –

'Well, good-bye, my brave scout. I must mention your name in my dispatches to the War Office.'

H. O. interrupted him to say, 'His name's Oswald Cecil Bastable, and mine is Horace Octavius.' I wish H. O. would learn to hold his tongue. No one ever knows Oswald was christened Cecil as well, if he can possibly help it. *You* didn't know it till now.

'Mr Oswald Bastable,' the Colonel went on – he had the decency not to take any notice of the 'Cecil' – 'you would be a credit to any regiment. No doubt the War Office will reward you properly for what you have done for your country. But meantime, perhaps, you'll accept five shillings from a grateful comrade-in-arms.'

Oswald felt heart-felt sorry to wound the good Colonel's feelings, but he had to remark that he had only done his duty, and he was sure no British scout would take five bob for doing that. 'And besides,' he said, with that feeling of justice which is part of his young character, 'it was the others just as much as me.'

'Your sentiments, sir,' said the Colonel, who was one of the politest and most discerning colonels I ever saw, 'your sentiments do you honour. But, Bastables all, and – and non-Bastables' (he couldn't remember Foulkes; it's not such an interesting name as Bastable, of course) – 'at least you'll accept a soldier's pay?'

'Lucky to touch it, a shilling a day!' Alice and Denny said together. And the Cocked-Hatted Man said something about knowing your own mind and knowing your own Kipling.

'A soldier,' said the Colonel, 'would certainly be lucky to touch it. You see there are deductions for rations. Five shillings is exactly right, deducting two-pence each for six teas.'

This seemed cheap for the three cups of tea and the

three eggs and all the strawberry jam and bread-and-butter Oswald had had, as well as what the others ate, and Lady's and Pincher's teas, but I suppose soldiers get things cheaper than civilians, which is only right.

Oswald took the five shillings then, there being no longer any scruples why he should not.

Just as we had parted from the brave Colonel and the rest we saw a bicycle coming. It was Albert's uncle. He got off and said –

'What on earth have you been up to? What were you doing with those volunteers?'

We told him the wild adventures of the day, and he listened, and then he said he would withdraw the word volunteers if we liked.

But the seeds of doubt were sown in the breast of Oswald. He was now almost sure that we had made jolly fools of ourselves without a moment's pause throughout the whole of this eventful day. He said nothing at the time, but after supper he had it out with Albert's uncle about the word which had been withdrawn.

Albert's uncle said, of course, no one could be sure that the dragon's teeth hadn't come up in the good old-fashioned way, but that, on the other hand, it was barely possible that both the British and the enemy were only volunteers having a field-day or sham fight, and he rather thought the Cocked-Hatted Man was not a general, but a doctor. And the man with a red pennon carried behind him *might* have been the umpire.

Oswald never told the others a word of this. Their young breasts were all panting with joy because they had saved their country; and it would have been but heartless unkindness to show them how silly they had been. Besides, Oswald felt he was much too old to have been so taken in – if he *had* been. Besides, Albert's uncle did say that no one could be sure about the dragon's teeth.

The thing that makes Oswald feel most that, perhaps, the whole thing was a beastly sell, was that we didn't see any wounded. But he tries not to think of this. And if he goes into the army when he grows up, he will not go quite green. He has had experience of the arts of war and the tented field. And a real colonel has called him 'Comrade-in-Arms', which is exactly what Lord Roberts called his own soldiers when he wrote home about them.

CHAPTER 14

ALBERT'S UNCLE'S GRANDMOTHER; OR, THE LONG-LOST

THE shadow of the termination now descended in sable thunder-clouds upon our devoted nobs. As Albert's uncle said, 'School now gaped for its prey'. In a very short space of time we should be wending our way back to Blackheath, and all the variegated delightfulness of the country would soon be only preserved in memory's faded flowers. (I don't care for that way of writing very much. It would be an awful swot to keep it up – looking out the words and all that.)

To speak in the language of everyday life, our holiday was jolly nearly up. We had had a ripping time, but it was all but over. We really did feel sorry – though, of course, it was rather decent to think of getting back to Father and being able to tell the other chaps about our raft, and the dam, and the Tower of Mystery, and things like that.

When but a brief time was left to us, Oswald and Dicky met by chance in an apple-tree. (That sounds like 'consequences', but it is mere truthfulness.) Dicky said –

'Only four more days.' Oswald said, 'Yes.'

'There's one thing,' Dickie said, 'that beastly society. We don't want that swarming all over everything when we get home. We ought to dissolve it before we leave here.'

The following dialogue now took place:

Oswald – 'Right you are. I always said it was piffling hot.'

Dicky – 'So did I.'

Oswald – 'Let's call a council. But don't forget we've jolly well got to put our foot down.'

Dicky assented, and the dialogue concluded with apples.

The council, when called, was in but low spirits. This made Oswald's and Dicky's task easier. When people are sunk in gloomy despair about one thing, they will agree to almost anything about something else. (Remarks like this are called philosophic generalizations, Albert's uncle says.) Oswald began by saying –

'We've tried the society for being good in, and perhaps it's done us good. But now the time has come for each of us to be good or bad on his own, without hanging on to the others.'

> '*The race is run by one and one,*
> *But never by two and two,*'

the Dentist said. The others said nothing. Oswald went on: 'I move that we chuck – I mean dissolve – the Wouldbegoods Society; its appointed task is done. If it's not well done, that's *its* fault and not ours.'

Dicky said, 'Hear! hear! I second this prop.'

The unexpected Dentist said, 'I third it. At first I thought it would help, but afterwards I saw it only made you want to be naughty, just because you were a Wouldbegood.'

Oswald owns he was surprised. We put it to the vote at once, so as not to let Denny cool. H. O. and Noël and Alice voted with us, so Daisy and Dora were what is called a hopeless minority. We tried to cheer their hopelessness by letting them read the things out of the Golden Deed book aloud. Noël hid his face in the straw so that we should not see the faces he made while he made poetry instead of listening, and when the Wouldbegoods was by vote dissolved for ever he sat up, straws in his hair, and said –

'THE EPITAPH

> The Wouldbegoods are dead and gone
> But not the golden deeds they have done
> These will remain upon Glory's page
> To be an example to every age,
> And by this we have got to know
> How to be good upon our ow – N.

N is for Noël, that makes the rhyme and the sense both right. O, W, N, own; do you see?'

We saw it, and said so, and the gentle poet was satisfied. And the council broke up. Oswald felt that a weight had been lifted from his expanding chest, and it is curious that he never felt so inclined to be good and a model youth as he did then.

As he went down the ladder out of the loft he said –

'There's one thing we ought to do, though, before we go home. We ought to find Albert's uncle's long-lost grandmother for him.'

Alice's heart beat true and steadfast. She said, 'That's just exactly what Noël and I were saying this morning. Look out, Oswald, you wretch, you're kicking chaff into my eyes.' She was going down the ladder just under me.

Oswald's younger sister's thoughtful remark ended in another council. But not in the straw loft. We decided to have a quite new place, and disregarded H. O.'s idea of the dairy and Noël's of the cellars. We had the new council on the secret staircase, and there we settled exactly what we ought to do. This is the same thing, if you really wish to be good, as what you are going to do. It was a very interesting council, and when it was over Oswald was so pleased to think that the Would-begoods was unrecoverishly dead that he gave Denny and Noël, who were sitting on the step below him, a good-humoured, playful, gentle, loving, brotherly shove, and said, 'Get along down, it's tea-time!'

No reader who understands justice and the real rightness of things, and who is to blame for what, will ever think it could have been Oswald's fault that the two other boys got along down by rolling over and over each other, and bursting the door at the bottom of the stairs open by their revolving bodies. And I should like to know whose fault it was that Mrs Pettigrew was just on the other side of that door at that very minute? The door burst open, and the impetuous bodies of Noël and Denny rolled out of it into Mrs Pettigrew, and upset her and the tea-tray. Both revolving boys were soaked with tea and milk, and there were one or two cups and things smashed. Mrs Pettigrew was knocked over, but none of her bones were broken. Noël and Denny were going to be sent to bed, but Oswald said it was all his fault. He really did this to give the others a chance of doing a refined golden deed by speaking the truth and saying it was *not* his fault. But you cannot really count on anyone. They did not say anything, but only rubbed the lumps on their late-revolving heads. So it was bed for Oswald, and he felt the injustice hard.

But he sat up in bed and read *The Last of the Mohicans*, and then he began to think. When Oswald really thinks he almost always thinks of something. He thought of something now, and it was miles better than the idea we had decided on in the secret staircase, of advertising in the *Kentish Mercury* and saying if Albert's uncle's long-lost grandmother would call at the Moat

House she might hear of something much to her advantage.

What Oswald thought of was that if we went to Hazelbridge and asked Mr B. Munn, Grocer, that drove us home in the cart with the horse that liked the wrong end of the whip best, he would know who the lady was in the red hat and red wheels that paid him to drive us home that Canterbury night. He must have been paid, of course, for even grocers are not generous enough to drive perfect strangers, and five of them too, about the country for nothing.

Thus we may learn that even unjustness and sending the wrong people to bed may bear useful fruit, which ought to be a great comfort to everyone when they are unfairly treated. Only it most likely won't be. For if Oswald's brothers and sisters had nobly stood by him as he expected, he would not have had the solitudy reflections that led to the great scheme for finding the grandmother.

Of course when the others came up to roost they all came and squatted on Oswald's bed and said how sorry they were. He waived their apologies with noble dignity, because there wasn't much time, and said he had an idea that would knock the council's plan into a cocked hat. But he would not tell them what it was. He made them wait till next morning. This was not sulks, but kind feeling. He wanted them to have something else to think of besides the way they hadn't stood by him in the bursting of the secret staircase door and the tea-tray and the milk.

Next morning Oswald kindly explained, and asked who would volunteer for a forced march to Hazelbridge. The word volunteer cost the young Oswald a pang as soon as he had said it, but I hope he can bear pangs with any man living. 'And mind,' he added, hiding the pang under a general-like severeness, 'I won't have anyone in the expedition who has anything in his shoes except his feet.'

This could not have been put more delicately and decently. But Oswald is often misunderstood. Even Alice said it was unkind to throw the peas up at Denny. When this little unpleasantness had passed away (it took some time because Daisy cried, and Dora said, 'There now, Oswald!') there were seven volunteers, which, with Oswald, made eight, and was, indeed, all of us. There were no cockle-shells, or tape-sandals, or staves, or scrips, or anything romantic and pious about the eight persons who set out for Hazelbridge that morning, more earnestly wishful to be good and deedful – at least Oswald, I know, was – than ever they had been in the days of the beastly Wouldbegood Society. It was a fine day. Either it was fine nearly all last summer, which is how Oswald remembers it, or else nearly all the interesting things we did came on fine days.

With hearts light and gay, and no peas in anyone's shoes, the walk to Hazelbridge was perseveringly conducted. We took our lunch with us, and the dear dogs. Afterwards we wished for a time that we had left one of them at home. But they did so want to come, all of them, and Hazelbridge is not nearly as far as Canterbury, really, so even Martha was allowed to put on her things – I mean her collar – and come with us. She walks slowly, but we had the day before us so there was no extra hurry.

At Hazelbridge we went into B. Munn's grocer's shop and asked for ginger-beer to drink. They gave it us, but they seemed surprised at us wanting to drink it there, and the glass was warm – it had just been washed. We only did it, really, so as to get into conversation with B. Munn, grocer, and extract information without rousing suspicion. You cannot be too careful.

However, when we had said it was first-class ginger-beer, and paid for it, we found it not so easy to extract anything more from B. Munn, grocer; and there was an anxious silence while he fiddled about behind the counter among the tinned meats and sauce bottles, with a fringe of hob-nailed boots hanging over his head.

H. O. spoke suddenly. He is like the sort of person who rushes in where angels fear to tread, as Denny says (say what sort of person that is). He said –

'I say, you remember driving us home that day. Who paid for the cart?'

Of course B. Munn, grocer, was not such a nincompoop (I like that word, it means so many people I know) as to say right off. He said –

'I was paid all right, young gentleman. Don't you terrify yourself.'

People in Kent say terrify when they mean worry.

So Dora shoved in a gentle oar. She said –

'We want to know the kind lady's name and address, so that we can write and thank her for being so jolly that day.'

B. Munn, grocer, muttered something about the lady's address being goods he was often asked for. Alice said, 'But do tell us. We forgot to ask her. She's a relation of a second-hand uncle of ours, and I do so want to thank her properly. And if you've got any extra-strong peppermints at a penny an ounce, we should like a quarter of a pound.'

This was a master-stroke. While he was weighing out the peppermints his heart got soft, and just as he was twisting up the corner of the paper bag, Dora said, 'What lovely fat peppermints! Do tell us.'

And B. Munn's heart was now quite melted, he said –

'It's Miss Ashleigh, and she lives at The Cedars – about a mile down the Maidstone Road.'

We thanked him, and Alice paid for the peppermints. Oswald was a little anxious when she ordered such a lot, but she and Noël had got the money all right, and when we were outside on Hazelbridge Green (a good deal of it is gravel, really), we stood and looked at each other.

Then Dora said –

'Let's go home and write a beautiful letter and all sign it.'

Oswald looked at the others. Writing is all very well, but it's such a beastly long time to wait for anything to happen afterwards.

The intelligent Alice divined his thoughts, and the Dentist divined hers – he is not clever enough yet to divine Oswald's – and the two said together –

'Why not go and see her?'

'She *did* say she would like to see us again some day,' Dora replied. So after we had argued a little about it we went.

And before we had gone a hundred yards down the dusty road Martha began to make us wish with all our hearts we had not let her come. She began to limp, just as a pilgrim, who I will not name, did when he had the split peas in his silly palmering shoes.

So we called a halt and looked at her feet. One of them was quite swollen and red. Bulldogs almost always have something the matter with their feet, and it always comes on when least required. They are not the right breed for emergencies.

There was nothing for it but to take it in turns to carry her. She is very stout, and you have no idea how heavy she is. A half-hearted unadventurous person (I name no names, but Oswald, Alice, Noël, H. O., Dicky, Daisy, and Denny will understand me) said, why not go straight home and come another day without Martha? But the rest agreed with Oswald when he said it was only a mile, and perhaps we might get a lift home with the poor invalid. Martha was very grateful to us for our kindness. She put her fat white arms round the person's neck who happened to be carrying her. She is very affectionate, but by holding her very close to you you can keep her from kissing your face all the time. As Alice said, 'Bulldogs do give you such large, wet, pink kisses.'

A mile is a good way when you have to take your turn at carrying Martha.

At last we came to a hedge with a ditch in front of it, and chains swinging from posts to keep people off the grass and out of the ditch, and a gate with 'The Cedars' on it in gold letters. All very neat and tidy, and showing plainly that more than one gardener was kept. There we stopped. Alice put Martha down, grunting with exhaustedness, and said –

'Look here, Dora and Daisy, I don't believe a bit that it's his grandmother. I'm sure Dora was right, and it's only his horrid sweetheart. I feel it in my bones. Now, don't you really think we'd better chuck it; we're sure to catch it for interfering. We always do.'

'The cross of true love never did come smooth,' said the Dentist. 'We ought to help him to bear his cross.'

'But if we find her for him, and she's not his grand-mother, he'll *marry* her,' Dicky said in tones of gloominess and despair.

Oswald felt the same, but he said, 'Never mind. We should all hate it, but perhaps Albert's uncle *might* like it. You can never tell. If you want to do a really un-selfish action and no kid, now's your time, my late Wouldbegoods.'

No one had the face to say right out that they didn't want to be unselfish.

But it was with sad hearts that the unselfish seekers opened the long gate and went up the gravel drive between the rhododendrons and other shrubberies towards the house.

I think I have explained to you before that the eldest son of anybody is called the representative of the family if his father isn't there. This was why Oswald now took the lead. When we got to the last turn of the drive it was settled that the others were to noiselessly ambush in the rhododendrons, and Oswald was to go on alone and ask at the house for the grandmother from India – I mean Miss Ashleigh.

So he did, but when he got to the front of the house and saw how neat the flower-beds were with red geraniums, and the windows all bright and speckless with muslin blinds and brass rods, and a green parrot in a cage in the porch, and the doorstep newly whited, lying clean and untrodden in the sunshine, he stood still and thought of his boots and how dusty the roads were, and wished he had not gone into the farmyard after eggs before starting that morning. As he stood there in anxious uncertainness he heard a low voice among the bushes. It said, 'Hist! Oswald here!' and it was the voice of Alice.

So he went back to the others among the shrubs and they all crowded round their leader full of impartable news.

'She's not in the house; she's *here*,' Alice said in a low whisper that seemed nearly all S's. 'Close by – she went by just this minute with a gentleman.'

'And they're sitting on a seat under a tree on a little lawn, and she's got her head on his shoulder, and he's holding her hand. I never saw anyone look so silly in all my born,' Dicky said.

'It's sickening,' Denny said, trying to look very manly with his legs wide apart.

'I don't know,' Oswald whispered. 'I suppose it wasn't Albert's uncle?'

'Not much,' Dicky briefly replied.

'Then don't you see it's all right. If she's going on like that with this fellow she'll want to marry him, and Albert's uncle is safe. And we've really done an unselfish action without having to suffer for it afterwards.' With a stealthy movement Oswald rubbed his hands as he spoke in real joyfulness. We decided that we had better bunk unnoticed. But we had reckoned without Martha. She had strolled off limping to look about her a bit in the shrubbery. 'Where's Martha?' Dora suddenly said.

'She went that way,' pointingly remarked H. O.

'Then fetch her back, you young duffer! What did you let her go for?' Oswald said. 'And look sharp. Don't make a row.'

He went. A minute later we heard a hoarse squeak from Martha – the one she always gives when suddenly collared from behind – and a little squeal in a lady-like voice, and man say 'Hallo!' and then we knew that H. O. had once more rushed in where angels might have thought twice about it. We hurried to the fatal spot, but it was too late. We were just in time to hear H. O. say –

'I'm sorry if she frightened you. But we've been looking for you. Are you Albert's uncle's long-lost grandmother?'

'*No*,' said our lady unhesitatingly.

It seemed vain to add seven more agitated actors to the scene now going on. We stood still. The man was standing up. He was a clergyman, and I found out afterwards he was the nicest we ever knew except our own Mr Briston at Lewisham, who is now a canon or a dean, or something grand that no one ever sees. At present I did not like him. He said, 'No, this lady is nobody's grandmother. May I ask in return how long it is since you escaped from the lunatic asylum, my poor child, and whence your keeper is?'

H. O. took no notice of this at all, except to say, 'I think you are very rude, and not at all funny, if you think you are.'

The lady said, 'My dear, I remember you now perfectly. How are all the others, and are you pilgrims again to-day?'

H. O. does not always answer questions. He turned to the man and said –

'Are you going to marry the lady?'

'Margaret,' said the clergyman, 'I never thought it would come to this: he asks me my intentions.'

'If you *are*,' said H. O., 'it's all right, because if you do Albert's uncle can't – at least, not till you're dead. And we don't want him to.'

'Flattering, upon my word,' said the clergyman, putting on a deep frown. 'Shall I call him out, Margaret, for his poor opinion of you, or shall I send for the police?'

Alice now saw that H. O., though firm, was getting muddled and rather scared. She broke cover and sprang into the middle of the scene.

'Don't let him rag H. O. any more,' she said, 'it's all our faults. You see, Albert's uncle was so anxious to find you, we thought perhaps you were his long-lost heiress sister or his old nurse who alone knew the secret of his birth, or something, and we asked him, and he

276

said you were his long-lost grandmother he had known in India. And we thought that must be a mistake and that really you were his long-lost sweetheart. And we tried to do a really unselfish act and find you for him. Because we don't want him to be married at all.'

'It isn't because we don't like *you*,' Oswald cut in, now emerging from the bushes, 'and if he must marry, we'd sooner it was you than anyone. Really we would.'

'A generous concession, Margaret,' the strange clergyman uttered, 'most generous, but the plot thickens. It's almost pea-soup-like now. One or two points clamour for explanation. Who are these visitors of yours? Why this Red Indian method of paying morning calls? Why the lurking attitude of the rest of the tribe which I now discern among the undergrowth? Won't you ask the rest of the tribe to come out and join the glad throng?'

Then I liked him better. I always like people who know the same songs we do, and books and tunes and things.

The others came out. The lady looked very uncomfy, and partly as if she was going to cry. But she couldn't help laughing too, as more and more of us came out.

'And who,' the clergyman went on, 'who in fortune's name is Albert? And who is his uncle? And what have they or you to do in this *galère* – I mean garden?'

We all felt rather silly, and I don't think I ever felt more than then what an awful lot there were of us.

'Three years' absence in Calcutta or elsewhere may explain my ignorance of these details, but still – '

'I think we'd better go,' said Dora. 'I'm sorry if we've done anything rude or wrong. We didn't mean to. Good-bye. I hope you'll be happy with the gentleman, I'm sure.'

'I *hope* so too,' said Noël, and I know he was thinking

how much nicer Albert's uncle was. We turned to go.
The lady had been very silent compared with what
she was when she pretended to show us Canterbury.
But now she seemed to shake off some dreamy silliness,
and caught hold of Dora by the shoulder.

'No, dear, no,' she said, 'it's all right, and you must
have some tea – we'll have it on the lawn. John, don't
tease them any more. Albert's uncle is the gentleman
I told you about. And, my dear children, this is my
brother that I haven't seen for three years.'

'Then he's a long-lost too,' said H. O.

The lady said 'Not now' and smiled at him.

And the rest of us were dumb with confounding
emotions. Oswald was particularly dumb. He might
have known it was her brother, because in rotten
grown-up books if a girl kisses a man in a shrubbery
that is not the man you think she's in love with; it
always turns out to be a brother, though generally the
disgrace of the family and not a respectable chaplain
from Calcutta.

The lady now turned to her reverend and surprising
brother and said, 'John, go and tell them we'll have
tea on the lawn.'

When he was gone she stood quite still a minute.
Then she said, 'I'm going to tell you something, but I
want to put you on your honour not to talk about it to
other people. You see it isn't everyone I would tell
about it. He, Albert's uncle, I mean, has told me a lot
about you, and I know I can trust you.'

We said 'Yes', Oswald with a brooding sentiment of
knowing all too well what was coming next.

The lady then said, 'Though I am not Albert's
uncle's grandmother I did know him in India once,
and we were going to be married, but we had a – a –
misunderstanding.'

'Quarrel?' 'Row?' said Noël and H. O. at once.

'Well, yes, a quarrel, and he went away. He was in the Navy then. And then ... well, we were both sorry, but well, anyway, when his ship came back we'd gone to Constantinople, then to England, and he couldn't find us. And he says he's been looking for me ever since.'

'Not you for him?' said Noël.

'Well, perhaps,' said the lady.

And the girls said 'Ah!' with deep interest. The lady went on more quickly, 'And then I found you, and then he found me, and now I must break it to you. Try to bear up ... '

She stopped. The branches crackled, and Albert's uncle was in our midst. He took off his hat. 'Excuse my tearing my hair,' he said to the lady, 'but has the pack really hunted you down?'

'It's all right,' she said, and when she looked at him she got miles prettier quite suddenly. 'I was just breaking to them ... '

'Don't take that proud privilege from me,' he said. 'Kiddies, allow me to present you to the future Mrs Albert's uncle, or shall we say Albert's new aunt?'

There was a good deal of explaining done before tea – about how we got there, I mean, and why. But after the first bitterness of disappointment we felt not nearly so sorry as we had expected to. For Albert's uncle's lady was very jolly to us, and her brother was awfully decent, and showed us a lot of first-class native curiosities and things, unpacking them on purpose; skins of beasts, and beads, and brass things, and shells from different savage lands besides India. And the lady told the girls that she hoped they would like her as much as she liked them, and if they wanted a new aunt

'It's all right,' she said

she would do her best to give satisfaction in the new
situation. And Alice thought of the Murdstone aunt
belonging to Daisy and Denny, and how awful it.
would have been if Albert's uncle had married *her*.
And she decided, she told me afterwards, that we
might think ourselves jolly lucky it was no worse.

Then the lady led Oswald aside, pretending to show
him the parrot which he had explored thoroughly
before, and told him she was not like some people in

books. When she was married she would never try to separate her husband from his bachelor friends, she only wanted them to be her friends as well.

Then there was tea, and thus all ended in amicableness, and the reverend and friendly drove us home in a wagonette. But for Martha we shouldn't have had tea, or explanations, or lift or anything. So we honoured her, and did not mind her being so heavy and walking up and down constantly on our laps as we drove home.

And that is all the story of the long-lost grandmother and Albert's uncle. I am afraid it is rather dull, but it was very important (to him), so I felt it ought to be narrated. Stories about lovers and getting married are generally slow. I like a love-story where the hero parts with the girl at the garden-gate in the gloaming and goes off and has adventures, and you don't see her any more till he comes home to marry her at the end of the book. And I suppose people have to marry. Albert's uncle is awfully old – more than thirty, and the lady is advanced in years – twenty-six next Christmas. They are to be married then. The girls are to be bridesmaids in white frocks with fur. This quite consoles them. If Oswald repines sometimes, he hides it. What's the use? We all have to meet our fell destiny, and Albert's uncle is not extirpated from this awful law.

Now the finding of the long-lost was the very last thing we did for the sake of its being a noble act, so that is the end of the Wouldbegoods, and there are no more chapters after this. But Oswald hates books that finish up without telling you the things you might want to know about the people in the book. So here goes. We went home to the beautiful Blackheath house. It seemed very stately and mansion-like after the Moat

House, and everyone was most frightfully pleased to see us.

Mrs Pettigrew *cried* when we went away. I never was so astonished in my life. She made each of the girls a fat red pincushion like a heart, and each of us boys had a knife bought out of the housekeeping (I mean house-keeper's own) money.

Bill Simpkins is happy as sub-under-gardener to Albert's uncle's lady's mother. They do keep three gardeners – I knew they did. And our tramp still earns enough to sleep well on from our dear old Pig-man.

Our last three days were entirely filled up with visits of farewell sympathy to all our many friends who were so sorry to lose us. We promised to come and see them next year. I hope we shall.

Denny and Daisy went back to live with their father at Forest Hill. I don't think they'll ever be again the victims of the Murdstone aunt – who is really a great-aunt and about twice as much in the autumn of her days as our new Albert's-uncle aunt. I think they plucked up spirit enough to tell their father they didn't like her – which they'd never thought of doing before. Our own robber says their holidays in the country did them both a great deal of good. And he says us Bastables have certainly taught Daisy and Denny the rudiments of the art of making home happy. I believe they have thought of several quite new naughty things entirely on their own – and done them too – since they came back from the Moat House.

I wish you didn't grow up so quickly. Oswald can see that ere long he will be too old for the kind of games we can all play, and he feels grown-upness creeping inordiously upon him. But enough of this.

And now, gentle reader, farewell. If anything in these chronicles of the Wouldbegoods should make you try to be good yourself, the author will be very glad, of course. But take my advice and don't make a society for trying in. It is much easier without.

And do try to forget that Oswald has another name besides Bastable. The one beginning with C., I mean. Perhaps you have not noticed what it was. If so, don't look back for it. It is a name no manly boy would like to be called by – if he spoke the truth. Oswald is said to be a very manly boy, and he despises that name, and will never give it to his own son when he has one. Not if a rich relative offered to leave him an immense fortune if he did. Oswald would still be firm. He would, on the honour of the House of Bastable.

THE CALL OF THE WILD
Jack London

This tale of a dog's fight for survival in the harsh and frozen Yukon is one of the greatest animal stories ever written. It tells of a dog born to luxury but sold as a sledge dog, and how he rises magnificently above all his enemies to become one of the most feared and admired dogs in the north.

LITTLE WOMEN
L. M. Alcott

The good-natured March girls – Meg, Jo, Beth and Amy – manage to lead interesting lives despite their father's absence at war and the family's lack of money. Whether they're making plans for putting on a play or forming a secret society, their enthusiasm is infectious. Even Laurie, the rich but lonely boy next door, is swept up in their gaiety. (*Good Wives*, *Little Men*, and *Jo's Boys* are also published in Puffin Classics.)

MOONFLEET
J. Meade Falkner

Most of the inhabitants of the tiny village of Moonfleet are either smugglers or fishermen, so it's no surprise when 15-year-old John Trenchard gets involved in the smuggling business. Eventually he is forced to leave the country with a price on his head, and only returns to England after a long and difficult period abroad.

OUR EXPLOITS AT WEST POLEY
Thomas Hardy

The story of two boys who discover how to divert an underground river and play havoc with the lives of the local Somerset villagers. But it's their own lives that are finally most in danger!

TOM BROWN'S SCHOOLDAYS
Thomas Hughes

One of the most famous of all school stories, it follows Tom's career at Rugby, from his first nervous day as a newcomer in an alien world to his last cricket match as Captain of the School eleven. Though nowadays they won't be tossed in a blanket or roasted over a fire, many readers will find that Tom's adventures and dilemmas strike a chord with them.

THE PRINCESS AND THE GOBLIN
George MacDonald

Princess Irene lives in a castle in a wild and lonely mountainous region. One day she discovers a steep and winding stairway leading to a labyrinth of unused passages, with closed doors – and a further stairway. What lies at the top? Can the Princess's ring protect her against the lurking menace of the goblins from under the mountain? An ageless story of mystery and magic.

PINOCCHIO
Carlo Collodi (translated by E. Harden)

The hair-raising adventures of a naughty wooden puppet. But he wasn't only naughty, he was also inquisitive and quite brave, and he had some astonishing adventures before he earned the thing he most desired – to be a *real* boy.

KING SOLOMON'S MINES
H. Rider Haggard

A story that has gripped generations of readers since it was first published. It tells of how three Englishmen made their perilous expedition over more than a thousand miles to the north of Durban, in search of a man. For his sake they faced the heat and flies, the long trek across waterless desert, the icy cold of the mountains. And ridiculous things saved them – a man's white legs, his false teeth, an eyeglass – and a half-shaved face! A classic adventure that has rarely been equalled.

LORNA DOONE
R. D. Blackmore

For generations the Doone family had been feared for their savage, marauding raids on innocent travellers crossing Exmoor and it had long been the family's intentions that Lorna should marry the ruthless Carver Doone. When John Ridd stole her away he brought down upon his head the enmity of the entire Doone family, bent upon revenge. A romantic tale of love, honour, bravery and treachery set in the time of James II and the Monmouth Rebellion.

WHAT KATY DID
Susan Coolidge

The moving story of how Katy Carr overcame her tragic accident and learned to be as loving and as patient as the beautiful invalid, Helen.

KIDNAPPED
R. L. Stevenson

A swashbuckling tale of kidnap and murder, set in the Scottish Highlands after the Jacobite Rebellion. It tells of the flight of young David Balfour after he is treacherously cheated of his rightful estate and then wrongly suspected of murder.

THE LOST WORLD
Sir Arthur Conan Doyle

Journalist Ed Malone is looking for an adventure, and that's exactly what he finds when he meets the eccentric Professor Challenger: an adventure that leads Malone and his three companions deep into the Amazon jungle, to a lost world where dinosaurs roam free and the natives fight out a murderous war with their fierce neighbours, the ape-men.